Derek Christian, Antichrist

A Collection of Short Stories

by

Robert R. Railey

Published by Biblio Publishing
The Educational Publisher, Inc.
1313 Chesapeake Ave
Columbus, OH 43212
Printed in the United States

ISBN: 978-1-62249-171-1

Contents

Derek Christian, Antichrist?

Prologue
"At the time of the end"

"In one instant, the sky will open up to reveal multiple shafts of fire and terrifying bolts of lightning which will emanate downward from the heavens. And from that time on, the average person will know that the time of the ancient Biblical Prophecy of Armageddon is upon us; and we will also know that the Earth will be consumed by fire."

But before the nations of Gog and Magog can be destroyed in the apocalyptic battle, and also well before Satan and the False Prophet can be thrown in a 'bottomless pit" for a thousand years, the people on Earth must first endure the second half of "The Tribulation."

It's been written that the first half of the seven years of "The Tribulation" will afford the people on Earth a full three and one half years of unprecedented peace and prosperity. We have also been told that during the second half of The Tribulations we will see war and pestilence not seen since the Biblical days.

Nowadays, the nagging question on many people's minds is just exactly how the true believers will be able to spot the Antichrist. Regrettably, this may not be an easy task for us to achieve; and that's simply because it's very doubtful that the Antichrist will show up sporting horns that protrude from his head; nor, will he most likely be dragging around a long tail. It's been said, however, that we'll know him by his deeds.

Though in recent times, more than a few people around the world have come to believe that the previously unknown preacher from the Western Kentucky area who'd just recently been recognized as being the absolute ruler of the televangelists might just be the Antichrist.

Chapter One

Within a few short years following the last battle of the American Revolution the wilderness tract of land known as Kentucky would officially become the fifteenth state of the newly formed United States of America; and since Kentucky lay directly to the west of Virginia some of the men who'd fought in America's War of Independence were given sizable land grants in the new state in lieu of payments for fighting on the line.

But then during those early pioneer days, there were very few courts of law to be found anywhere in the state of Kentucky; and the U. S. Military posts were even more scarce which left the early settlers of the region no choice then but to resort to the only type of law that was readily available to them; and which then meant that frontier justice would have to prevail.

So for that reason, it was not unusual for the different groups of vigilantes to have to expel the violent and the antisocial individuals from their frontier communities; and on certain other occasions it even became necessary for them to hang somebody.

Consequently, myriads of myths and legends have greatly abounded concerning the early frontier days in Kentucky. And in a film from yesteryear, which was titled, "How the west was won," there was one particular scene filmed in the Western Kentucky area that quite accurately depicted a notorious family of river pirates that made its living by robbing and killing the unassuming and trusting boaters who were traversing the Ohio River. Thus after having practiced their murderous ways of luring the people into there lair, the killers would then dump their victim's bodies down in a deep hole in the floor of a cave which was located in the side of the riverbank.

That same part of Western Kentucky was also home to the infamous Harp brothers and their brother in-law, who just happened to be the duly elected Sheriff of the district, but who was also the leader of a real life gang of murdering thieves that robbed and killed the people living in the Western Kentucky communities; until, that is, when the vigilantes and the local militia made the fateful decision to put a stop to it.

And as it has been previously noted in some of the published accounts of the aforementioned incident, the militiamen proceeded to shoot and kill the renegade Sheriff as he sat comfortably in a chair in the gang's ferry office on the Kentucky side of the Ohio River. Then shortly thereafter, the vigilantes captured one of the Harp brothers at a nearby crossroads where they proceeded to place his severed head in a fork of a tree which was forevermore known as "Harp's Head." It's long been said that the militiamen left the man's head in the tree to serve as a warning to the people in the area to show just exactly what would happen if they ever decided to embark upon a life of crime.

Then following that rather impromptu execution of one of the Harp brothers, a few of the militia members trailed the other Harp brother all of the way down the Natchez Trace to the city of New Orleans, Louisiana where they just happened to find him enjoying himself in a brothel. And after first dragging the man to the outside, the militiamen proceeded to execute him right there on the sidewalk.

Chapter Two
Modern-day Kentucky

With three years of military service in the U. S. Air Force behind him, and also with twenty-five thousand dollars of questionably procured money in his pocket, you would think that a person's first thoughts would be of home; and yet, Derek Christian wasn't so sure about that.

His home was in Western Kentucky, that is, if he ever decided to return; but what was waiting for him there? What with the ever-increasing number of high sulfur coalmines being shut down every year, and then too, there was the mean spirited woman who was under the impression that they were betrothed to be married, Derek wasn't any too thrilled with the idea of going back home; but he probably would.

His wife to be was a fairly new transplant to that particular part of Western Kentucky. Her name was Barbara Holton of the Holton Clan from the Pattyville, Kentucky district. In Derek's opinion she was without a doubt the sexiest and the most sensual woman he'd ever met. But marrying into the Holton clan would necessarily cause Derek to undertake some very deep considerations; for the rumors abounded that if a person were to ever betray a member of the Holton clan in any way, then they would just as likely take you down to the river and (drowned-ye). They were a rowdy bunch, alright, and they were most generally inclined to settle their arguments with knives and guns.

According to the local legend, the Holton clan had migrated to Derek's part of Western Kentucky after a group of vigilantes had driven them out of the Pattyville district following a fiasco which had occurred at a funeral home. For years, the Holtons had had a longstanding feud with another clan from the Pattyville area; and the melee' which had ensued inside a funeral home had purportedly come about after the elder Holton had deliberately urinated on the body of a dead man while he was lying in a casket. Then once the fight had begun in earnest, the patriarch of Holton family had proceeded to cut off one of the dead man's brother's ear.

Although later on that same day, Uncle Clinton Holton would become another casualty of the feud when he became involved in a barroom brawl with a member of the enemy clan and wound up getting shot in the stomach; amazingly, though, Uncle Clinton somehow survived that particular ordeal.

Eventually, though, both sides began to tire of the constant fighting and the leaders of the clans agreed upon a tentative, if somewhat fragile truce. But when the feud broke out anew, all of the other families in the area that weren't personally involved in the mayhem formed a vigilante posse that immediately banned the entire Holton clan from the Pattyville area upon pain of death should the warning not be heeded.

Babs Holton, as Barbara preferred to be called, was a dark-haired beauty of about five feet and four inches of height; but when those black eyes of hers were on fire, she gave the impression of being seven feet tall and bullet proof.

According to their family's history, before migrating to Western Kentucky the Holtons were some of the first settlers to pioneer and then homestead the mountainous regions of Tennessee; and during those early days, the legend states further that a few of the Holton men had married into a Native American family which might have given Babs her coal black hair and high cheekbones; plus the inability for her to be able to successfully drink any alcoholic beverages at all.

At times, Babs could be as sweet and gentle as a newborn lamb, but then on other occasions she could be just as volatile as her four brothers, who without a doubt, were some of the meanest fighters who'd ever come out of the mountains.

So as a result, Derek had made it a steadfast point to never drink any alcoholic beverages with the Holton clan. On the other hand, his decision not to socialize with the Holtons was brought on by the fact that not only was the Holton clan a too violent of a group to drink with, but he also thought that the drinking of liquor was a foolish waste of good money. In reality, though, that particular line of thinking had more to do with what Derek was really all about; and that was his desire to become extremely wealthy.

Chapter Three

The Christian family had migrated to Western Kentucky in order to help lay some of the first railroad tracks ever constructed in that area. Ultimately, though, they fell in love with the beautiful and fertile land of Western Kentucky which included the gently rolling hills and lush meadows which surround the community of Clay, Kentucky, which in their opinion, was one of the most beautiful parts of the whole of Webster County.

Then once settled in, the Christian family decided to homestead a tract of bottomland in the Tradewater River region; and subsequently, they've been living in that particular district ever since. Then again, who wouldn't love the beautifully wooded hills which at times will block the mist covered meadows until the late morning sun creeps up high enough to cause the fields to come alive with the bright vistas of Kentucky Bluegrass and the flowering goldenrod plants which just happen to be the state flower.

And even though more than a few of the Christian family men were still employed by the same railroad company that their ancestors had worked for back in their home state of West Virginia, some of the members of the Christian family had opted to work in the coalmines of Western Kentucky. Then too, quite a few of their clan had answered the call to serve their Lord by becoming Baptist Ministers.

Yet when it came to physical labor, Derek Christian didn't particularly care for any of the types of the work that many of his family members favored; instead, he planned on searching for a vocation that would allow him to amass a small fortune, while at the same time doing as little work as humanely possible. Derek also felt that he was extremely fortunate to have an overabundance of a certain type of acid in his body, which he believed, would not only cause him to suffer severe muscle cramps while performing manual labor, but it also caused his jewelry, and even those small metal screws in his reading glasses to turn green. Also oddly enough, one of the very worst effects of his strange ailment was that his condition would not allow him to remain out of doors for any extended amount of time because of an overabundance of a particular chemical in his body which seemed to attract mosquitoes and chiggers.

Indeed, there were times when Derek felt that he was blessed to have such a fortunate and God given excuse that would allow him to forgo any type of physical labor without receiving a lot of criticism from his family and neighbors. Derek had also excused himself from ever working in the coalmines, when after on three separate occasions, the roofs of the mines had caved in on both his father and his grandfather.

Chapter Four

A distant cousin of Derek's, who just happened to be one of his childhood heroes, was a very interesting character to say the least. For at one time in the past Harold Hanson had been one of the biggest bootleggers and whiskey runners in the entire Western Kentucky area. Though after he'd decided to go straight, he eventually ended up owning a great number of successful businesses and productive farms in the Western Kentucky area.

One of Harold's claims to fame was that he'd been wounded several times by members of the notorious Shelton gang which included Blackie Harris, who was another infamous bootlegging gangster member of the brethren. At that particular time, the Shelton gang operated primarily out of Southern Illinois; but its tentacles reached deeply into the neighboring states which included Kentucky and Indiana. Supposedly, it was one of Harold's old lieutenants from the illegal whisky business who'd shown Derek a few of the sites along a Southern Illinois highway where some of the causalities of the whiskey wars had allegedly been buried.

Generally speaking, Derek suspected that the majority of Harold's war stories were mostly true; and especially since Derek just happened to personally know one of families which had lost five of their sons in the whiskey wars. Then again, it wasn't only the bootlegging business which had caused the people living in the Western Kentucky area a great deal of trouble; for two of Derek's own family members had been killed in the coalmine strikes which had taken place during the early parts of the twentieth century.

In one particular confrontation, the owners of a local coalmine had allegedly hired a trainload of strikebreakers from the city of Chicago, Illinois in order to try prevent the coalminers from Western Kentucky from joining the United Mineworker's Union. And in the gun battle which followed, one of Derek's distant cousins was killed by one of the strikebreakers; while at the same time another of his cousins had died at the hands of a local deputy sheriff.

To Derek, it seemed as if violence had always plagued this particular part of the country; and even his hometown of Clay, Kentucky had seen its own share of mayhem. For when Derek was but a child he just happened to be downtown Clay one day when an armed and dangerous man had blatantly refused to surrender his weapon to the town Marshal who then had no other recourse but to employ deadly force. Then later on, the local courts would declare that the marshal had simply been upholding the law; and therefore, the shooting was a case of justifiable homicide.

Nonetheless, a similar fate might have befallen Derek's three hundred and thirty pound uncle Vernis Curry Paulson, who after first imbibing an enormous quantity of moonshine liquor, had shown up in downtown Clay on Election Day with a large hog leg pistol strapped to his waist. Although luckily for uncle Vernis, the same Town Marshall who'd just previously shot and killed a man in downtown Clay was able to disarm the drunken uncle Vernis who was then allowed to sleep it off in the local jail.

Chapter Five

"Booster," as Derek Christian was affectionately known to his family and friends owned a lanky and rawboned six-foot four inch frame which was handsomely topped off by an unruly shock of dark brown hair that hung loosely above an affable smile. Some people remarked that he reminded them of the loveable Will Rogers of old who'd hailed from Oklahoma and was quite the celebrity back in his day. Rogers had appeared in several Hollywood films as the loveable old cowboy who could perform amazing rope tricks. Rogers primarily enjoyed being in the spotlight where he could effectively deliver his political barbs which were usually aimed at the office holding politicians.

And even though Will Rogers was a very popular and entertaining satirist and political activist back in his day, his brand of humor would not necessarily be out of style today since it would be strikingly similar to a few of the same types of stand up comics who regularly appear on television.

For the most part, though, the people who knew Booster certainly didn't believe that he was a satirist or even an activist like the Will Rogers of old: instead, they thought of him more as a pitchman for he always had something going on which he hoped would make him rich. But in order for him to fully implement his latest money making scheme, he would not only need the co-operation of his rather large and extended family, but he would also need the assistance from quite a few of the other people who lived and worked in the region.

Nevertheless, there was always something new and exciting going on when Booster was around and about: and a person could always bet that whatever was going on with Booster it would certainly be entertaining. Even so, the locals always hoped and prayed that Booster's latest venture wouldn't cost them too much money.

It wasn't so much that the people didn't trust Booster: moreover, when they first learned about one of his latest exploits, they would usually just shake their heads and smile; then again, they would also be a bit curious as to what the newest scheme was all about.

On the other hand, though, they would also have to admit that there'd been a few people around the area who'd actually made a great deal of money from Booster's varied and sundry enterprises.

Chapter Six

It's also a well-known fact that Derek Christian wasn't the only colorful character to have called Western Kentucky his home for there was another man who'd hailed from the same general area and had gone on to accomplish even greater things. When Booster's father was a child growing up in the town of Clay, there was a local businessman there by the name of Hunky Blueford who at the time had owned a tiny ice-cream shop in the downtown area that would serve you up a tremendously large scoop of ice cream on a cone for only five cents.

In time, however, Mr. Blueford would go on to own several dairy farms in the general area as well as many other related businesses, until eventually, he would amass enough money to afford him a chance to run for the U. S. Congress. Unfortunately, though, the man failed in his attempt to win a seat in the U. S. Congress. However, the man's financial successes had definitely made an incalculable impression on young Derek Christian for it'd shown him just exactly what money can buy.

But then after having spent some quality time with his family and his fiancé, Babs Holton, Booster decided to look up an old childhood friend of his. Whenever Booster thought about his early childhood days it would invariably include the memory of the day that he and his friend Tug Whitledge had shown up in downtown Clay with blood streaming from their faces and arms where they were forced to confess to the town Marshall that not only had they'd been caught stealing watermelons from Mr. Winstead's patch, but also that he'd peppered them with some rock salt loaded shotgun shells; and so naturally, everybody in town had a good laugh over that particular incident.

Derek and Tug had spent many a memorable day while swimming and "hogging" for fish, turtles and the occasional copper belly water snake which, from time to time, could be found in the hollowed out spaces below the water line and beneath the roots of the large trees that lined the banks of the Tradewater River.

Hence, at that point in time, Booster's most immediate problem was how best to locate his friend Tug. Eventually, however, he was able to find him working in the fields alongside his father and his two brothers. Then after sharing a few moments of genuine emotions with one another, the two friends made plans to meet up later that evening at an eating-place in downtown Clay.

Then after finishing their evening meal, the two friends hopped into Tug's pickup truck and then headed down the old state highway number 109 towards Providence, KY where they'd planned on picking up Clifton E. Raleigh III who was the third part of the trilogy of their lifelong friendships.

Cliff was a pleasure, alright, for he was joyous, happy, and free most of the time; and that was in spite of having to live with the loss of his mother when he was a mere child. Of course it wasn't only the loss of his mother which had hampered his emotional maturity, for just shortly after Cliff's mother had passed away, his father had married a woman many years his junior; and then later on, that impromptu marriage had proved to be a big mistake when shortly thereafter the new bride began an affair with a young farmhand who worked for Cliff's father.

In time, the young wife and her lover devised what they thought was a foolproof plan whereby they could do away with the older gentleman in order to acquire his rather sizeable estate which included a large productive farm in addition to the money he'd earned in his younger years when he was a professional prizefighter.

And in addition to the property that Mr. Raleigh owned outright, he'd also invested tens of thousands of dollars in the various diamond rings that he wore on the fingers of both hands. Evidently, those outward signs of luxury and wealth had been too much for the young bride and her lover to resist.

So when the full story of that terrible event was eventually revealed, every soul in town would learn that the young bride had suggested to her elderly husband that the two of them should embark upon a lusty and sensuous twilight romp atop the highest hill on their farm; and unfortunately for the elderly man it was there that Mr. Raleigh was lured into an encounter which had almost proved to be fatal. It seems that after first disrobing while standing on the hilltop, the young bride had easily gained Mr. Raleigh's rapt attention, while at the same time, the young farmhand had crept up behind the older gentleman from where he proceeded to shove him off of the top of a high cliff to what should have been his death.

Then immediately following the hilltop assault, and being that the young couple honestly believed that the older man was indeed dead, the two lovebirds hurriedly returned to the farm where they took their time in cleaning out the entire household of everything that was of any value. During the following day, however, the situation had changed drastically when the young wife received word from their bank that the joint bank accounts that she'd shared with her husband had been closed.

It seems as if Clifton Raleigh II had somehow managed to drag his beaten and bloodied body all of the way into the town of Morganfield, KY where a shop owner had observed him buying firearms which he said he direly needed in order to exact the revenge that he felt he had coming to him because of the terrible wrong which had just been done to him. Then fortunately for the young Mrs. Raleigh, someone from town was sent out to the Raleigh farm to tell the young couple that they'd better clear out of the area before the older man returned home.

So by the time that the elderly Mr. Raleigh was able to return to his home, the two would-be murdering thieves had absconded with all of the personal property that they could possibly load onto their two pickup trucks. Meanwhile, some of the townspeople of Morganfield, Kentucky reported that they'd heard that the two lovebirds were headed for California. So by practicing a lot of patience and tolerance, the young Clifton Raleigh III had somehow managed to rise above the turmoil and trauma that he'd been faced with throughout much of his life. More importantly, though, Clifton, had developed into what most people considered to be a normal and responsible young man.

Chapter Seven

As most of the people in the area were inclined to say, Booster Christian was a dreamer of elaborate designs: and as such, his number one dream was that he would someday be able to sell a one-dollar Hula-Hoop to every single person in China for a princely sum of five dollars apiece; and with well over a billion Chinese on the planet, it would seem as if a scheme of that magnitude would surely return a rather healthy profit.

Yet no one could say that Booster had not been successful in several of his previous ventures: for at various times he was heavily invested in the pyramid types of businesses which had included the original phone cards, and then later on he'd become part of the herbal revolution. And during the three years in which he'd served in the military, he was able to continue on with many of his business interests back home in Kentucky. For example, he'd been able to add several hundreds of new clients to his various pyramid businesses because of the thousands of U. S. servicemen and women he'd come into contact with while serving in the U. S. Air Force.

Still, there was a well hidden side of Booster's personality and character that he didn't necessarily want people to know about: and that very simply was the fact that he always kept an unknown plan of attack and agenda under his hat until such time that he was fully ready to spring it upon the unassuming public.

And since satellites had begun to circle the globe, he knew that a person needed only to own a computer, and then to also subscribe to an internet service provider in order to send electronic e-mails to any of his thousands of business associates which were scattered throughout the world; so naturally, Booster's various Pyramid schemes had expanded exponentially. Then again, that was mainly due to the thanks of the hundreds of new pyramid members which he'd brought on board while serving those three years in the U. S. military.

Back in the latter part of the twentieth century, Booster was one of the first people in the Western Kentucky area to become a distributor for the very popular pre-paid phone cards; and within a short period of time, the selling of those phone cards would end up being a most lucrative business for him. For when the phone cards first appeared on the market they'd created a land rush type of commerce. Those cards were especially coveted by the people who didn't have access to long distance calling. Eventually, though, the cards would end up being sold out of practically every convenience store in the country.

Nevertheless, it'd been a tremendous learning experience for a young businessman such as Booster: so from then on, he would learn that in order for a person to become successful in any of the pyramid types of schemes, an individual needed only to bring together a group of people who were interested in making some fast money. Derek also discovered that the only way for the original distributors in any pyramid plan to make any real money would be for them to continue to bring new people on board. This then would ensure that those who were climbing to the top of the distributors list would benefit financially from the newest members of the scheme who were still on the bottom of the ever expanding list.

Then once the phone card game was finally over and done with, the next pyramid type of program that Booster became involved in was put together by a group of attorneys, who theoretically, would accept an inexpensive prepaid fee if any of the paid-up members of the plan were to ever find themselves in need of some good, professional legal advice. In a way, this program was very similar to the prepaid phone card plan to the extent that the main purpose of the plan was to continually bring new people on board who wished to become distributors.

It seemed as if Booster had always been involved in one scheme or another; and at one time in the past he was member of a pyramid plan that distributed various health food supplements such as herbs, vitamins, diet pills and natural health products. Of course it must be said that the main objective for anyone involved in those types of pyramid schemes is that it's not necessary for a member to personally sell the products, although they may do so if they wish, but the main goal is for the original members of the plan to continually bring new distributors into the fold; for when all the smoke clears, that's how they make their big money. It's really quite simple; a distributor is paid a commission for every new person he or she brings on board.

So as a rule, the only people who ever make any real money in a pyramid scheme are the ones at the top of the distributor list; and from then on, the newest members of the scheme will simply help to enrich the pocketbooks of the people who were already at the top of the list.

Chapter Eight

Since Booster knew practically every single farmer in the area by his first name, it seemed only logical to him that he should devise a plan that would help them make some extra money; of course it goes without saying that the plan would also have to help him out financially. So after much due consideration, Booster was ready to launch a new business venture that would give the farmers a way in which to harvest a quick and easy cash crop: by the same token, the scheme would not require of them to put up a lot of front money; or at the very least, they wouldn't be required to make an enormous investment.

Then as luck would have it, the timing for Booster's newest adventure couldn't have come at a better time for it was about that same point in time when the tobacco production in the state of Kentucky had begun to sharply decline. And since most farmers could always use another cash crop to supplement their incomes which usually come from the sales of their grain crops and livestock, Booster sincerely hoped that they would be open to a brand-new moneymaking type of proposition.

So after first consulting with some fish farm owners from the deep South, Booster came up with a plan that would require of each local farmer to make an annual investment of only twelve hundred dollars in order to restock their newly acquired fish ponds. His figuring was that once the fully grown fish were sold to the distributors in the East and Midwestern parts of the country, the farmers could expect to show a profit of three thousand dollars a year; and that was after having worked on the project for a period of only eight months. Those four months off would allow for the inclement winter weather which a person could expect if you lived in the Western Kentucky area.

Derek's plan also required of the farmers to dig their own fishponds; but if there was one thing that he knew for sure about farmers was that they certainly weren't afraid of a little hard work.

The problem was, however, Booster had no real evidence to support the facts relating to the annual dollar amount of profit that the farmers could expect to earn from the fish farms: for in all actuality he'd manufactured those numbers in order to fit them into his somewhat overblown sales presentation; but as Booster was fond of saying, "Absence of evidence is not absence of fact".

Nonetheless, the first ten farmers that Booster had approached with the fish farm plan seemed quite receptive to the idea; and as such, each of them had come up with the twelve hundred dollar deposit. Although the next man on his list of prospects was a farmer by the name of Grant Tolliver who just also happened to be a Baptist Minister. Reverend Tolliver had listened attentively and politely to Booster's sales pitch, but then when Booster asked him for the twelve hundred dollar deposit, the reverend answered him with a statement of his own.

"When pigs fly," he said, and that'd pretty well ended the conversation. "And besides," as the pastor continued, "God always has and always will provide for us."

It was also at that point in time when the reverend inquired about Booster's spiritual condition; and since the reverend was obligated to carry the Gospel to the sinners he wouldn't take no for an answer until Booster agreed to attend Reverend Tolliver's Southern Baptist Church on the following Sunday morning.

To his credit, however, Booster did indeed keep his word to the preacher: for he actually did attend the pastor's church service on the following Sunday morning; and at the end of the service, as was customary, the pastor asked everybody in the church to bow their heads and to close their eyes.

Of course the bowing of heads would just naturally be followed by a musical arrangement called the "Altar Call" which is a fairly common practice in many of the Baptist Churches. And as the more frequent visitors are aware, that particular part of the service is an open invitation to the people who may wish to come forward so that they might receive God's forgiveness for their sins; and if they feel the need to be saved, then it also affords them the opportunity to accept Jesus Christ as their personal savior.

Then somewhat amazingly, it was at that very moment when a strange and wonderful feeling came over Booster; and even stranger was the fact that he couldn't seem to resist the urge to rise up and then walk towards the altar where he kneeled and began to confess his sins before God, Reverend Tolliver, and all of the rest of his friends and neighbors.

At that very moment, Booster had not only asked God to forgive him for all the mistakes that he'd made while involved in the pyramid schemes, but also for all of the wrong things that he'd done while stationed in the Philippine Islands. Eventually, though, Booster was able to rise up from his knees; and then once he'd regained his composure he pleaded openly with the preacher for permission to share his confession and testimony with the entire congregation.

Then right there in front of God and the parishioners, Booster vowed that the monies that the farmers had invested with him to furnish the seed stock on their uncompleted fish farms would be returned to them with interest. Then after the entire congregation had said amen in unison, the preacher asked Booster to please come back for both the Wednesday night prayer meeting and the following Sunday's service just so he could once again share his testimony with the congregation; for in the preacher's eyes, it was beginning to look as if God might have called Derek to serve.

Chapter Nine

Ever since they'd first migrated from West Virginia to Kentucky, religion and hard work were certainly nothing new to the Christian family; and of course Derek was well aware of the fact that he'd come from a long line of farmers, railroaders, coalminers and Baptist Ministers. So in keeping with the family's traditional few of Derek's family members had always insisted on staging their own personal Tent Revival Meetings in and around the Western Kentucky area.

And more often than not, it was Derek's mother who played the piano during those church revivals while his father did most of the singing. Though as a rule, it was his grandfather, Samuel Christian, who did most of the preaching. To a child, those summertime revivals were exciting and most pleasurable; and Derek had many a fond memory of the times when he'd sat on a front row bench beneath that huge tent while at the same time dangling his bare feet in the sawdust which had just recently been scattered upon the bare earth.

Then at the end of the revival service, the nice ladies of the area would more often than not serve the Christian family a box lunch of chicken dinners along with warm milk which had come straight from a cow; and on certain occasions the ladies might even bring along some fresh homemade pies or some apple pan dowdies.

In those days, the love of religion was definitely a passion in the Western Kentucky region: and not only was Derek expected to attend church services every Sunday morning, but he'd also been commanded to attend the Wednesday evening prayer service. So while growing up, attending church was as much a part of his normal routine as was his schooling and farm work. And even when he'd traveled along with his high school basketball team to the Kentucky State finals he was expected to attend church at least one time while there.

For Derek, his new way of living had left him feeling free and clean. And then once all of the fish farm money had been returned to the farmers, it wasn't long before some of the leaders of the area churches started asking Derek to speak at their churches. So when the Southern Baptist Conference announced that they would schedule their next annual convention in the city of Nashville, Tennessee nobody in the area was any too surprised when the local ministers nominated Derek and Reverend Tolliver to represent them at the convention. Of course only Reverend Tolliver would have the authority to be able to vote on any of the many policy changes they could expect to confront that year.

Although just as surprisingly, Reverend Tolliver was determined to try to convince the convention committee members to allow Derek to speak to the entire audience of ministers; and this was in spite of the fact that Derek had not as yet been ordained. Even so, Reverend Tolliver was convinced that Derek Christian had been called to serve the Lord.

Nonetheless, until it was actually time for the two men to head off to the convention in Nashville, Derek would continue to work on his father's farm; and naturally, he would also try to spend as much time as he could with finance' Babs and his two childhood friends, Tug and Cliff.

Chapter Ten

On the day before the Southern Baptist Convention was scheduled to begin, Derek and Reverend Tolliver loaded their luggage into one of the church's old gray vans before heading on down towards Nashville, Tennessee. Thus with Derek's brand new Sunday-go-to-meeting suit hanging in the rear of the vehicle, he related a story to Reverend Tolliver about the almost daily joke that his school chums had played on him while he was still in school. It seemed as if one of his childhood friends could almost always be counted on to ask him how long he'd been a Christian: then of course, he would just naturally tell them that he'd always been a Christian. Now, however, it was actually true and not just because his surname was Christian.

After arriving in Nashville, the two men would then, of course, become actively involved in the day-to-day work at the conference. They would also discover that it would take a full five days of routine and sometimes quite boring discussion meetings before the Southern Baptist Conference member's committee would get around to voting on the newly recommended changes in policy. Then once back home in their respective states, the ministers would submit the recommendations to their own parishioners and church deacons who would either accept or reject the suggestions.

At the conference, the two men would discover that Saturday was always one of the most important days of the entire convention: for as a rule, that's generally the day that the guest speakers engage the audience with what the organizers hope will be their splendid oratory gifts; and so naturally, Reverend Tolliver thought it would be only fitting if Derek were allowed to stand before the convention members and deliver his well rehearsed speech on that fateful Saturday afternoon.

The placing of Derek's name on the roster along with the well-known dignitaries from around the country had not been an easy task; but then primarily because of Reverend Tolliver's lifelong association with the organization, and also quite possibly because of his persistence, the members of the board had no choice then but to relent. Nevertheless, the real shocker came later on that same day when a representative from a newly formed Christian Television Broadcasters network approached the two men and offered to buy them dinner. Then after the normal dinner conversation had subsided, the man who claimed that he presented a well-respected religious broadcasting network hinted that he might just have a very interesting offer for them to consider.

Unfortunately, though, Derek and Reverend Tolliver would have to return back home to Western Kentucky and then wait another several more days before they would eventually receive the long-awaited phone call from the president of the Christian Television Broadcasting Corporation with whom they'd dined when they were in Nashville. And when the phone call finally came, the two men were pleasantly surprised when they received an invitation to travel to Atlanta, Georgia in order to discuss a possible contractual agreement with the president of the network.

Of course it was only natural that the two men should be excited about making the trip to Atlanta; for as Reverend Tolliver was fond of saying, they were just simply trying to do God's work. But then after arriving in Atlanta, they were immediately directed to the office of the president of the broadcasting corporation, a certain Mr. Fergus K. Denton, who produced a voluminous file, which he said, had been painstakingly compiled by a team of private investigators. The file also included some documents from various law enforcement agencies.

From then on, Mr. Denton hardly ever mentioned the investigative file again; he did, however, explain in great detail just exactly what the corporation would expect of Derek if the broadcasting company decided to prep and then train him for a life that would be spent primarily in front of their television cameras.

It soon became apparent to Derek and Reverend Tolliver that Mr. Denton was a man of very few words: for he almost immediately went straight to the point by telling them that his religious broadcasting network already had millions of daily viewers; and also that, they owned dozens of affiliate television stations spread out across the U. S. and Canada. Even so, Mr. Denton had to concede the fact that his broadcasting network might not be as well-known as the Pat

Roberts or the Jerry Falwell networks. Then again, he said that he honestly believed that if they were to find the right T. V. personality then his corporation would be capable of attracting a much larger portion of the religious broadcasting television audience.

Whether such a statement was intended as flattery or not, Derek had no way of knowing. Derek was also told that since he was blessed with a photogenic countenance, and that he also owned a pleasant and resonating voice, Mr. Denton believed that those two qualities alone would help to attract new viewers: or at the very least, it would help for a while. "Of course on down the road a new T. V. personality had better have some other qualities or else he couldn't expect to last very long in a medium such as television," Denton said.

Lastly, Mr. Denton stated that his corporate people had polled the Nashville audience following Derek's thirty minute speech at the convention and they'd discovered that the majority of those interviewed said that they could feel the sincerity flowing out of Derek's soul.

Denton then said that he would be terribly disappointed if Derek didn't eventually become one of the most influential televangelist in the entire country; that is, of course, once after he'd been properly trained and refined by his corporation's promotional teams.

Even so, Derek and Reverend Tolliver were somewhat taken aback when Denton handed them a rather lengthy contract to read. And not so surprisingly, the very first paragraph in the contract said that in order for Derek to become a televangelist for Denton's Christian Broadcasting Corporation, he must first become an ordained minister. On the other hand, though, Derek was told that for the time being he needn't worry himself too much about such minor details; and especially since it'd already been arranged for him to attend some classes in theology and public speaking at a well respected Seminary located in the Midwest.

The next paragraph in the numerously paged contract was something that the men from Western Kentucky had already expected; it stated that the executives of the corporation most definitely desired that Derek should immediately get married. Mr. Denton then said that, "he already knew all about Derek's finance' Barbara Holton and her volatile family, but that he considered the situation to be a minor problem which could be resolved by simply keeping her out of the lime light."

The wording in the contract also affirmed that Derek would immediately begin to receive a base salary from the corporation; but then after the program had been on T. V. for a while, his annual income would be commensurate with the total dollar amount of donations and membership fees that were almost surely bound to follow. Even so, both Reverend Tolliver and Mr. Denton were somewhat stunned when Derek slid the contract back across the desk while politely declining the offer.

"Before I could even think about doing God's work I would first have to feel that I am properly qualified. Likewise, I would also have to feel in my own heart that I have truly been called to serve the Lord," Derek said.

But then after carefully picking up the papers from the desk, Mr. Denton began to read aloud the last paragraph of the contract. "Derek Christian will submit a ten thousand word essay to this corporate office by no later than fourteen days from the date of this interview. In the essay, he will outline his views on religion and on the role he thinks that the church should play in the lives of all men and women."

"We too, want to be sure that you have been chosen to serve the Lord," Denton said.

Chapter Eleven

Then after returning back home to Kentucky, Derek began to put on paper just exactly what he thought the churches of today needed to achieve in order to better serve all of humanity. Thus, while writing in his personal journal, he avowed that he would ask God to deliver unto us everything that was good for mankind. He'd also decided that his essay would define his own opinions on man's three main concerns while here on earth.

In the essay, Derek wrote that in his opinion God was the absolute beginning and the end: for without God there would be no humans or churches. Secondly, would be Derek's opinion of mankind which he considered to be nothing more than the children of God. Thirdly, he would spell out his own personal opinions of the churches of today: which he regarded as a total entity; and by doing so, Derek felt that he could best define God by using just two words; omnipresent and infinite.

Nevertheless, Derek was more than a little surprised to find that the study of mankind could be a far greater challenge to master than he'd previously believed; for without some kind of divine guidance in his life he was limited to just one man's experience, his own.

Derek would find that defining the church would prove to be the most difficult part of trying to honestly describe the trilogy; and this was particularly evident in his writings which had so glaringly exposed the fact that his religious education had been limited exclusively to the study of the protestant persuasion of religion.

Nonetheless, after only a few more days of intense prayer and meditation, a feeling came over Derek that a power greater than himself had entered his very being; and also, that the power had actually begun to direct his thinking.

So when he was writing the essay for Mr. Denton, Derek tried his level best to describe in detail what he knew about the world's major religions by listing a few of their accomplishments and their failures. Thus what little Derek had learned about the history of the church in general, his understanding was that Christianity had first begun in the Middle-East and Asia Minor as a faction of Judaism. Then later on, it'd evolved into a completely separate religion which was eventually embraced by an Eastern Roman leader. In the end, however, Christianity would become the official religion of the Roman Empire; and from there, it would be spread out across much of the rest of the world. To Derek, it appeared as if Catholicism must have evolved from the early Christian Church.

Islam, Derek had discovered, is a very old religion that's best defined by the teachings of the Prophet Mohamed and which is similar to the way that Christianity has been influenced by the life of Jesus Christ; and as Derek had come to discover, both of those religions continue to serve the same God; albeit, some nations prefer to use different names when describing their deities.

Then too, both the Hindu and Buddhist religions are also very old; and then along with some of the other major religions of the world they still continue to satisfactorily serve their millions of their followers.

In any case, Derek was beginning to think that all of the religions of the world have one major drawback; and that simply is the fact that they don't have a central clearing house which could be used for the discussion of their religious views and differences.

Therefore, he thought that what the world needed most was some sort of a united nations of religion; or perhaps even, a new world order which could be called something as benign as "The Spiritual House of Worship" or "The House of Spirituality". Derek honestly felt that the major religions of the world should focus on trying to become more alike rather than trying to prove how differently they believed in their own version of God.

Yet when Mr. Denton had the chance to read Derek's rather lengthy essay, he at first was struck with a strange feeling that he was reading something from a book called Mein Kamp, (My Struggle), which was written many years ago by a person named Adolph Hitler. For in his book, Hitler had outlined his plans for Germany's Nazi Party to completely dominate the world.

Although initially, Mr. Denton was moved to dismiss the thought that Derek was attempting to promulgate such a controversial idea of having all the leaders of the world's churches under one organization's control; and especially since the views expressed by Derek in his somewhat dark essay might have had more to do with the arrogance of youth. He also suspected that Derek might have simply been trying to impress the board members with his revolutionary ideas. That said, Denton was confident that his future T. V. star's thinking would level out somewhat after his sojourn at the seminary.

Chapter Twelve

Then somewhat prophetically, on the very day that Derek was scheduled to graduate from the seminary, the dean invited him into his office just so he could personally award him the diploma. Yet all throughout the one-on-one meeting with Derek, the learned Doctor of Theology certainly didn't believe that the graduation certificate he was about to hand over to Derek should be considered a legitimate diploma. For in his opinion the entire thing was nothing but a charade; and that it was also more akin to the honorary degrees which on certain occasions are handed out to some of the more famous politicians and actors.

By the same token, the dean had only to assume that the broadcasting company in Atlanta must have made a sizeable contribution to the board of directors of the seminary in order for them to be able to coerce the leaders of such a prestigious school of theology into considering such an outrageous act of actually graduating this pretender.

Then too, the dean must have mightily regretted the fact that his retirement date was still so far ahead in the future: for if his retirement date had only been a little nearer he would have simply stepped down from his post rather than lower his school's integrity and dignity by having to personally offer up such a phony diploma to someone he considered to be nothing more than a smalltime conman.

Yet when the unpleasant conversation with Derek was thankfully over and done with, the dean began to wonder if his first estimation of this future televangelist might have been off target. For when their conversation had finally ended, it'd become patently clear to the dean as to why the people at the broadcasting corporation were so keen on this young man.

But what was also truly amazing to the dean was that he'd completely forgotten to ask Derek any of the questions which he'd previously planned on presenting to him: and therefore, the only singular thing that he could think of at the time was to ask Derek if he believed in God. Then somewhat surprisingly, Derek replied that he did indeed believe in some type of God. Then almost unbelievably, Derek had the audacity to ask the dean the following question, "To whom does God pray?"

The dean was completely aghast by what he considered to be the most sacrilegious statement that he'd ever heard; in fact, it was all he could do to just shove the graduation completion certificate into Derek's waiting hands before then hurriedly exiting the room.

Chapter Thirteen

Then once back home in Kentucky Derek decided that he desperately needed a few days of rest and relaxation before he and Babs would allow Reverend Tolliver to marry them in his small, wood framed church. Eventually, though, the marriage ceremony was finally scheduled to take place; and it would, of course, be well represented by both sides of their large families. But then just as some of their family members people had feared would happen, all four of Bab's brothers showed up smelling strongly of alcohol; thankfully, though, nobody got their ears sliced off.

Regrettably, though, their somewhat shortened honeymoon could have just as easily been called a busman's holiday: for as soon as the wedding ceremony was officially over and done with, the two newlyweds would then once again be headed back to Nashville where they hoped to catch a few shows at the Grand Ole Opry before driving on down to Atlanta, Georgia where Derek was planning on introducing his new bride to Mr. Denton.

Of course the time that they were to spend in the city of Atlanta could be called anything but a vacation; and especially since Derek was required to spend the first two days in the city by visiting a barber shop and various men's clothing stores. On the third day, however, he began a new regimen which consisted of sitting in front of a live television camera for a period of no more than two hours in the morning and then once again in the evening.

Amazingly, though, after only a week's time from the date of Derek's very first telecast, the phone calls, the emails, and the letters began to pour in by the tens of thousands. Then also luckily for both Derek and the broadcasting corporation, most of the comments were deemed quite favorable. By then, however, another very strange phenomenon had come to pass. That being that dozens of pastors from around the country were calling the network to ask if Derek would be available to speak at their churches.

In time, the newly minted televangelist would become so popular that the recently formed Christian Television Broadcasting Corporation would have to hire additional clerks just to open the mail; and not so surprisingly, a few of the letters from the T. V. audience had even included some marriage proposals.

The broadcasting company's motto must have been, "Let's make hay while the sun shines," for after only a month following Derek's first televised program the corporation came up with cleverly named revival which was to be called "The Great American Crusade" which was scheduled to embark upon an extended tour of sixty some odd American cities. And in the event that the domestic crusade proved to be a rounding success, it was hinted that a European tour might even be in the offing.

Thus with the upcoming crusade in the front of his mind, Derek's sermons were ever so slowly beginning to be based on the themes of peace, unity and harmony; and not so surprisingly, it seemed as if the public just couldn't get enough of his style of preaching. Apparently, Derek had that remarkable and unique ability of being able to speak out against the most controversial subjects, such as war and discrimination, without offending even the most ardent war hawk generals in the Pentagon, or any of the members of the minorities or the majorities.

So without a doubt, the latest televangelist to grace our modern-day airways would almost assuredly feel the need to speak out about the importance of practicing more patience and tolerance towards one another. Though on other occasions, Derek would implore the leaders of the wealthiest nations of the world to do more to help the less fortunate. And even though a few of the world's best known religious leaders had made similar statements in the past, Derek's speeches didn't seem to fall on deaf ears as theirs had done.

For when the global television audiences began to take note as to what Derek Christian was actually saying, then they too began to believe that something as simple as feeding the hungry people of the world might just prevent some of the future wars.

Unfortunately for Derek, however, more than a few people around the world were beginning to believe that he'd already crossed that invisible line which theoretically separates the church from the state: and so naturally, it was being reported that he'd already ruffled more than a few feathers when he began asking the people of the world to vote only for the leaders who promised them peace and prosperity instead of more violence.

What's more, just immediately following one of Derek's more vocal diatribes against the slaughter of the innocents of the world, the citizens of some of those counties which had previously been ruled by a long line of despots and dictators had begun to demand their right to choose their own religious and democratic leaders. Then shortly thereafter, several new leaders were installed in a few of those countries which had never before known democracy.

Though what happened next could have almost been prophesied: for in a very short period of time, an amazing phenomenon had begun to take place. It seemed as if the citizens of the world had decided to depose of all the warmongering egomaniacs and dictators who'd led them down the path of ruin and destruction; and if any of those tyrannical dictators chose not to peacefully step down from office, then they were disposed of by violent means. However, those isolated instances of violence were immediately denounced by, "The House of Spirituality and Harmony," which by then was what Derek's brand-new nondenominational broadcasting network was being called.

So in view of the latest happenings it was beginning to look as if the citizens of world were no longer willing to accept the politics of old; and it also appeared that they were no longer willing to tolerate the dictators of any cut of the cloth.

Hence, for the millions of the members of Derek's nondenominational mega-church, it must have seemed as if the day of reckoning was upon them: and as a direct result millions of people around the world were beginning to sing the praises of the new prince of peace; and this was particularly true of the younger people of the world who'd elevated their new religious leader and spiritual advisor into an almost cult type of figure.

Then too, owing to the rapid advance of new developments in the electronics' industry, Derek's daily televised program was able to feature a segment whereby electronic e-mails from around the world could be flashed on the television screen where they would instantly be translated into the language of the local television viewing audience.

Moreover, the arenas and the stadiums in the major cities of the U. S. where Derek's organization chose to appear were always filled with a standing room only crowd; this then made the American Crusade a huge success. Furthermore, every single one of the corporation's productions would not only be televised around the world live, but they would also be available on same-day-tape via the commercial satellite networks. So naturally, it was no small wonder that Derek Christian was beginning to replace some of the modern-day sports heroes as one of the world's best known personalities.

Chapter Fourteen

Yet regardless of the tremendous success that the crusade had produced so far, Derek was hearing some distant rumblings coming from his hometown in Western Kentucky; and yet, those rumblings weren't emanating from any of the leaders of the churches back home, or at least not yet.

Instead, the rumblings in the Western Kentucky area were being caused by a completely different set of circumstances; for as the scientists around the world were well aware of, there's a large crack in the earth's crust in the middle of the United States which had aptly been named the New Madrid Fault. This particular fault runs mainly from north to south and then all throughout the Midwestern states of Missouri, Arkansas, Illinois, Indiana, Kentucky and Tennessee with the epicenter being centered in New Madrid, Missouri.

Although luckily for the people who live in that region, the area surrounding that particular fault hasn't been subjected to a major earthquake in a very long time. In fact, the last serious quake in that part of the country occurred during the winter months of the years eighteen hundred eleven and twelve with one of the quakes being so powerful that the Mississippi River had actually been forced to flow backwards; and then also according to the scientist, the quake was responsible for creating an enormous new lake in the northwest corner of Tennessee which the officials had named Reelfoot Lake.

Yet also just as amazingly, when the historic quake occurred it was recorded in the newspapers that the people who lived on the Eastern Seaboard of the United States could feel the earth move.

Still, Derek wasn't too terribly concerned with the possibility of lightening striking in the same place twice. In fact, Derek was about to discover that the latest rumblings back home weren't actually being caused by the New Madrid Fault Line in Missouri. But since the quakes were occurring close by to their homes in Western Kentucky, this caused Babs to firmly insist that they should immediately return to their homes in case they had to evacuate their families from the region.

Anyway, the worry over the minor quakes back home might have been a blessing in disguise since "The Great American Crusade Tour" had taken such a physical and mental toll on the two of them they'd already decided that a well earned vacation was definitely in order. Then too, Derek was also anxious to return home just so he could check up on the progress of the construction project that was currently underway on the church he'd attended as a child.

Chapter Fifteen

Once back home in Western Kentucky, then the first thing that Derek had planned on doing was to inspect a part of the new construction that he was especially proud of; and that primarily had to do with the structural changes in the eastern part of the church where the apse and altar were to be located. And per his instructions, the contractor had installed a wall to wall viewing screen which extended from the floor to the top of the newly heightened ceiling.

Unfortunately, though, in order to display the immensely large screen properly, it meant that the baptismal tank and the choir's seating arrangements would have to be removed from the area directly behind the pulpit; this then meant that the only remaining symbol of a Christian church would be the twenty-four by forty-eight inch, gold plated metal cross that weighed just over forty-two pounds and was scheduled to be hung high upon the front of the apse but then directly above the podium. It seems that Reverend Tolliver had found that particular cross for sale on the internet and had commented to Derek that he must have it.

Also as luck would have it, none of their new office buildings, or even the newly remolded church, had suffered any major damage from the recent minor earthquake; and therefore, Derek and Babs decided to travel on to Atlanta where they could help the network complete the preparations that were already underway for the upcoming world tour that would include a stopover at many of the world's capitals.

Of course it goes without saying that both Derek and the executives at the broadcasting corporation were cognizant of the enormous logistical problems that they would encounter while on the upcoming world tour; for just the moving of the hundreds of tons of equipment around the globe, and then along with, of course, the making of the hotel reservations for the dozens of people that would accompany the tour would require a tremendous amount of planning and effort.

But since money was no longer an issue, and also if the organizers didn't come across any other insurmountable problems, the world tour would take place as planned. For according to the latest poll which had been conducted by a well respected business magazine, Derek's broadcasting network was already in control of a sizeable percentage of all the monies of the world.

As a matter of fact, even Reverend Tolliver was amazed to discover that a single televangelist could amass as much wealth as some of the smaller Third World Countries had in their treasuries; and yet, he knew it to be true because he'd personally seen the broadcasting companies' bank statements. And even though the world had become a much smaller place, it was still rather difficult for Reverend Tolliver to believe that one person could leave such an indelible mark on the politics of the world as Derek had done.

Chapter Sixteen

In order to guarantee the success of the upcoming world tour, a maelstrom of publicity would just necessarily have to precede the crusade. And of course, all of the pre-planning would be extremely helpful in filling the tens of thousands of seats in the various arenas and stadiums in the cities which Derek and his team had selected to visit.

Also at that point in time, Derek was beginning to believe that it was the substance of his sermons which had caused the multitudes to come over to his way of thinking. On the other hand, though, not every one of the world's political and religious leaders had rushed out to endorse his somewhat controversial message. That said, many of the world's leaders were somewhat reluctant to criticize him publicly. As such, a situation of that nature must have caused some of the world's leaders to feel as if they were walking on egg shells. But from what they'd already seen of Derek, some of those same leaders had become more than a little leery of what the future might hold for them and the rest of mankind.

Though still not wanting to be outdone by anybody, the Civil Life's Union had made a decision which had puzzled everybody in the country including Reverend Tolliver. For years, the Union had primarily been terrorizing the churches and the communities across the United States with their incessant lawsuits concerning the legal rights of the county authorities to display certain monuments such as the Ten Commandments or anything else that had to do with religion on their courthouse lawns. Now, they were actually threatening to take Derek's organization to court over of the fact that his broadcasting corporation was named "The House of Spirituality and Harmony."

In the Union's opinion, the broadcasting corporation that owned, "The House of Spirituality and Harmony" was seducing people into handing over their hard-earned money in the guise of donating to a religious organization, when in fact, nowhere in name or deed did Derek's broadcasting company ever claim to be connected with any church whatsoever. Therefore, the Union postulated the opinion that since Derek's organization didn't meet the basic foundation of law which governs houses of worship, then they should not be entitled to a tax-free exemption which was normally only granted to a regularly established church," or so said the Union.

Then around that same point in time, another very interesting Op-Ed had begun to appear in some of the free presses of the world when shortly after one of the Union's leading members stated publicly that Derek's broadcasting company should henceforth declare whether or not the entity was a legitimate church; and if not, then they should be forced to pay taxes like any other business.

Apparently, the news of this religious and political wrangling and infighting had made its way into Washington, D. C. where the newly elected President of the United States was a member of a brand-new and truly independent political party who also just happened to be an avid supporter of Derek's organization. Accordingly, then, when the President of the United States threatened to nominate two new judges to the Supreme Court that weren't particularly partial to the views of the Civil Life Union, the leaders of that organization went on back to their old game plan of harassing the politicians who manage the county courthouses across the country.

So with that particular crisis out of the way, the world crusade would continue to travel around the globe, until, that is, when it made its last planned stop which just happened to be in the Middle East where many hundreds of years ago numerous other religious crusades of quite a different nature had occurred; but since this particular crusade had instituted a theme of peace and harmony, and not of violence, it ended up being very well received in the part of the world which has historically been known as the Levant.

The world tour was a monumental success: and since Babs was eight months pregnant, the Christian family decided that they would immediately return to the Western Kentucky area in order to await the birth of their first child.

Chapter Seventeen

"It's good to be home," Derek thought, for it'd been three long years and six months since he'd last preached in the church where he'd spent much of his childhood. He was also looking forward to dedicating his newly remodeled church so that he and Babs could have an ideal place in which to baptize their first child.

In the meantime, however, there was a tremendous amount of church business that required Derek's immediate attention. For in addition to the issues concerning the remodeling project, he was almost totally absorbed with the training of the dozens of new employees who desperately needed his help with the planning of the upcoming "Second Great American Crusade."

So expressly because of the labor intensive training projects that he was involved in, Derek was forced to spend an inordinate amount of time with his new office staff: and one of which just happened to be an attractive young woman by the name of Olivia Morton who'd originally been hired to be his private secretary. And even though many of the other employees considered that particular lady to be a godsend to the organization, she'd developed a habit of overzealously safeguarding Derek's time to such a degree that made Babs feel as if she needed an appointment just to get in to see her own husband.

In fact, it was during those extremely busy times when Derek was forced to spend the better part of his waking hours in the newly remodeled church office building that Babs would occasionally walk the short distance between their home and the newly constructed office building just so she could have a face-to-face conversation with her husband. Babs knew, of course, that the upcoming crusade would demand an ever increasing amount of his time and efforts; and so naturally he wouldn't be able to share much of his time with her.

On one particular occasion, however, when the outer office receptionist was away from her desk, Babs had entered Derek's private office without first knocking where she surprised Derek and Olivia who appeared to be involved in a very intimate conversation but had ended suddenly when they realized that someone else was in the room.

Then later on that same evening, Babs made it perfectly clear to her husband that she was very upset over what she believed she'd witnessed earlier that day when she'd entered his private office. So from then on, their agreement was that he would either move his private secretary to one of the other offices, or at the very least he would stop working so closely with her.

So in order to keep the peace in the family, Derek just naturally agreed to his wife's most earnest demands; but in the days following that particular incident Babs had noticed that anytime that Derek had to work late at the office Olivia's Red Ford Taurus automobile was almost always parked in the lot behind the church.

For Babs, the situation at home had become almost unbearable; and even though she was greatly concerned about the real possibility of Derek having a relationship with Olivia she'd forced herself to concentrate mainly on having a normal delivery of their yet unborn baby. Babs had decided that she would cross that other bridge when she got to it; but Derek also knew that the Holtons weren't the kind of people that could take a personal affront lying down.

Chapter Eighteen

Thankfully, though, the delivery of their first child came off without incident and the couple was blessed with a healthy and handsome baby boy. Babs was also grateful that her husband was spending less time at the office which she'd primarily attributed to the arrival of their newborn son. But she also suspected that his desire to avoid the people at the office was due in part to the discouraging news reports that were appearing almost daily on all of the major television networks.

For during that terrible period there were frequent accounts of the brand new wars that were being fought all across the globe; and then along with the wars, there were a record-breaking number of famines and other disasters which seemed to be springing up from all around the globe. And during one particular day while Derek was suffering a case of severe depression, he told Babs that he was beginning to wonder if "The House of Spirituality and Harmony" Broadcasting Network might be facing doom and disaster.

The dire situations at home and around the world were having such a profound effect on Derek's disposition that Babs was forced to ask Reverend Tolliver to have a little talk with him. She knew, of course, that if Derek would listen to anybody it would be Reverend Tolliver. Babs considered Reverend Tolliver to be one of the best men that she'd had ever known. In fact, the very worst thing that she'd ever heard him say was when he admitted that after hearing a fire truck's siren in his neighborhood he'd silently prayed for the fire truck to stop at someone else's home and not his church.

So then later on that very same evening, but only after some additional prodding from Babs, Reverend Tolliver showed up at their home where the two men prayed together for several hours straight before they even began to discuss the plans for the upcoming all new American Crusade.

Reverend Tolliver had always felt that he knew his protégé better than anybody else on earth. Nevertheless, even Reverend Tolliver was beginning to worry about Derek's mental condition. For as a matter of fact he'd told Babs that there were subjects being discussed between him and Derek that were better off left unsaid.

In the end, however, Reverend Tolliver said that he wasn't overly concerned about Derek's momentary lack of discretion: "for as we all know, promiscuity is a condition that many a good man has fallen prey to."

Reverend Tolliver sincerely believed that infidelity is such a common human frailty that he was willing to overlook Derek's case of temporary insanity; and particularly since lust is most generally just "the lack of opportunity or the fear of oppression" that keeps most men on the straight and narrow.

That said, Tolliver was more than a little concerned about Derek's spiritual condition; and particularly since the newest line of sermons which Derek had written for the upcoming American tour had so many maxims and pithy statements inserted into the text that the entire context of the speech sounded more like the dictates of a despot or a Czar than those of a prince of peace.

Yet luckily for all those involved, Derek was gracious enough to allow Reverend Tolliver to tone his sermons down somewhat; and in addition to that, Reverend Tolliver made Derek promise that in the upcoming crusade he would speak only of love, patience, and tolerance.

Chapter Nineteen

Fortunately for Derek's broadcasting corporation, the entire east coast portion of the Second Great American Crusade had ended on a high note: and it was beginning to look as if the total attendance for the west coast revivals might even outpace the huge numbers which had been posted by the first American Crusade; then again, it helped immensely that the broadcasting network had added some additional affiliate T. V. and radio stations to its ever-growing family.

Nonetheless, the executives at the broadcasting corporation had only to assume that Derek's message was becoming more popular throughout the global community. For by then, it was sincerely believed by all that the recent high numbers of natural disasters from around the world had frightened everyone so badly that they were even more inclined to believe that the people of the world needed someone like Derek Christian to pray for their safety and salvation. Yet to Derek's way of thinking it seemed as if the entire plethora of those natural disasters was necessary in order to make the average person even more keenly aware of his or her own mortality.

So in order to capitalize on the modern-day misfortunes of the citizens of the world, Derek had begun telling his millions of followers that they should depend wholly on the one person in the world who could successfully pray for their salvation. But in addition to the prayers, Derek had also suggested that they needed somebody who knew what was best for them; and then of course, that person would be Derek Christian.

Thus, during that tumultuous period in history there seemed to be no limit to Derek's power and popularity around the globe and at home; and since "The House of Spirituality and Harmony" had no enemies, per se`, there was never any doubt in Derek's mind that his loyal followers would continue to do his bidding. In fact, Derek's power and popularity had become so immense that one of Europe's leading newspapers was forced to shut completely down when after the publisher had so brazenly denounced Derek's broadcasting network as being just one more money grabbing entity.

Though what was so truly amazing to Derek's friends and enemies alike was the fact that only three and one half years had passed since Derek had first begun to preach his themes of love, peace, and tolerance; and yet, Derek's magnetic personality had somehow managed to conquer more human minds and souls than all of the previous televangelists put together.

Ultimately, though, the faint rumblings of discontent could be heard from the members of Derek's own supporters: and that noise was particularly loud at the end of the west coast crusade when Derek told the members of The House of Spirituality and Harmony that they should insist that their governments issue an International I. D. card which a person would need in order to obtain any types of food stuffs; and then following that almost unbelievable edict from the so-called prince of peace, Derek very strongly then suggested that the I. D. cards should only be issued to the loyal members of "The House of Spirituality and Harmony".

Then almost unbelievably, tens of millions of people from around the world had decided to honor Derek's most outlandish request by inundating their respective governments with so many phone calls, letters, and e-mails that the leaders of those countries had seriously begun to consider that most bizarre suggestion.

The question is, however, how in the world could a group of supposedly normal and well educated people allow such a thing to happen; then again, similar tragedies had occurred in certain parts of Europe both before and during the Second World War

Yet regardless of the recent criticism which had been leveled against Derek and his so-called church, there were still plenty of people around the globe who'd begun to wonder if the end of the world really was at hand. But to make matters even worse, that particularly alarming situation was then immediately followed by statements from a few of the world's more respected religious leaders who'd begun to speak openly about the real possibility of an actual Antichrist and the resulting battle of Armageddon which has long been prophesized as being the last conflict that will ever be fought on this earth.

Even so, a growing number of people from around the globe had steadfastly refused to believe that the battle of Armageddon would take place anytime in the near future. In fact, some of the world's more learned historians had previously stated that according to the Bible, the end of time on Earth will not come about until David's Temple has been completely rebuilt in the city of Jerusalem. It's also been said that the Israeli historians know where each and every stone from David's Temple is located.

In fact, the situation had deteriorated so badly that a few of the world's most trusted leaders were now saying that Derek Christian might just possibly be the most dangerous man on earth. And since it was almost impossible to keep the news reports away from Derek, both Babs and Reverend Tolliver were highly concerned that Derek might just be having a nervous breakdown. As a matter of fact, Derek's depression had worsened to such a degree that the people nearest to him were wondering if he might be in need of some psychiatric help.

Chapter Twenty

Then once finally back home in the sanctity and the security of their well protected enclave in Western Kentucky, Babs decided that the time had come for them to christen their son. But because of the structural changes in the newly remodeled church, this rite would have to take place without the benefit of a baptismal tank.

Hence with the wondrous event scheduled to take place during the following Sunday morning's service, and also since this would be such a momentous day for all those involved, both sides of their extended families would just naturally be invited to attend the service.

The long-awaited Sunday morning church service had finally arrived; and as soon as Reverend Tolliver had finished baptizing the child, he then handed the boy over to Derek, who at first, began to speak like the man they'd known for years. Suddenly, though, the words that were coming from Derek's mouth weren't recognizable to anybody. Of course that was primarily due to the fact that he wasn't speaking standard English.

Yet for a while longer, Derek continued to speak in a tongue which made him sound as if he were a man possessed. Eventually, though, Derek began to speak in a normal fashion. It was then, however, that Derek shocked the entire congregation by saying that he was baptizing his son in the name of The Father, The Son, The Holy Spirit, and Satan.

By pure instinct, Babs tried valiantly to wrench her son from her husband: but then just as she was about to successfully pull her son away from Derek's grip, she stumbled and fell forward off of the front of the stage. Luckily, though, two of her brothers just happened to be sitting in one of the front row pews and were able to come to her aid.

Then suddenly, all of the people in the church were frozen in their tracks. For at that very instant the floor of the church had begun to sway back and forth with such force that it caused the entire building to shake so violently that even the walls of the church were beginning to disintegrate.

The violent shaking of the building had also loosened the bolts that secure Reverend Tolliver's forty-two pound metal cross to the top of the wall that projects out from the semicircular apse which is located directly above the pulpit. And in an almost surreal way, the cross descended the twenty feet, or so, on a straight downward path until it struck Derek squarely on the top of his head with such force as to cause his immediate death. Amazingly, though, out of the destruction which had been visited upon the church, Derek Christian was the only person injured in the disaster.

For many years to come, the people in that part of the country would just naturally come to their own conclusions about what'd actually caused the destruction of their church: then of course, practically every person who lived in that area was well aware of the potential danger of living so nearby to the New Madrid Fault Line. Consequently, then, many of the locals were just naturally in agreement that an earthquake had most likely caused Derek's death.

Nonetheless, a great many of the local people, and even a good percentage of the people from around the world, would come to believe that Derek's death, and the destruction of his church, was simply the act of a vengeful entity that was restoring the earth and its people back into God's good graces. "Absolute power corrupts absolutely;" except, that is, when it's God's power.

Turtle Doves

Ever since the 9/11, 2001 terrorist attacks on New York City, the Pentagon building in Washington, D.C., and the tragic plane crash in Pennsylvania, the National Security Agency has increased the number of American spy agencies to over a dozen different organizations. Consequently, the need to hire tens of thousands of brand new employees meant there was always an outside chance that a few of those people would be woefully under qualified.

Murphy's Law would once again prove to be alive and well when just shortly after a division manager at the C. I. A. made the fateful decision to transfer Jeff Colburn out of the accounting department and into a more visible and overt department of the National Security Agency where the employees were not only encouraged to experiment with new and exciting ideas on how best to listen in on suspected terrorist's telephone conversations, but the bosses at the N. S. A. had actually approved a few of those high school science lab types of experiments whereby the newly chosen superspies were allowed to field test some of their most improbable ideas.

This transfer and promotion had suited Jeff just fine, and especially since for the past several years the former accountant had been toying with the notion of planting microchips into the bodies of a squadron of domesticated turtle doves which could be used to eavesdrop on our enemies. Yet even Jeff was surprised when his superiors at the N. S. A. approved this bold new venture of his.

Though in light of the tremendous successes that the highly valued squadrons of Carrier Pigeons had achieved during both of the World Wars while delivering literally thousands of vital military messages to the generals in the rear, the idea of using birds to spy on suspected foreign nationals had suddenly sounded quite plausible.

Jeff's working theory was that a plethora of the highly trained turtle doves would be loosed in the general area of a suspected terrorist's residence so that the birds could place themselves upon the exact and proper telephone wires that were known to be used by the people under surveillance. Of course, the people on Jeff's team would have needed to have previous knowledge as to just exactly which telephone line was being used by the suspected terrorists in order for the birds to know where to position themselves.

And since a good many of the foreign embassies are located in the Washington, D. C. area, Jeff's superiors decided to field test this new theory in the Nation's Capital. Accordingly, then, the turtle doves would be released just a short distance away from the targeted address where they would hopefully alight upon the telephone wires which were directly above the electronic-laden, but nondescript white van, which had previously been parked in the front of the selected embassy.

Then just shortly thereafter, a person on the embassy's roof commenced to raise the flag of the Tsar of Russia which proudly displays the two-headed eagle that stands as a symbol of Russian strength and fortitude. Then unbelievably, the man on the roof unleashed a full squadron of eagles of the rapture variety which attacked and then ate Jeff's highly trained turtle doves, microchips and all.

Alas, the Cold War had once again escalated to the point of an all-out conflict.

A Magnificent Donnybrook

A few months after the last presidential inauguration an historical event of unprecedented proportions was about to take place. For the first time ever America could boast of having eight living ex- presidents which consisted of four Democrats and four Republicans. And not so surprisingly, all eight of them were then summarily invited to attend a photo-op session which was scheduled to take place on our nation's birthday, the Fourth of July.

Naturally, the party was scheduled to take place in the Oval Office at the White House where all eight of the ex-presidents could be posed by the official White House photographer in such a way that would be somewhat familiar to those of us who had participated in a high school photo-op which would be to place the taller of the men in the rear. That said, the only other notable difference in the lineup was that the photographer had staggered the men in the front row so as to allow the camera to catch a full body shot of each man.

At first, the room was filled with much laughter and gaiety. Unfortunately, though, a few resentments from the past came bursting forth which changed the otherwise friendly ethos of the group into a snarling and bitter convention of some very mean acting old men. But since this untoward circumstance had not been anticipated from our highly respected former leaders, the Secret Service men had been posted in the hallway outside of the Oval Office.

Amazingly though, even after the first punch had been thrown, the official White House photographer kept screaming most vociferously to his able assistants for them to keep their cameras rolling. Then later on, it would come to light that the official photographer had voted for the runner-up in the last presidential election, and not for the duly elected president; it was also learned that he'd felt mightily spurned when his request to fill an open vacancy at the U. S. Embassy in Venezuela had been turned down. Apparently, the photographer had always dreamed of visiting the country that just happened to be the birthplace of his beloved and deceased father.

Ultimately, though, we were to learn that the main reason for the photographer's instant dismissal from his cushy job at the White House was simply the fact that he'd misguidedly used the opportunity to distribute his secretly taken cell phone photographs of the otherwise clandestine brawl around the world by-way-of YouTube and Facebook.

Nonetheless, the next scene in this most unforgettable drama could have only been surpassed by the bungling and the ineptness of the old-time silent motion picture stars, The Keystone Cops, for upon hearing what must have sounded like a barroom brawl, our brave members of the Secret Service went rushing wildly through the closed office doors with their guns drawn. Though as it turned out, it might have been bad timing for at that exact moment the lone Texan in the room had just hurled a straight back chair at the ex-president from the state of Georgia. Luckily, however, the thrown chair missed it mark; although it did take out a few of our brave Secret Service men.

Then not to be outdone, the two ex-presidents from the great state of Illinois most brutally attacked the wild man from Texas, who by then, was being somewhat protected by the former governor of California.

All in all it was quite a donnybrook: but nobody could have ever guessed what would happen next. For when it looked as if the brawl might be winding down, the lady Madam Secretary of the United States came rushing into the room with nothing less than a rolling pin in her hand with which she very deftly used to clobber one of the ex-presidents with!

Mirror Image

After a grueling fourteen hour day of continuous auditioning, Consuela Imelda Sanchez was extremely grateful to once again be back home in her small but comfortable New York City apartment. The day had gone extremely well for she'd just landed a leading role in a major Broadway musical production that was ready to go into rehearsals. Consuela knew full well that the landing of this particular role would ultimately be a major turning point in the career of any highly trained operatic singer and actress. She also knew that she'd fought long and hard to achieve this well-earned success.

Nothing in the world could upset her on this fine day, she thought. And even though the electronic opener on the front door of her lower East Side apartment building was still broken, at least the elevator was in good working order. Still, one would think that a thirteen hundred a month apartment would afford a person a safer and more secure place in which to dwell.

But then after exiting the elevator on the fourth floor of her apartment building she couldn't help but notice that the painters in the empty neighboring apartment had once again left the door wide open. Normally, an empty apartment on her floor wouldn't be too much of a concern to her, but with the front door buzzer still out of order she knew that it would be entirely too easy for a complete stranger to gain access to the empty apartment.

She was, however, extremely thankful to finally be alone in the quite confines of her own apartment where the first order of business would be to remove the heavy makeup that she'd been obligated to wear while auditioning for the leading role. The cleansing cream and the soapy water on her face seemed to revive her almost immediately. But then all of sudden a disturbing image seemed to flash across the deepest background of her medicine cabinet mirror.

At first, the image in the mirror appeared to be an exact representation of her own face. It was her face that she was seeing in the mirror, but then again it wasn't. And for some strange reason Consuela remembered reading a few vague verses from Leaves of Grass which was Walt Whitman's collection of poetry.

It seems that while riding the trains all throughout New York City, Whitman would posit the theory that every single person on the train was exactly like him, and that, he was exactly like everybody else on that same train. "I am him and he is me," or something like that, Consuela thought.

However, the images that Consuela was observing in her very own medicine cabinet mirror did not match concisely with her exact movements or expressions. As a result, she was left with the strangest feeling that she was reliving an old T. V. commercial in which the people who lived in the next-door apartment might actually be able to see, or even to speak with their neighbors if they just happened to open their own medicine cabinet door at the exact right time. Of course Consuela clearly understood the improbability of something like that ever happening. Nevertheless, she was also well aware of the fact that the neighboring apartment door had been left wide open.

"Was it possible that the workmen next-door were simply playing games with her," she wondered. If so, then there was nothing left for her to do but to go next door and check it out.

So with her house keys and a small canister of mace in hand, Consuela decided to thoroughly investigate what she feared were mighty strange goings on in the neighboring apartment. But upon entering the empty apartment she very quickly discovered that not only was there a light burning in the bathroom, but that the medicine cabinet door had been left standing ajar. Yet after taking a closer assessment of the readily apparent facts, she very quickly then determined that there was nothing else out of the ordinary to be found anywhere in the empty apartment.

She did, however, have to wonder if perhaps somebody had actually removed and then replaced the medicine cabinet in the next-door apartment. So after a bit of brainstorming, Consuela decided to return to the empty apartment where she thoroughly coated the medicine cabinet screws with some clear fingernail polish. Her figuring was that if anybody were to remove the screws, then she would certainly be able to recognize the ruse.

Then once back in her own bathroom, Consuela proceeded to place a small stepstool in front of her bathroom sink just so she could keep an eye on the medicine cabinet mirror while she sipped on the glass of Madeira wine that she was drinking while eating her micro waved spaghetti dinner.

Though what happened next was totally unexpected. The image in the mirror began to speak to her. "So Consuela, I imagine that you're feeling quite proud of yourself for landing that wonderful role in that brand new musical, aren't you?" The mirror image said. "And oh by the way, I personally feel that you butchered the intro in the first act.

"You know, I'm not quite sure that I'm supposed to be having a conversation with you; and especially since you are not really a live person," Consuela said. "Well that certainly strikes me as funny: do you then actually mean to say to me that you don't remember asking for my opinion during those myriad numbers of times that you had an important decision to make?" The image said.

"I wasn't necessarily talking to you, I was just thinking out loud," Consuela said. "We'll see," the image said. "But for now you'd better be getting yourself off to bed because tomorrow I don't want to have to drag your lazy butt all around the stage," the mirror image said.

Yet as she was trying to doze off to sleep, Consuela couldn't help but to continue to think about the strange conversation that she'd just had with herself; and it was her own self, wasn't it? For the time being, though, she wasn't too sure about anything. "Perhaps I'm just tired," she thought, as she fell into a very deep sleep.

Then early the next morning, Consuela was very rudely awakened by the loud buzzing of the alarm clock that she kept in her bedroom. She was, however, about to be suddenly and completely mystified by what she was seeing on the other side of the medicine cabinet mirror. Incredibly, the image in the mirror appeared to be wearing the very same clothing that Consuela had laid out from the evening before.

"Consuela, you'll just have to trust me on this; and please believe me when I say that it's all for the best," the image in the deepest part of the medicine cabinet mirror said.

"This can't be happening to me: and besides, I've always thought that I was doing a pretty good job at living life," Consuela said.

"To tell you the truth you were almost always wrong in the decisions you made; and therefore, I cannot allow you to mess up our lives anymore than you already have," the bathroom image said.

"So beginning today I plan to replace you in that musical production that you have worked so diligently to obtain; and thank you for that." "Unfortunately for you, however, you are to be banished to the confines of the medicine cabinet mirror for eternity," the new Consuela said.

Decibels Can Kill:
A Murder Mystery

Chapter One
Cause and Effect

Mitch Simmons had always been quite fond of reading Shakespeare, but then one day as he was leafing through the play "Macbeth" he found himself more than a little impressed with the following verse, "It will have blood; they say, blood will have blood." Then again, it wasn't so much that Mitch really needed any outside encouragement in order to commit the acts of revenge that he'd seriously been contemplating. This of course was the unfortunate death of his seven year old granddaughter who'd been run over and killed by a hit and run motorcyclist who Mitch suspected of not only driving recklessly at the time of the incident, but of also operating a motorcycle while intoxicated.

Unfortunately, however, by the time the Tulsa, Oklahoma Police Department had discovered that the suspected driver in the hit-and-run accident was an active member of a local motorcycle club from the North Tulsa area, the bike in question had already been reported stolen. Moreover, when the police located the bike that was alleged to have been involved in the hit-and-run fatality, they found that the bike in question had already been completely rebuilt with new parts. This then would almost certainly negate any real possibility of finding any incriminating blood or DNA evidence that might have been present on the damaged parts of the motorcycle.

Then to make matters even worse, when an impromptu news conference was held on the steps of the Tulsa County Courthouse, the prosecuting attorney, a certain Mr. Marion West, would cite the lack of any credible evidence as the main reason for not further pursuing a case of negligent homicide against the motorcyclist from the North Tulsa area. On the other hand, though, a spokesman for the Tulsa Police Department stated that, "in his opinion, the investigation against the suspected driver of the bike, one, Jeremy Ragland, should go forward even if the state decided not to prosecute the suspected hit-and-run biker."

From then on, the Tulsa Police Department would continue to consider Jeremy Ragland as a person of interest in the tragic death of the seven year old Tulsa girl who'd been run over and killed by a motorcyclist while playing in her grandfather's front yard. Although in hindsight, the investigation into the death of the seven-year-old girl seemed doomed to fail from the very beginning; and particularly since the owner of the bike had filed a police report stating that his motorcycle had been stolen from his home in North Tulsa on the very same day that the young girl had been run over and killed.

Consequently, then, without any eyewitnesses that could positively identify Mr. Ragland as being at the scene of the crime, and also without having any access to the damaged parts of the motorcycle which had purportedly been involved in the tragedy, the police were deprived of any forensics evidence.

Mitch knew, of course, that life must still go on; and after only a few months following the tragic death of his granddaughter he decided to seek some solace and peace of mind by doing a little solitary fishing at Skiatook lake which was a very popular lake that was located to the northwest of Tulsa and only about an hour's drive away.

Yet to his chagrin, a lone member of a local motorcycle club that was located in the Tulsa area just happened to also be visiting the lake on that very same morning. Of course Mitch knew that the smartest thing for him to do would be to climb back into his pickup truck and vacate the premises just as quickly as possible. However, he was so overcome with such an intense hatred of the motorcyclist who'd run over and killed his granddaughter that he thought very seriously about retrieving the fully loaded twelve gauge shotgun stored behind the seat of his pickup truck and then purposely firing all six rounds into the motorcyclist until he was quite certain that the stranger was dead.

Just the thought of murdering an anonymous motorcyclist did not seem to unnerve Mitch as much as he thought that it should have; and if he were to be completely honest with himself, then his only concern at the time would have been to pick up the ejected shotgun shells from the ground and then hurriedly drive away from the scene. Then once Mitch had driven a safe distance from the edge of the lake to the main entrance road he would have had a clear view of the surroundings behind him which would have made it easy for to determine if anybody was attempting to follow him.

Nonetheless, Mitch was so shaken by the event that he decided that the only sensible thing left for him to do would be to relocate to another part of the country. Accordingly, then, the first thought that came to mind was that he would move to the city where his sister and brother-in-law had just recently moved in order for his sister's husband to take on a new job at a fairly large newspaper in the Midwestern metropolis of River City.

Then luckily for Mitch, the next two months of his life were mostly peaceful and uneventful; that is, if you don't count the time that he had to spend with the realtors, the bankers, and a moving company. Eventually, though, he was ready to leave the life that he'd known in Tulsa, Oklahoma behind him. There was, however, one major drawback; and that simply was the fact that in the future he would be unable to make his almost daily visits to the Tulsa cemetery that was home to both his deceased wife of some thirty-odd years, and his granddaughter. On the other hand, though, the decision to relocate to another city was made somewhat easier by the fact that his two daughters and their extended families had decided to remain in the Tulsa area where they would be able to tend to the family plots at the one of the local cemeteries.

Nevertheless, Mitch knew full well that he would almost certainly bring along with him all of the anger and hatred that he'd acquired since the untimely death of his young granddaughter. But then once he'd made the final decision to pull up stakes and move to a community that was located well to the east of the Mississippi River, he found that the adage of, "old habits die hard," was indeed true because he still desperately felt a need for revenge.

Chapter Two
Subterfuge

The historic Farmer's Market in River City is located directly across the street from a beautiful old library that's listed in the National Register of Historic Places. Then too, the old market is also located fairly close by to Haynie's Corner which is a much older part of town that has just recently been developed into a modern-day art colony. Then by coincidence, the old market place is most easily assessable by way of the north side entrance which is situated directly across the street from a building that houses one of the city's largest motorcycle clubs. And during recent times, the people in this area have witnessed more than a few heated exchanges between the local artists and the bikers; and sad to say, quite a few of those confrontations have turned violent.

An outsider could only venture to guess as to what had originally caused the long-standing rift between the two completely diverse groups of people; and particularly since the male members of both tribes tend to wear their hair in ponytails. Yet when a River City Herald newspaper staff writer decided to interview one of the art colony's insiders, the lady artist in question was quoted as saying that, "the feud between the two groups had first begun when one of the so called, Biker Babes, switched teams and then took up with one the male artists that just happens to live and work in the Haynie's Corner District."

Though when asked, the majority of the artistic types that call River City their home would most likely state that they usually feel as if their personal safety is in jeopardy anytime that they are forced to be in the presence of the bikers. That said, it's a foregone conclusion that the artists would never give up on shopping at the Farmer's Market since it's one of the few places in town where the Hippies, as many of the locals are prone to call the writers and the artist, can still find the organically grown produce that they prefer.

But to be completely fair to the bikers, the feud between the two warring parties has never been entirely one-sided; and consequently, the local authorities are forced to keep a constant close eye on the activists from both camps. This would be especially true of one particular lady artist and painter by the name of Lavern Ouster, who not only claims to speak for the entire artistic community, but who also has written numerous articles to the editor of the River City Herald newspaper stating that if any of the local residents were to ever be deemed a nuisance to the city, then in her opinion, it would definitely have to be the motorcyclists, who, with their loud muffler pipes were a constant nuisance to the community at large.

Ms. Ouster was also quick to state that she was in total agreement with a few of the other residents of the city who'd written to the editor saying that perhaps there should be an arbitrary bounty placed on the heads of the members of the motorcycle clubs. And in one particularly vicious letter to the editor, Ms. Ouster had the gall to point out the fact that the early homesteaders out west had very successfully eliminated the frightening wolves and various other varmints from their farmlands and ranches by initiating a bounty system in order to rid their land of what they considered to be troublesome pests. Ms. Ouster closed her most outrageous letter to the editor by suggesting that perhaps the local authorities should make available to the public a fifteen dollar varmint permit which would allow the holder of the license exterminate one of the motorcyclists.

The situation had certainly gotten out of control, alright, and in what they considered to be an act of self-preservation a few of the bikers had begun to write some scathing letters of their own to the editor in which they argued that the entire Haynie's Corner Art District was nothing but a safe haven and domain for the city's prostitutes and drug addicts. This then was immediately answered in kind by a slew of letters to the newspaper from the members of the artistic community which stated the following; "Well, isn't that just like the old proverbial pot calling the kettle black?"

Chapter Three
Un-serene Retirement

As a retired electrical engineer who'd just recently sold his home in the Tulsa, Oklahoma area, Mitch Simmons was fortunate in the sense that he could afford to purchase a very nice condominium that just happened to be located in the near downtown area of his new hometown; and what with a view of the beautiful Ohio River from his balcony, he hoped that he could once again learn how to be happy.

However, he did have a few regrets about the location of the condo which he'd had so hastily chosen for his new home. In fact, Mitch had done something completely out of character for him because he'd failed to drive by his prospective new address on a late Friday or Saturday evening in order to check out the neighborhood for noise pollution. For if he'd done so, then he might have noticed that there was an inordinate number of motorcycle riders that continually traversed the streets surrounding his new apartment complex; and also that the motorcycle traffic was especially heavy on weekend evenings between the hours of ten and twelve o'clock P. M. as the motorcyclists traveled through a nearby intersection that not only was adjacent to a near downtown city park, but was also located fairly close by to his new living quarters.

Therefore, it was quite understandable that Mitch was still somewhat perturbed and even a little angry with himself for not first checking out the neighborhood a little more closely before buying the condo. Ultimately, though, it required of him to simply take a leisurely drive through the near-downtown area before he was able to pinpoint the cause of the abnormal amount of biker traffic in his part of town. Then much to his dismay, he discovered that an older building that was located nearby to the Farmer's Market was being used as the headquarters for a local motorcycle club. This would, of course, account for the excessive amount of motorcycle traffic that he'd noticed all throughout his neighborhood. This would also help to explain the large numbers of weekend bikers that he had seen traveling through a particular intersection that just happened to be within earshot of his new residence.

It was also true that the loud noise generated by the baffle-free style of drag-pipe muffler systems that many of the motorcyclists seemed to favor nowadays was extremely irritating to many of the city's inhabitants. Moreover, Mitch knew that by living in the close proximity to so many of the two-wheeled devils, as he now preferred to think of the motorcyclists, might cause him to despise the bikers even more than he already did; that is, if that was even humanely possible to do so. More importantly, though, Mitch had begun to wonder if he should continue to fight the impulse to extract revenge upon the bikers of the world; or perhaps, he should just surrender to the overpowering urge to kill off as many of them as he possibly could in the remaining years of his life. So with that thought in mind his new hobby consisted of trolling the local lakes, parks, and all of the rest of the recreational areas that were located in and around River City while he patiently, and even somewhat hopefully, searched for an unsuspecting biker that would be an easy prey.

Then while visiting a few of the places where the motorcyclists were likely to congregate, Mitch knew that he could have very easily dispatched at least three of the bikers to their deaths. Yet what was truly amazing about the entire situation was the fact that he could have done so without attracting any undue suspicion to himself. Mitch also knew that if he ever decided to start killing off the bikers in earnest, then the deed would almost assuredly be accomplished by using the same 12 gauge pump shotgun that he always carried along with him in his pickup truck.

Still, Mitch had begun to wonder what would happen if someone were to be able accurately describe his pickup truck to the authorities as he was driving away from one of the crime scenes. So naturally, he knew that if and when he ever made the decision to put his plan into action he would have to choose his killing fields very carefully.

Mitch was well aware of the fact that if a person continued to randomly gun down the hated bikers in public places, as he was seriously thinking about doing, then the odds of getting caught would be stacked heavily against him. Therefore, it was around that time when he was seriously thinking about exterminating every single one of the hell-raising bikers on this earth that he decided upon a completely new method of vengeance. And being that he was a retired electrical engineer, he knew that it was within his realm of experience to design an experimental motion censoring and triggering device known as a, "SASER."

Theoretically, a device of that nature could be programmed to fire a shotgun shell toward a particular target, that is, if the sound reaching the built-in sound detector in the experimental device were to be equal to, or even exceeded the 110 decibel range. So after a quick trip to the intersection at the nearby city park that just happened to be located just a few short blocks from his residence, Mitch fervently believed that his idea for a stand-alone killing machine was as least somewhat feasible. To make matters even simpler, a few of the metal overhead streetlight poles at the intersection were already adorned with some yellow metal boxes that housed the, "walk and don't walk," signs that told the pedestrians when it is safe to cross the street. This made Mitch think that one more yellow metal box would not look all that out of place or even suspicious.

On the other hand, though, Mitch didn't really wish to harm any innocent travelers. So he decided that if he ever got around to implementing his own personal design of a remote killing machine, it would require of him to integrate a timing device into the system that would allow the battery powered apparatus to remain inactive and dormant until after ten o'clock P. M. when there is usually an increase of motorcycle traffic at that particular intersection.

And even though Mitch had allowed his brother-in-law the journalist, Tom Petty, to examine the finished schematic for his newly designed SASER device, he'd never actually shown him the finished product which clearly suggests that the SASER device is quite capable of firing a shotgun shell at a specific target.

Yet because of the tremendous amount of biker traffic in the near downtown area, Mitch was beginning to have some misgivings about living in the proximity of the biker club. Hence just prior to the unpleasantness that he was presently experiencing because of the noise created by the excessive numbers of biker traffic, he'd previously believed that living near a park was a blessing. For during nice weather, Mitch had noticed that a person living in this beautiful Midwestern metropolis could almost always expect to find a few of the local neighborhood mothers and their children enjoying themselves in this near downtown city park. And on certain occasions, a person might even find a few of the local retirees from a nearby assisted living complex that were just simply passing the time by sitting around at one of the numerous picnic tables.

Yet early one Saturday morning that would have certainly not been the case since the area of the park nearest to a major intersection had been cordoned off with that all too-familiar, yellow police crime-scene tape. So instead of the hordes of citizens that would normally be enjoying themselves in the park that morning the area closest to a busy intersection was all abuzz with several uniformed police technicians and a squad of detectives who were all actively scouring the grounds, the immediate trash cans, and even the nearby sewers for any evidence that might help to identify the person who'd shot and killed a motorcyclist during the previous evening.

Of course an autopsy would eventually be performed: and when finished, the coroner would estimate that the time of death for the twenty-six year old male motorcyclist to be somewhere between ten o'clock on the previous evening and two o'clock on the following morning; and which then had coincided perfectly with the account which had been given to the police by a local bread-truck driver who'd called 911 after having driven upon the carnage at approximately 10:15 on the previous evening.

Then almost prophetically, the eventual autopsy would prove that the young biker had been struck multiple times with double ought twelve gauge shotgun pellets. Then by using forensics' science, it was presumed that the victim has fallen off the bike almost immediately after being struck by the blast. Also just as characteristically, after the rider had fallen to the pavement on the north-easternmost portion of the intersection, the rider-less bike proceeded on a southwesterly course before eventually colliding with a metal light pole on the far corner of the intersection.

But since the tragic event hadn't been reported until after the fact, the police were left without any known eyewitnesses to the crime. Hence, it would be up to the investigating officers to canvass the entire neighborhood in hopes of finding someone who'd seen or heard something out of the ordinary during the previous evening. Then as was usual in those types of cases, the facts concerning this incidence would not only be broadcast over the air by the local television and radio stations, but the facts would also be displayed in the local newspapers in hopes of finding someone who might have been in the general area at the time of the event. And since the average motorcycle produces at least 100 decibels of sound, and a shotgun blast produces approximately 140 decibels, it was hoped that someone might have heard the crime being committed.

Tom Petty, who was one of the staff writers at the River City Herald newspaper, and who was also a brother-in-law to the retired electrical engineer, Mitch Simmons, just happened to be working late on a story that same evening when he suddenly became lot more interested in a report on his police scanner when a River City police officer advised dispatch to have his supervisor rendezvous with him at a near downtown city park. A request of that nature was certainly nothing out of the ordinary but then shortly thereafter the situation appeared to be a lot more serious than Tom had at first believed when the same officer suggested that dispatch might want to also contact the coroner's office.

After having worked as a staff writer and crime reporter for a period of fifteen years, which included fourteen years for a newspaper in Tulsa, Oklahoma, and then another year or so with the River City Herald, Tom suspected that another tragedy had occurred in his newly adopted hometown. It seemed that yet another person had apparently died, but then once on the scene at the city park he had only to assume that this most recent homicide victim would almost certainly qualify as the fourth local motorcyclists in the past several months to have been killed by a blast from a shotgun.

And even though each of the three previous victims had been slain with double-ought twelve gauge shotgun pellets, the stark difference between the murders from the past and this most recent homicide was simply the fact that the first three victims had all been gunned down in sparsely populated areas, and not in a public venue, as was the case in this apparent homicide.

Also just as regrettably for Tom it was beginning to look as if it might be another difficult assignment for both his newspaper and the River City Police Department to investigate. Nonetheless, if the newspaper was unable to find any answers to the recent rash of murders of the local motorcyclists, then it wouldn't be for the lack of resources since the paper had a daily circulation of over two-hundred and fifty thousand subscribers; and that figure didn't even include the newspapers that the Herald published for some of the smaller communities in the surrounding area.

Yet after having spent over an hour at the scene of the crime, Tom felt as if he had uncovered most of the available facts on this particular case; until, that is, when he was finally able to speak privately with a homicide detective named Walter Sessions, who as fate would have it, had been part of the original investigating team who'd worked the three previous homicides of the motorcyclists who'd all been gunned down in the River City area. So by daybreak, the story that Tom was planning on writing for his newspaper would describe in detail just exactly how their city's latest homicide victim had died; and because of the real possibility of there being a serial killer running amok on the streets of River City, the story might even end up being distributed to the wire services. This then would almost guarantee that the story would be published by a vast majority of the Midwestern newspapers.

"Walter, would you be kind enough to help me out here with a few of the details?" Tom said.

"Well Tom, there's really not much more that I can tell you about this case excepting to say that the facts in this case are strikingly similar to the other three homicides that we are currently working. Of course we won't have any definite answers for you until after the autopsy has been performed," detective Walter Sessions said.

"When you say similar to the other cases are you referring to the entry wounds on both the torso and on the right side of this victim's head?" Tom said.

"That's right, Tom, I am, but until we hear from the coroner's office I won't be able to make a more definite connection between this case and the other three homicides that are lying unsolved on top of my desk. Yet having said that, I can tell you that I did see what appeared to be a double-ought buckshot pellet protruding from the right side of the victim's temple; but that's off the record," detective Sessions said.

Thus after working at his desk for a few more hours, Tom was more than ready to call it a long day and night, but then just as he was preparing to exit the newspaper's parking lot he was only a little surprised when his brother-in-law, Mitch Simmons, pulled his pickup truck up alongside his automobile.

"How's it going, Tom?" Mitch said.

"Well, other than being exhausted from having to work all night I'm suppose I'm doing alright," Tom said.

"That's right; you are right in the middle of covering that huge city budget deficit, aren't you?" Mitch said.

"I sure am Mitch, but that's not the reason that I had to work all-night; it seems as if another local motorcyclist has been murdered," Tom said.

"Wow! That's about the third one this year, isn't?" Mitch said.

"Actually, Mitch, this is the fourth homicide of a local motorcyclist that I have personally investigated within the last year," Tom said.

"Well Tom I won't keep you, but please say hello to my sister Beth for me," Mitch said.

"Will do, Mitch, and don't forget that you're still invited over to our house for Sunday dinner," Tom said.

Then immediately following his conversation with Mitch, it was straight home for Tom where he hoped to catch a long nap before the reading of the opening minutes of the city's annual budget committee meeting that was scheduled to take place that evening at city hall where the elected city leaders would once again be arguing over the city's fiscal matters.

But since that Mitch was no longer actively employed, and also since he had no other pressing commitments for the remainder of the day, he decided to drive on over to the city park where the police technicians were still conducting their investigation into the shooting which had claimed the life of yet another one of the city's motorcyclist.

Chapter Four
Chasing Ghost and Lies

Detective Walter Sessions of the River City Police Department's Homicide Division wasn't any different than his colleagues in the law enforcement field in as much as he was used to hearing mostly lies from the people he investigated. So when he and his partner decided to follow-up on an attempted murder case which had just recently crossed their desks he was tempted to dismiss the biker's official statement to the police as nothing more than pure imagination.

For in this particular case it was extremely difficult for Walter to believe that a young and apparently healthy motorcyclist could have seriously believed that he was about to be overpowered by the middle-aged, and frail-looking longhaired artist that was still recuperating in the intensive care unit at one of the local hospitals. Unfortunately, however, the main obstacle that the police had to overcome in that particular case was the fact that the person who was still laid up in the hospital had never regained consciousness; and therefore, the police were only getting one side of the story. Moreover, the biker, one James Forrester, had a lengthy police record which included several assault and battery offences along with some misdemeanor drug charges.

Although luckily for the police, a non-partial bystander had witnessed both the initial confrontation and the eventual altercation between the biker and the middle-aged artist. Thus, in her official statement to the police the witness swore that after first being harassed in the Farmer's Market parking lot by the much younger biker, it was actually the artist who'd thrown the first punch. Then notwithstanding the facts of that particular case, a person would most generally be tempted to believe that the artistic types who are most generally portrayed as being mild-mannered pacifist would be sitting ducks for the motorcyclists, who as a rule, are thought of as being more aggressive than the so-called Hippie types.

Furthermore, that same case scenario would seem to be particularly truer if the biker in this case happened to belong to one of the more notorious motorcycle gangs. Nevertheless, if a person were to total up the number of assaults which had occurred in the River City area over the past year it would appear as if the artists/Hippies were far ahead in the body count which stood at four deaths to none. Then too, that running count number of four deaths to zero would largely depend on whether the artist that was currently fighting for his life in the intensive care unit at one of the local hospitals lived or died.

Also somewhat interestingly, in the past year alone the River City Police Department had recorded a total of nine cases of assault and battery which had taken place in the general vicinity of the Farmer's Market's parking lot; and that number didn't even include the most recent attack which had sent a man to the I. C. U. unit at one of the local hospitals. Oddly enough, though, only three of the nine people who'd been arrested during those previous violent episodes were known to be active members of the motorcycle club that was located directly across the street from the old market place. Therefore, these facts seemed to substantiate detective Sessions' belief that sometimes looks can be deceiving; and also, that practically any person is capable of doing serious bodily harm to another human being.

Detective Walter Sessions knew, of course, that racial profiling and the common act of lumping groups of people together in order to make them fit into a certain stereotype have been around for a very long time. Yet for the life of him, he just couldn't fathom the idea of any one of the artistic types that he knew personally would be capable of using a baseball bat on another human being; much less summon up the necessary courage it would take for someone to be able to use a knife or a gun on another person.

That said, Walt's new partner, Detective Sergeant Mathew Morris, who before migrating south to the Midwestern Metropolis of River City had previously worked for the Chicago Police Department where not only had he been a highly decorated member of the Homicide Division, but he'd personally investigated more crimes against humanity than Walter could have ever dreamed of. This then made Walter think that Matt might be a little too jaded to fit successfully into a much smaller metropolitan police department such as the one in River City.

Then again, it was also true that when it came to the solving of homicide cases that Detective Sergeant Mathew Morris had benefitted immensely from his family's long history of service in the field of law enforcement which had produced four generations of excellent and dedicated homicide detectives for the city of Chicago. Even so, if a person were to ask Matt to pinpoint any one common thread that had run all through those twenty years of service on the force in Chicago, he would most likely say that the only people who'd never lied to him were the medical examiners and the coroners.

"Walt, before we head off to the hospital to checkup on that assault victim's recovery I'd like to stop by Lavern Ouster's art studio," Matt said.

"That's a good idea Matt, for if there's one person in town who could fill us in what the biker James Forrester might have been up to it would be the lady artist, Ms. Ouster," Walt said.

"Then following our interview with the lady artist I would also like to speak with the person who'd witnessed the assault in the Farmers Market parking lot," Matt said.

Then as a matter of luck, Ms. Ouster's art studio was located in the very heart of the Haynie's Corner District which meant that her studio was not all that far removed from the bronze historical marker which stated that the original land owner, a certain Mr. Haynie, was a pioneer who not only had lived and farmed in the immediate surrounding area, but he'd also been quite fond of raising geese. This then is what had prompted the locals to name a certain part of the neighborhood, Goosetown.

Then by walking just a few short blocks due west from Haynie's Corner, a person could expect to find another historical marker which stated that the land inside of the Riverside Park area had once been used as a campsite for a great many of the Southern Refugees who'd migrated north across the Ohio River in order to distance themselves from the death and destruction which had been bestowed upon the South during the disastrous American Civil War.

And even if a person were to disregard the numerous art festivals which are held annually in the Haynie's Corner District, the neighborhood is almost always a lively place to visit; and that would be especially true during the annual Art Gala and the various other street carnivals that are usually held in the pie-wedge shaped intersection whose center is decorated with a sculptured and antique looking water fountain. Then also quite understandably, some of the street festivals that are held in the square are so large that they occasionally end up being carried over onto the sidewalks and the neighboring yards of the surrounding homes and businesses.

Then also during the times in which the Arts & Crafts Fairs are held in the Haynie's Corner District, there are usually some very talented artists on hand that, for a fee, would paint your portrait in about an hour or so. Of course the annual street carnivals are held primarily as moneymakers for the local non-profit 501(c)3 Arts & Crafts Guild. Nonetheless, the regional exposure that the street carnival provides is usually more than enough to compel the members of the local bands to donate their time and talents.

So after having located the art studio where the elderly lady artist was known to hold court, the two investigators identified themselves as detectives for the River City Police Department. From then on they would learn that Ms. Ouster was indeed a real pleasure to speak with. For even though she claimed to be nothing more than a simple working artist of some eighty-odd years of age, Ms. Ouster could be both gregarious and gracious. She was, however, most generally fond of saying that her main purpose in life was to further the interest of her beloved art colony.

"Ms. Ouster, do you happen to know a man by the name of James Forrester?" Matt said.

"No, I don't believe that I know that man personally, although it's entirely possible that I've heard his name mentioned at one of our guild or board meetings; but why do you ask?" Ms. Ouster said.

"You might recall that he was the motorcyclist who was involved in a recent altercation at the Farmer's Market with a man by the name of Thomas Pirtle," Matt said.

"Oh that's right: I knew that I'd heard that name before; and now of course, I do remember that he's the one who's guilty of hurting our dear old sweet Tom, isn't he?" Ms. Ouster said.

"Well that'll be up to the courts to decide as to which of the two combatants is actually guilty of an assault; but for now, Mr. Pirtle is still a coma," Matt said.

Thus by sensing that Ms. Ouster might be more than a little biased toward the artistic types, the two detectives decided to excuse themselves from her company. And also being that it was getting late in the afternoon they hoped that their sole eyewitness to the most recent assault at the Farmers Market would be at home. And then luckily for the two detectives, the purported witness to the most recent altercation in the parking lot at the Farmers Market just happened to live within the same general boundaries of the Haynie's Corner District.

At one time in the past, Helen Marks could have been what some people might refer to as an old maid. However, she was not an artist and she definitely wasn't one of the Hippie types, she just happened to live in the very same house where she'd grown up. In fact, Helen had just recently inherited the two-and-a-half story, seven-gabled, Victorian style of house just shortly after her parents had passed away. Though generally speaking, a person trying to live on a third-grade schoolteacher's income would almost assuredly find it prohibitively expensive to heat and cool such a large house; that is, of course, if a person were to occupy the entire house. On the other hand, though, Ms. Marks had managed to live quite comfortably in just three of the downstairs rooms plus the kitchen. The other parts of the house were intentionally closed off; and as such, they were only heated by the naturally rising heat from the boiler in the basement and the radiators on the first floor.

"Ms. Marks, my name is Detective Sergeant Morris and this is detective Sessions of the River City Police Department, and if you don't mind, we'd like to ask you a few questions about the altercation that you recently witnessed in the Farmers Market parking lot," Matt said.

"Well detective, like I told the uniformed policemen at the Farmers Market, Jimmy Forrester was a former third-grade student of mine," Ms. Marks said.

"Actually, Ms. Marks, we'd like to know just exactly how the fight got started," Matt said.

"Well to tell you the truth detective it happened so fast that it's rather difficult for me to remember all the details but I do believe that the person who got injured real badly had just exited the rear door of the market when at the same time Jimmy was turning his bike around in the parking lot; and from then on everything seemed to happen in slow motion. For if memory serves, it seems that Jimmy startled the older man by driving so closely to him. This then caused the older man to drop his sack of produce while at the same time connecting with a punch to the side of Jimmy's head," Helen said.

"So then there's no doubt in your mind as to which one through the first punch," Matt said.

"None whatsoever, detective, it was the older man alright: but when the incident was finally over and done with I made it a point to tell Jimmy that in the future he should not be using the parking lot as a place to turn his motorcycle around in," Ms. Marks said.

"Well thank you for your help," Matt said.

On the way back to the police headquarters Matt thought that he had a pretty good idea as to what had transpired in the parking lot. So therefore, the case file would be turned over to the district attorney's office for further review. Of course there was a good chance that the state's attorney would file an assault charge against the older man. However, there was also an outside chance that the prosecutor would decide that the biker, Jimmy Forrester, had overreacted and had used more force than necessary to protect himself from the older man. In all actuality, however, Matt seriously doubted if any decision would be made until they learned whether Mr. Pirtle would live or die.

Chapter Five
New Surroundings

Not only did it take Mitch Simmons a substantial amount of time to learn how to properly navigate his way around the one-way streets and the expressways of his new hometown, but he also had to get used to the quaint customs and the mentality of the local people. And being that River City is located in the southernmost part of a Midwestern state, and also being that it's located on the Ohio River which acts as a natural boundary to the state of Kentucky, Mitch soon realized that the community he'd chosen to be his new hometown was significantly influenced by the Southern way of life. In fact, it seemed as if the local populace could be counted on to fiercely extol the independent ways of the Southern people; and some of the most apparent ways that they succeeded in expressing their love of the great outdoors was through the riding of horses and motorcycles.

What's more, just shortly after Mitch had purchased his condo in the near downtown business district he discovered that the love of hunting and fishing in that particular part of the Midwest was more than just a sport, it was a passion. And from what he had heard about the past, only a few decades had passed since the General Assembly of his new home state had made it illegal to openly transport firearms in a vehicle; for up to that point in time it was commonplace to see gun racks being displayed prominently in the rear windows of pickup trucks.

However, just knowing that a goodly portion of the local inhabitants chose to own firearms did not discourage Mitch from wanting to remain in River City; and especially since the right to bear arms had been practiced quite liberally back in his home state of Oklahoma where the majority of the people that he knew personally had not only kept firearms in their homes, but a right smart percentage of them had elected to carry side arms on their persons.

However, there was, a distinct segment of the local population that would take some additional getting used to; and those were the people that the locals most commonly referred to as, "Rednecks." And as Mitch had subsequently learned, the term Redneck had originated in the early parts of the twentieth century when the soon to be unionized coalminers of West Virginia, Eastern Kentucky, and Pennsylvania most commonly wore a red bandanna around their necks while fighting with the members of the various detective agencies which had been hired by some of the coalmine owners in hopes of keeping the workers from joining the union.

Of course nowadays this term has taken on a somewhat derogatory meaning when it's used primarily to define the heavy drinking and the hard fighting young men who tend to frequent the bars and saloons on any given Friday or Saturday evening in search of what they most likely consider to be the three most important goals of their life.

That would be to chase women, drink as much alcohol as they possibly could, and then finish up their evening by getting into a fistfight. For during one particular Friday evening as Mitch was having a sandwich at one of the local coffee shops he just happened to overhear a trio of young males discussing their plans for the rest of the evening which included, getting drunk, getting into a fight, and then just possibly ending up in jail.

A declaration such as the one that Mitch had overheard coming from those three young men in the restaurant would almost certainly have sounded out of place in a town such as Salt Lake City, Utah or in any other city that Mitch was familiar with. As a result, Mitch was beginning to think that the town he'd chosen as his new place of residence could just as easily be named the, "Mean City," instead of River City. Though some of his perception of the community might have been clouded by the numerous reports on the local television stations and the River City Herald newspaper that seemed to suggest that

nothing but violence and mayhem could ever live and thrive in this teeming community on the Ohio River.

In reality, however, there was never any doubt in the local people's minds that River City had a well-earned reputation of being an extremely violent place in which to live. Or at least that was certainly the case according to an old-timer who just happened to live in the same condo complex as Mitch. For according to that particular gentleman, River City had at one time been designated as the murder capital of America; and as some of the older residents loved to say, you haven't really lived unless you were living in River City during the World War II era when the vices such as gambling and prostitution were allowed to run rampant. For back in the good old days they say it was very commonplace for the local authorities to find dead bodies strewn haphazardly about in the river-bottom and on the banks of the Ohio River.

"Well so much for brotherly love," Mitch thought, but all of the stories of the past had simply strengthened his already firm resolve to keep a loaded twelve gauge pump shotgun hidden behind the seat in his pickup truck. And since his brother-in-law Tom Petty the journalist seemed to be on such close terms with a few of the local police officers, Mitch had asked Tom to meet up with him at the main police headquarters on the upcoming Monday morning so he could apply for a personal protection permit which would give him the right to carry a concealed handgun. Of course even if the local chief of police were to approve his application for the right to carry permit, the paper work would still have to travel north to the state police headquarters in the state capital for final approval.

Chapter Six
The Facts Don't Lie

Detective Sergeant Matt Morris had been a member of the River City Police Department for only a short period of time when he and his new partner, detective Walter Sessions, caught the assault with intent to kill case which had just recently taken place in the old Farmers Market parking lot. Unfortunately for Matt, however, the violence that we human beings insist upon inflicting on one another was beginning to appear normal to him. This seemed to be particularly true to Matt since he'd just spent the last twenty years of his life working as a homicide detective on the streets of Chicago.

Unfortunately, though, there were times when even he wondered if he wasn't becoming a bit too casehardened and jaded? In fact, matt had always worried that he might become too inured to other people's misfortunes. Yet all throughout his long career as a homicide detective Matt had found that murder is murder and that it really doesn't matter if the homicide takes place on the mean streets of a big city like Chicago, or in a much smaller Metropolis such as River City.

Yet for some strange reason, the new case that Matt was currently working seemed to remind him of a similar case that his father had once worked while chasing the bad guys up and down Michigan Avenue in the heart of Chicago's famous Magnificent Mile. In that particular case, Matt's father, who'd served on the Chicago Police Department as a homicide detective for a great number of years was forced to weave his way through the brotherhood of the Long Blue Line in order to help convict a fellow homicide detective of several murders.

Of course Matt and his partner didn't have any reason to believe that any of the River City officers were involved in a cover-up on the case that they were currently working. Or at least, it certainly didn't appear to be that way. But what they did have to contend with was the fact that the people from both camps, I. E., the bikers versus and the Hippies and the artistic

types had not only closed ranks against the police department, but one of the staff writers at the River City Herald had also stopped cooperating with the police department.

To Matt, it was beginning to seem as if the members of the two local warring parties must have been related to the famous families that were involved in that long-standing Hatfield and McCoy feud that took place many years ago in the hills of West Virginia and Eastern Kentucky. For just like the participants in that age-old terrible struggle from the long forgotten past, the bikers and the artists had apparently decided that they would rather fight their own battles than ask for help from the local authorities. Ultimately, though, the two detectives would discover why Tom Petty the journalist had made the decision to join ranks with the artistic types from Haynie's Corner.

Consequently, this new development in the case had begun to seriously interest Matt. Even so, he wasn't any too surprised to learn that someone whose name had come up during their extensive investigation into the latest violence at the Farmer's Market had a very interesting past. In fact, this latest piece of information had surfaced when Matt was searching through the archives of one of Tulsa's old newspapers and he accidently uncovered the fact that not only was Tom Petty related to the seven year-old girl who had been run over and killed by a hit-and-run motorcyclist in the city of Tulsa, Oklahoma, but that another recent arrival to the River City area was none other than Mitch Simmons, who as it turned out was Tom's brother-in-law; and who also just happened to be the grandfather of the seven year-old girl who'd died at the hands of the hit-and-run motorcyclist in Tulsa.

Yet for Matt, the clincher would come later when he bumped into Tom Petty at the main police station while the staff writer was there to gather some information on a story that he was writing for the River City Herald. Then curiously enough, as Tom was taking care of his newspaper's business at the police station he'd elected to show Matt a diagram of a theoretical device that his brother-in-law, Mitch Simmons, had supposedly been working on which included something called a "SASER," which was a device that once perfected would be comparable to a laser.

Then according to Tom, the device that Mitch Simmons had allegedly designed could also be used as a sound detector. This then meant that after the device had received a jolt of at least one hundred and ten decibels it could cause the device to discharge a shot gun shell when aimed towards the source of the sound.

Normally, just the thought of having that kind of information at his disposal wouldn't be all that beneficial to Matt; but since he and his partner Walt were already deep in the process of investigating the city's most recent homicide case where the person's death was caused by his being struck with double ought shotgun pellets, the idea of a remote killing machine had begun to interest him immensely. For as a matter of fact the latest development in the case had prompted him to ask the chief of detectives for permission to send the C. S. I. technical squad back out to the near-downtown city park just so they could search for any additional evidence that might still be present at the scene.

Even so, while the C. S. I. team was re-visiting the crime scene at the city park they failed once again to find any hidden sound detectors or any other unexpected foreign devices in the park. On the other hand, though, when one of the members of the police department's forensic team decided to re-evaluate the angle of penetration on the right side of the victim's head and torso, they came to the conclusion that the fatal shotgun blast must have come from the area immediately surrounding the metal street light pole nearest to the intersection. Hence by luck or design, a police technician just happened to dab the street side of that particular light pole with a cotton swab. Then later on, when the sample was subjected to a lab test it indicated the strong presence of potassium nitrate which is one of the main ingredients in the manufacture of gunpowder.

Now, the two detectives had a working theory as to how the latest murder of a local motorcyclist might have been carried out; they were, however, nowhere closer to solving the crime than they had been at the beginning. If anything, this new information concerning the likelihood of a remote killing machine had tended to cloud their thinking even more so; that is, until Matt decided to discuss the possibility of developing a sound detection device with an electrical engineer at one of the local universities.

Then oddly enough, a person by the name of Brett Parks, who was the head of the engineering department at one of the local universities, had also been trying to perfect a device that incorporates the theoretical SASER device, and a sound detector into an invention that would fulfill the needs of many of today's industries. His thinking was much along the same lines as Matt's in as much as there was a real possibility that a remote killing machine of that nature could actually fire a shotgun shell in the direction of a motorcycle if the amount of decibels it produced was in the one hundred and ten range. Admittedly, though, the main drawback in creating such a device would be the SASER'S system's inability to differentiate between the noise made by a baffle free muffler system on a motorcycle and the high-pitched sound that the squealing brakes on a dump truck might produce.

Nevertheless, both Matt and his partner Walt honestly believed that they had the proof-in- the-pudding when some minute traces of nitrate were found on the light pole at the city park. Then too, they also had the body of a dead motorcyclist which they thought was pretty solid evidence that such a remote device could actually be put together. Still, the desire to believe that it was actually possible to create such a device consisted primarily of physical evidence. The problem was, however, the evidence did not point directly to any one of their persons of interest.

To Matt's way of thinking if motive was the only criteria for building a solid case against any one of their many suspects, then he would certainly not have a problem. For up to that point in time practically everybody's name who'd come up during the murder investigation appeared to have a possible motive. What with the need for revenge that the artists and the Hippies from the Haynie's Corner District were most likely feeling after their artist friend, Thomas Pirtle, had been so badly injured that he was still in a coma.

Then too, there was the staff writer, Tom Petty, who along with his brother-in-law, Mitch Simmons the retired electrical engineer from Tulsa, seemed to possess more than enough expertise to be able to design a remote killing machine such as the one that was suspected of having killed the young motorcyclist at the city park. So they certainly weren't lacking in suspects.

"Let me ask you something, Walt: why would Tom Petty go out of his way to show us the drawing of that SASER device that his brother-in-law Mitch Simmons had allegedly designed?" Matt said.

"Well Matt, there's no way to know for sure just exactly what Tom Petty was thinking but it could be that he was trying to take the heat off of himself by placing it squarely on his brother-in-law's shoulders," Walt said.

"That's the way I see it too. So let me ask you outright; do you think that the journalist is good for the city park murder?" Matt said.

"He could be: but anyway that you look at it we should probably ask Mr. Petty to make an official police statement at the stationhouse just so we could have him on record in case he ends up being more involved in the murders of those four motorcyclists than he would like for us to believe," Walt said.

"I completely agree with you, Walt: but, it might even be wiser if we spoke with Mitch Simmons first," Matt said.

For Walt, it was simply a matter of making a quick call to a good friend of his who worked at the local gas and electric company in order to verify the retired engineer's address. And as it turned out, the man's condo was located a mere eight blocks from the main police headquarters. So then luckily for the detectives, not only was the engineer from Tulsa at home when they called on him, but he was also receptive to the idea of granting them an unofficial interview. At first, however, Mr. Simmons appeared to be at a loss as to why the two homicide detectives wanted to discuss the theoretical SASER device which was such a new invention of his that he hadn't even found the time to apply for a U. S. Patent.

"Mr. Simmons, you might recall awhile back when one of our local motorcyclists was found shot dead in the intersection that's nearby to a downtown city park," Matt said.

"Yes I do remember when that happened, and from what I've read in the local newspaper, River City has just recently experienced a sudden spike in the number of unsolved homicides," Simmons said.

"That's true: but the only murder that concerns us here today is the one that just took place over in the city park. And to tell you the truth Mr. Simmons we'd very like much to take a look at the laser type of device that you've purportedly been working on; and we would also be especially interested in knowing if a device of that nature could have possibly been used to kill that unfortunate motorcyclist," Matt said.

"Well I doubt very seriously if anyone has been able to build an actual working model of an experimental SASER device, I know I haven't," Simmons said.

"But what about that diagram of a SASER device that you just recently showed to your brother-in-law, Tom Petty, what was that all about?" Matt said.

"Oh that, well the truth of the matter is that all throughout the last several years, Tom and I have enjoyed sharing engineering ideas with one another; and even though Tom hasn't had any formal training as an electrical engineer, he has probably read more engineering trade journals than I have;

and in all probability, he's as knowledgeable about that particular type of science as I am," Simmons said.

So then as a result of what Simmons had just told them, the detectives realized that they'd hit another dead-end. Therefore, the detectives thanked the engineer for his time and then headed on over to the River City Herald newspaper where they hoped to have another chat with the staff writer Tom Petty; instead, however, they were dispatched to an active crime scene which was located on the side street that faced the north side of the old Farmers Market parking lot.

Then once on the scene, the first thing they noticed was that the entire area was so crowded with the specialty-type of emergency vehicles from the police and fire departments that the two detectives were forced to park a half block away from the epicenter of the blast which had created a small crater in the gravel parking lot of the tavern which sat cattycornered from the Farmers Market. Although strangely enough, the building that housed the motorcycle club which was located next door to the tavern's parking lot had suffered only minor damage.

Now, of course, it would be up to the local police and the A. T. F. agents from the Bureau of Alcohol, Tobacco, and Firearms to identify the person who'd detonated what appeared to a homemade bomb. Then shortly thereafter, a representative of the local fire department stated that in his opinion the bomb had been made from a type of farm fertilizer. Yet if Matt had learned anything during his twenty years as a big city cop in the city of Chicago, it would be that a detective should always try to locate the uniformed police Sergeant who was in charge of the crime scene.

"What's you got, Sarge," Matt said

"Well detective, it appears that whatever type of explosion that was used to create this crater in the parking lot has certainly done some considerable damage to the fence and a few of the automobiles that were parked close by.

Fortunately, however, we haven't come across any causalities," the sergeant said.

"So what do you make of the situation?" Matt said.

"Well normally I wouldn't have a clue, but then luckily for us, this particular bomber was nice enough to leave us a note," the sergeant said.

Regrettably, though, most of the glued on lettering had been so badly damaged by the blast that Matt had a very difficult time in trying to decipher the exact meaning of the words which apparently had been cut out of the local newspaper and a few magazines and then pasted onto a piece of artist construction paper. But then regardless of the fact that some parts of the note had been partially destroyed by the force of the blast, Matt was able determine that the heading on the piece of paper had most likely read, "This is for Thomas Pirtle."

Matt knew, of course, that Thomas Pirtle was the middle-aged artist who'd just recently been severely beaten in the Farmers Market parking lot by a twenty-six year old biker named James Forrester. And even though Forrester was currently out on bond, Matt knew that he would automatically be picked up by the police if Mr. Pirtle were to pass away. So at that point in time the significance of the so-called SASER device didn't seem to be quite as important to Matt as he stared down into the small crater which had been created by the homemade bomb.

But then according to protocol, the investigation into who'd planted the bomb in the tavern parking lot which was adjacent to the motorcycle club, would of necessity, be turned over to the Federal agencies such as the A. T F. and the F. B. I.

Matt was contented to let the Feds work the bombing: and besides, he and his partner felt as if they already had enough on their plate by trying to figure out who was using a twelve gauge shotgun to kill off as many of the River City bikers as they possibly could. For at that point in time it really didn't seem to matter if the recent biker deaths had been caused by a SASER device, or just a run-of-the-mill twelve gauge shotgun that could easily be purchased at any local retail store. For as Matt had learned on the streets of Chicago, no matter how the act is accomplished, dead is still dead.

Chapter Seven
An Arrest

Out of all the different tactics which are usually employed by the various groups of law enforcement across the country the law that gives the authorities the legal right to arrest, and then hold an individual for a period of up to seventy-two hours is by far one of the scariest. This somewhat shameful holdover from a much earlier time gives the authorities the power to keep a suspect under lock and key for a period of up to three days without having to charge the individual with a crime. Of course any lawyer worth his salt can file a writ of habeas corpus which would give the authorities no more than two business days to "produce the body" in a court of law so that a judge could then determine whether there was enough credible evidence to warrant an arrest.

So when the River City Police Department began to seriously harass the members of the motorcycle club that owned the building across the street from the Farmers Market parking lot where the young biker had assaulted the much older artist, the bikers immediately hired a lawyer by the name of Sean Loudermilk, who not only was a well known and much feared local civil rights activist, but he was also a weekend motorcycle enthusiast.

In Loudermilk's opinion, conspiracy to deny a person his basic civil rights of freedom is tantamount to forbidding that same person from enjoying the fruits and the benefits of our constitution; and therefore, the act of unlawfully interrogating one of his clients without probable cause would be paramount to throwing the baby, the bath water, and all of the civil rights laws out the window. And even though Mr. Loudermilk had never actually argued a case in front of the state Supreme Court, he was still somewhat feared because of his constant threats to do so. For as we all know, no city administration wants, or needs, the negative headlines that such a case could engender.

Subsequently, then, it didn't take too long for the River City Police Department to realize the error of their ways. So instead of continuing to harass the bikers, as the police had been doing for quite some time, the police embarked upon a new campaign in which the chief had hoped would keep the bikers and the artist from killing each other off.

In the police chief's new program, which the editor of the River City Herald had so handsomely labeled "separate but equal," it was highly suggested that the artistic types from the Haynie's Corner District should shop for their produce at the Farmers Market on week days only; and accordingly, the motorcyclists would then, of course, have the market to themselves on weekends. Then too, another brand-new city ordinance was proposed that would make it illegal for the bikers to use the parking lot in the rear of Farmers Market as a place for them to turn their bikes around in.

In the meantime, however, another strange turn of events in this unprecedented local saga had suddenly appeared. It seems as if the F. B. I. and the A. T. F. agents had alerted the local authorities to the fact that they'd received some detailed information from an informant concerning the recent explosion in the tavern parking lot that was adjacent to the motorcycle club's headquarters. Apparently, the Feds had detained a woman who not only had made routine book deliveries to the old historic library, but it was also believed that the woman who was currently in Federal custody for detonating the bomb in the parking lot was also one of the local farmers that regularly supplied the Farmers Market with fresh produce.

And according to an account in the River City Herald newspaper, the woman accused of placing the bomb in the parking lot next to the biker's clubhouse was supposedly related to the elderly artist who'd been attacked while shopping at the market. This then was immediately followed with an official statement from the River City Police Chief which stated that the present situation had gotten so far out of hand that he was tempted to ask the mayor and the governor to send in the National Guard.

Moreover, Major William Hardin, who was the current River City Chief of Police stated that he'd not seen a feud such as the one presently being played out in River City since his childhood days back home in West Virginia where a few of the better known feuds had lasted for several generations.

In the end, however, it was readily agreed by all that something had to be done to quell the violence. So with a federal grant of a little over hundred thousand dollars, Chief Hardin was able to completely envelop the entire area surrounding of the Farmers Market with surveillance cameras. It was said that not even a mouse could cross that particular parking lot without being detected. And within only another few days following the installation of the surveillance cameras, a disturbance in progress was caught on tape which showed several of the artistic types pummeling one of the bikers.

Chapter Eight
Biker Number Five

Eventually, however, common sense replaced bravado and the bikers very wisely then made the decision to sell their old clubhouse across the street from the Farmers Market. Of course the determining factor which had prompted them to remove their club from the area was simply the fact that yet another one of their brethren had just recently been gunned down in a park that was located in a rural part of the county.

Yet during an exclusive interview with one of the staff writers from the River City Herald, the club's former president, a certain Mr. Josh Morley, cited the ever-increasing expense of keeping up an older building as the main reason for them to abandon the headquarters that they'd called home for years.

Of course if anyone had a reason to feel grateful for the club's closing then it would definitely have to be Mitch Simmons who was now able to relax on his balcony that overlooked the beautiful Ohio River. It also goes without saying that Mitch welcomed the newfound peace and quiet that he'd found in his new hometown. Most notably, though, was the absence of those late night, window rattling, and bone jarring interruptions that he'd endured from those baffle-free muffler systems on the motorcycles that many of the local bikers preferred.

Though if asked, Mitch would have been hard pressed to feel any empathy for the five bikers who'd been murdered since he'd migrated to River City from the Tulsa area. For up to that point in time he could still vividly remember the scene of his granddaughter being run over and then dragged down the street by a monstrous looking motorcycle which had been ridden by an equally evil looking man.

Robert R. Railey

Death at the Wheel

aggie Fortune's hometown was Toledo, Ohio, but on a stunningly beautiful spring day in the early part of the twenty-first century she could have been found motoring along on the westernmost portion of the Indiana Toll Road. For on that particular morning she'd made previous plans to attend to some urgent business matters in the city of Chicago Ridge, Illinois which is a suburb located to the south of Chicago, Illinois. And interestingly enough, just moments before she was about to crash her automobile into a solid concrete wall, one of the more pressing questions on her mind might have been, "where in the world did that pungent odor of rotten eggs suddenly come from?"

According to the surviving mechanical evidence, and also being that the possibility of suicide had been ruled out by her closest family members, the investigators couldn't find any logical reason to explain why Maggie had been unable to prevent her late model automobile from plunging headlong into a concrete wall which had just recently been installed as part of the newly remodeled three lane section of roadway located on that particular part of the westbound Indiana Toll Road which was nearby to the city of Gary, Indiana.

Of course nowadays an autopsy is most generally mandated for the majority of our modern-day automobile accidents that involve a fatality. Yet in that particular highway accident, the Lake County Indiana coroner had no trouble in identifying the primary cause of Maggie Fortune's death which was due to blunt force trauma. The coroner did, however, discover some extremely high concentrations of more than a few toxic chemicals in Maggie's bloodstream; but since the majority of our states are primarily concerned with the blood alcohol content, or else the presence of illegal drugs in an accident's victim's system, coroners don't generally run additional test for other types of toxic chemicals.

So initially, no red flags were raised as the result of Maggie Fortune's tragic and untimely death in an all too common highway automobile accident; but then further on down the road there would be plenty of those who would suspect that her death might have been the very first beginnings of the next pandemic to strike the industrialized world.

In fact, some of those same observers, would in time, become so concerned with the sudden increases in the total number of fatal accidents on our roadways that a few of the experts had begun to compare the tens of thousands of additional modern-day automobile deaths to the horrendous Spanish Flu pandemic of 1918 that took an estimated fifty million human lives worldwide.

Even so, it would take several additional months of intensive investigations before the researchers could even hazard a guess as to why we were experiencing such a large and sudden increase in the number of deaths on our nation's highways. Accordingly, then, by the time that the experts were finally able to get a grasp on the significance of the situation, there would be thousands more of additional victims added to the already rapidly climbing numbers of Americans and others from around the world who were dying a lot more frequently on our roadways.

Could it be an act of terrorism? The authorities were prone to ask: and with that thought in mind practically every one of our national defense organizations sprang into immediate action. Unfortunately, though, the infighting amongst the various government agencies had become so intense as to require the chairperson of the House Subcommittee on Oversight and Investigations to oversee the entire investigation which, by that time, had included members of the Homeland Security Agency, the F. B. I., the N. S. A., and the C. I. A.

Though at first glance, this elite group of spy chasers seemed quite intent upon tripping over each other's feet, until finally, the House Committee Chairperson made the recommendation that the representatives from all of those various agencies should congregate in the southern U. S. city of Atlanta, Georgia where they could avail themselves upon the services of the Center for Disease Control and Prevention which is a government agency that's better known as the C. D. C.

Then as quickly as the investigators could gather themselves at the C. D. C. in Atlanta, Georgia, they immediately began to overwhelm the scientist and the medical doctors at the center with such questions as to what kinds of evil forces were killing off America's motorist by the tens of thousands. For by then, each and every one of the investigators, plus the majority of our American protectorates, were beginning to believe that any one of our numerous enemies in the Middle East could have easily been behind such a well orchestrated scheme of killing off us Westerners.

Ultimately, though, the days turned into weeks as that very special group of government investigators continued to pour over the thousands of pertinent documents which had not only been collected from each and every one of our fifty states, but there were also hundreds of similar types of reports coming in from practically every other industrialized country on the planet.

Yet in the end, the investigators were forced to admit that whoever or whatever was responsible for the steadily growing numbers of people who were dying in their automobiles was not just a concerted effort to kill off us Americans, but that the mysterious illness, if that's what it really was, seemed to also be killing off people from other countries as well.

This then meant, of course, that there would have had to have been a logical and practical system of cause-and-effect in order to produce the staggering numbers of recent automobile related deaths which had occurred in both the United States and in the rest of the world.

So in order to solve this grave mystery, the scientists had to first eliminate, as suspect, all of the known chemicals of mass destruction from their list of possible causes. Of course it goes without saying that the bacterium anthrax was among the first on the list that would have had to have been be excluded. Then along with the anthrax, there was a whole litany of other lethal agents such as, blood agents, nerve agents, incapacitating agents, and even riot control agents.

Ultimately, though, it was only at what had seemed to be a very late date that the medical people in Atlanta had finally gotten around to checking the blood of the tens of thousands of the "Death Car" victims for signs of possible carbon monoxide poisoning. For after all, the investigators had known that a great many of the highly suspicious road fatalities had taken place in high-speed crashes. That said, a small percentage of the deaths had also occurred while the victims were parked in semi closed in areas with their engines running.

Though for the most part, the likelihood that the deaths had been caused by carbon monoxide poisoning had initially been ruled out. Especially being that practically every single fatality had taken place in an automobile that was less than two years old; and which then meant, of course, that the exhaust systems in the death cars should have been intact and in good shape.

But then during one of the mini conferences which had taken place between the scientists from the C. D. C. and the representatives from the Homeland Security Agency, an investigator just happened to ask one of the leading scientists to please demonstrate to her just exactly how the exhaust system and the catalytic converters are supposed to operate on a gasoline engine.

Then just moments later, the investigator who'd posed that particular question to the panel of scientist was invited to watch a demo film which included a detailed schematic of just exactly how an internal combustion engine is able to safely discharge the toxic fumes which are the direct result of the burning of petroleum products such as gasoline and oil.

Consequently, then, it was at that very moment when the investigators and the scientists had what could have only been called an epiphany. For the investigator's very next question to the panel of experts was, "well with all of these safeguards on the modern automobile engines supposedly in place, could someone please tell me why the catalytic converters on the so-called death cars didn't remove the harmful chemicals from the exhaust systems in which they'd been engineered to do?"

Then interestingly enough, a collective hush fell suddenly over the entire room; and for just a moment or two that one singular and poignant question had apparently stumped practically every one of the investigators and the scientists alike. Of course the obvious answer would be, if the catalytic converters had done the job that they'd originally been designed to do, then the platinum, the benzene, and all of the other carcinogenic poisons which had supposedly been applied to the converters in the factories would have prevented anyone who was driving an automobile built in the United States from 1975 on from being accidently poisoned.

For it stands to reason that if the appropriate minerals, elements, and chemicals had been properly applied as a wash coat to the catalytic converter's ceramic core in the factories, then there should not have been any leaks. So then luckily for the investigators, it appeared as if Pandora's Box might have been inadvertently opened.

Thusly, it would now be a simple matter for the experienced investigators to ask the local F. B. I. agents to take a look at some of the wrecked automobiles which had just recently ended up in a salvage yard on the outskirts of Atlanta.

Then next on the agenda was a question posed by the very same investigator who'd previously asked for a detailed explanation of how a catalytic converter is supposed to work by asking for the names of the manufactures which had produced the majority of the aforementioned converters that'd ended up in the so-called death cars.

Then also luckily for the investigators at the C. D. C., the newly obtained information showed clearly that the largest manufacturer of catalytic converters in the entire country was located right there in the city of Atlanta, Georgia. Even so, just exactly how they were supposed to proceed was a pertinent question which was on everybody's mind. But since the representative from the Department of Homeland Security felt as if his office held sway over the entire group of investigators and scientists, he suggested that they should covertly take possession of a few of the finished products that were being shipped daily from the local factory which had already produced a great many of the catalytic converters in question.

That done, then their next concern would be to simply take the converters apart in order to inspect the interiors of the devices. Though not knowing just exactly what they were supposed to be looking for, both a local mechanical engineer and a chemist from the Atlanta area were brought in to advise the team as to what they should expect to find once they'd cut open one of the newly manufactured catalytic converters.

Though at first glance, the wash coat on the ceramic cores from the newly manufactured catalytic converters appeared to be a silver white substance which would be consistent with what a coating of the chemical element platinum should look like. Nonetheless, once the grayish materials had been carefully removed from one of the brand-new converters and then also subjected to a chemical analysis, it was readily apparent to the chemist that the minerals and the elements which had been applied to the ceramic core in place of the extremely expensive platinum were nothing more than cheap imitations which consisted mostly of, cyanides, sulfur and caustic alkalis.

Of course the United States Department of Justice would then ultimately take control of the case. And then once their investigation had been completed, it was determined that the person who'd served as the superintendent of the catalytic converter factory in Atlanta for the past two years had substituted the highly expensive platinum with the less expensive minerals.

Then later on, when a representative from the Homeland Security Agency was called to testify before a United States Congressional Committee, the agent stated that the data collected by the C. D. C. had failed to prove definitively that the plant superintendent's theft of the valuable platinum was the single, or even the primary cause, of the mysterious deaths at the wheel.

On the other hand, though, it was duly noted that since the thieving plant manager had been incarcerated in a Federal Prison, the total number of highway deaths in the U. S. had plummeted dramatically. That same agent also then stated that there was no evidence of any foreign nationals having been involved in the theft of the platinum.

Robert R. Railey

A Man Named Park

Contrary to popular belief, not all of the famous boxing gyms are located on the northeastern coast of America; in fact, one of the most successful gyms in the United States can be found in the very Southern town of Memphis, Tennessee.

For if a modern-day fight fan were to ever enter that relic of an old building which is partially hidden away in a waterfront alley in the old part of Memphis, then the hundreds of photographs that line the walls of Mort's Gym would attest to the fact that practically every single one of the great boxing champions from the past sixty years had spent at least a portion of their time training at Mort's Gym; and it's also quite possible that Mort had personally been involved in their training.

The legend of Mort's Gym began when a retired boxer and wrestler from the Memphis, Tennessee area was able to scrounge up enough ready cash to buy an old rundown warehouse building that not only was located close by to the Mississippi River, but it was also well hidden in an alley directly behind S. Front Street and not too far removed from Beale Street where some of the world's greatest blues singers had honed their talents.

Then eventually, the rickety old building which sat partially hidden away in an alley would be named Mort's Gym in honor of the new owner, Mortimer Manuel Philo, who'd migrated to the United States from the Middle East just shortly after the hostilities of the Second World War had ended. This was also right after the United Nations had ceded a portion of Palestine to the European Jewish people who'd been displaced by the Nazis government of Germany.

Yet all throughout the lean years while Mort was still struggling financially just to keep the doors open, he was forced to diversify his business by catering to an entirely new generation of athletes who preferred to combine their traditional boxing skills with a new sport called kickboxing, or mixed martial arts. Though in Mort's opinion the new sport was nothing more than a combination of street fighting, karate, kickboxing, and the good old-fashioned pugilism.

But then after having converted a fair amount of his business to a completely different type of sport, Mort would still concentrate primarily on the training of the more traditional type of fighters who compete for rankings in the World Boxing Association. At any rate, the fight game that Mort had known and loved had suddenly become quite vexing to him.

For not only did it require of him to visit a multitude of different venues and fight clubs in search of superior talent, but to his way of thinking the new sport would produce even a greater number of fatalities in the ring. Still, it was his business to entertain, and as such, he was willing to travel to the far edges of the world in order to find the necessary talent that he so desperately needed in order to stay at the top of the fight game; and he would continue to search for exceptional talent even if his latest prospect happened to reside in an outlaw country such as North Korea.

Yet as Mort was about to learn, it's a whole lot easier to enter a rogue nation like North Korea than it is to leave their country; and especially if your assemblage is trying to smuggle an internationally ranked twenty-three year old North Korean kickboxing fighter out of his homeland.

Nonetheless, after arriving at the international airport in Seoul, South Korea, Mort and his assistant, Kim Jong-Soo, were fortunate enough to be able to procure the services of a friendly South Korean civilian medical helicopter pilot who was happy to accept both the challenge and the large amount of cash that he could earn by risking his life and freedom.

However, the helicopter pilot felt obliged enough to warn the human smugglers that even though they would be flying below the North Korean radar, there were other dangers that they would inevitably have to face. One of which was the numerous groups of North Korean soldiers that routinely patrol the northern side of the border that separates North and South Korea.

For the most part, though, the incursion into enemy territory went smoothly for Mort and the so-called Memphis Boxing Mafia who then hurriedly gathered their little group of compatriots together for the long flight back home to Memphis, TN. In retrospect, however, Mort had only to wonder just exactly how they'd been able to get away with their little ruse so easily without being detected; and particularly since the North Koreans had a lengthy history of almost never allowing dissidents of any type to escape across their heavily guarded border.

Once back home in Memphis, Tennessee, then the next step in Mort's master plan would be to schedule a contest between the current American kickboxing champion, a certain Mr. Kyle Mansard, who was a twenty-six year old fighter from Kansas, and the newly arrived North Korean champion, Li Park. Of course it goes without saying that Mort would just naturally insist that the fight had to take place in his own gym in Memphis.

And regardless of the fact that Li Park had been a highly ranked fighter back home in North Korea, he would almost surely be rated much lower in the U. S. where the competition is much greater. Yet according to Mort who'd already produced a long and envious list of contenders and champions in his world-famous gym, he honestly believed that Li Park was destined to become one of the greatest fighters who'd ever stepped into the ring.

"The Fight of the Century," was the title that Mort had chosen for the upcoming contest. Of course that was simply a manifestation of his own personal way of promoting the upcoming epic battle between Li Park and Kyle Mansard; but it also took a ample degree of Mort's well-known guile and persuasion to convince the sponsors and the promoters to hold the contest in little old Memphis, Tennessee. Admittedly, though, he was only able to do so by agreeing to hold the inevitable rematch in Las Vegas, Nevada where the gate receipts and the probable pay-for-view T. V. revenues would almost assuredly be astronomically high.

"Hey-Days and Pay-Days": was one of Mort's most favorite phrases: and he always tried valiantly to espouse the virtues of his beloved fighters anytime that he felt the need to instill in them a few words of encouragement. Then just because of who he was, Mort would go out of his way to comfort and console his fighters, if by chance, one of them just happened to be lying prostrate in the middle of one of the sparring rings.

"Nothing but sunny skies are in your future," was another of Mort's favorite pep-talk types of themes that he frequently enjoyed using; and particularly if one of his fighters just happened to be going through a particularly dark period of time. At one point in time Mort had even gone so far as to quote Shakespeare to one of his fighters by saying, "Either victory, or else a grave." This was also very similar to another one of his favorite phrases which was, "Never, ever, give up."

Yet with only ninety days left in which to work with his new fighter, the time constraints would be extremely harrowing for both Mort and his able assistant Kim Jong-Soo, who not only would have to take turns in instructing Li Park about all of the various rules and regulations that any American kick boxer would have to be knowledgeable of, but they might also have to guard against the real possibility of having to fend off some nosy agents from the U. S. Immigration and Customs Enforcement Agency.

So by thinking ahead, Mort had previously released a media package to the World Kickboxing Association wherein he stated that he'd personally rescued an orphan known as Li Park, from the mean streets of San Francisco, California.

Then not so surprisingly, many of Mort's friends, and then along with, of course, the municipal authorities in the city Memphis, all got together and decided to proclaim the night of the upcoming fight as one of the greatest events to ever take place in the fabulous city of Memphis, Tennessee. The other, of course, was the day that the King of Rock and Roll, Elvis Presley, had decided to make Graceland his home.

Ultimately, then, the day of the fight would come and go: and thanks mostly to the efforts of Mort, the great event in Memphis had been a rousing success with Mort's fighter, Li Park, winning the contest by a very narrow margin. Just naturally, though, all eyes would then immediately be focused on city of Las Vegas, Nevada where the rematch between Li Park and the former world champion, Kyle Mansard, was expected to produce an even greater amount of interest; both at home and internationally.

On the other hand, though, the attention that Mort's gym was attracting was becoming somewhat unnerving to him; and that was mostly due to the fact that he wasn't sure whether the interest in his latest champion had to do with his ethnicity, or his talent. Furthermore, Mort had begun to wonder about the motives of some of the newly arrived Asians and Americans, who as a rule, were usually dressed in their Brooks Brothers business suits.

Nevertheless, the questions concerning the motives and objectives of the recent visitors to the Memphis area was a matter that would ultimately be settled when Li Park was arrested in the Memphis Memorial Cemetery while accepting some classified government documents from another Asian who just happened to be employed at the Oak Ridge National Laboratory in Tennessee where he worked as a technician in the fusion energy division.

In retrospect, Mort could understand why the normally ever watchful North Korean Military had allowed him and his assistant to exit their country with such a prized athlete in their grips. Apparently, Li Park had been recruited by the North

Korean government to help their spies smuggle some vital nuclear secrets out of the U. S. and then back home to North Korea.

Passkey

If asked, practically every single tenant in a near-downtown River City apartment complex would agree that Gary Phillips was the absolute best building superintendent in the entire city. And being that River City was one of the fastest growing metropolises to be found anywhere in the Midwestern part of the United States, that was certainly saying something.

In fact, until just recently Gary's apartment complex had been such a safe place to live that it was almost as if crime had taken a holiday; and that was somewhat due to the fact that Gary ran an extraordinarily tight ship, for when he was on the job crime was almost nonexistent. Of course Gary preferred not to count any of the minor disagreements that can occur almost anywhere; and especially when you have such a large group of people living under one roof. Besides, those minor incidents were almost always initiated by a visiting friend or relative of the people who inhabit the building and not by any of the residents. So for many a year Gary's apartment complex had been a relatively peaceful place in which to live.

Then too, it helped tremendously that Gary had an apartment in the same building as his tenants; and therefore, he was more readily available to handle the majority of their emergencies. To Gary, it mattered not whether it was night or day. More importantly, though, Gary was the type of maintenance man that preferred to immerse himself deeply into the personal lives of the building's residents. As a matter of fact, the tenants knew that not only would he be available to handle the majority of their maintenance problems, but they also knew that he would do his level best to protect them from any harm.

Consequently, then, during the ten years that Gary had been employed as the head maintenance man at the near downtown apartment complex, he could be counted upon to inject himself into the minor fracases that only rarely would necessitate the need to call in the River City Police Department for assistance. For as a rule, Gary would just simply show the troublemakers to the door.

Even so, life in any modern-day metropolis will almost certainly have its downside; and as such, a given number of those inhabitants can be expected to pass away on a regular basis. Of course death by natural causes, or even from accidents, will generally constitute the greater majority of those unfortunate but somewhat expected deaths; and that's particularly true if the establishment happens to be home to a high percentage of the elderly.

Nevertheless, there will always be exceptions to this inexact formula. For instance, if a person happens to live in one of the larger American cities that has a troubled history of gang violence, then it wouldn't be all that unusual to have some innocent bystanders become injured in one of those gangland types of shootouts.

Though this certainly wouldn't be the case in River City: for as a matter of fact just prior to the unprecedented spate of the three recent murders in Gary's retirement village, the complex had not recorded a single case of homicide in the previous twenty-five years of its existence.

So naturally, Detective Sergeant Frederick Engle of the River City Police Department's Homicide Division was deeply concerned over the sudden rise of homicides which were currently taking place in his hometown; and particularly since the murders were occurring at one of the city's largest and most popular retirement complexes. The problem was, however, there were no eyewitnesses to any one of the three separate and seemingly unconnected homicides, which had taken place during the previous six months.

Accordingly, then, it was quite understandable for detective Engel to feel as if it might be the proper time for him to employ a completely different approach in order to try to uncover some new evidence. So in the end, he decided upon a rather unconventional method of investigating the murders of those three elderly residents who'd all been killed in broad daylight, and in their own apartments.

His new theory was that he should try to work forwards instead of backwards which was the more conventional way of solving homicides. In other words he would concentrate primarily on the current residents and the employees of the complex. This then meant, of course, that he would ultimately have to re-interview the friends and the families of the three murder victims.

And since there'd been no forced entry in any of the three separate homicide cases, detective Engle had only to assume that the victims had willingly granted their killer or killers free access to their apartments. So naturally, it stands for reason that the person or persons responsible for the deaths of those three elderly people would have to be someone that the victims knew and trusted.

Although reasoning of that type would do nothing except to open up a brand new can of worms; for then, it meant that detective Engle would have to take a look at anyone who might have had a reason to be in the apartment complex on the days of the murders. But then somewhat coincidentally, all three of the homicides had occurred between the hours of 1:00 and 5:00 o'clock P. M.; and strangely enough, all three of the murders had taken place on Friday afternoons.

So then along with interviewing the residents, the investigators had also planned to question the people who work in the manager's office; and which then meant that they would also have to include the man in charge of the building's maintenance, Gary Phillips, who so far had been a great deal of help to detective Frederick Engle. Furthermore, the detective was actively counting on Gary's intimate knowledge of the personal lives of the more than one hundred residents in order to help him compile a Ben Franklin type of suspect list which is a list that would accentuate the positive and the negative traits of any potential suspects.

Hence with Gary's immeasurable help, detective Engle was able to assemble a detailed list of all of the previous complaints and the resentments which had been filed with the management. Incidentally, though, the facts of each incident had also been duly recorded in Gary's personal journal. Though when pressed by detective Engle as to why he'd found it necessary to keep such a complete record of his goings and comings, Gary professed the need to keep a journal of his daily routines in case he might someday be accused of misappropriating an item from any of the resident's apartments.

All the same, when all of their fine detective work had failed to identify even one viable suspect, Detective Sergeant Engle, and his partner, detective Dan Murray, decided that perhaps they should begin their investigation anew by taking a fresh look at the first of the trilogy of murders which was an eighty-four year old man, who at the time of his death, had been a resident of the complex for a little over ten years.

Unfortunately, though, the detectives were still unable to uncover any significant new leads in the rather brutal slaying of that first victim. Excepting for the fact that they remembered seeing the deceased's name listed as a witness on a formal complaint which had been duly registered with the manager's office. It seems that the first murder victim, whose name was Ed Milner, had sided with another resident who'd filed a minor complaint against no other than their beloved and deeply trusted maintenance man, Gary Phillips.

A common thread, perhaps? Even so, detective Engle couldn't help but to notice that certain parts of these horrible events were beginning to make him feel a little creepy. Thus when Engle and his partner decided to take a fresh look at the second and third homicides, they noticed that there might just be a connection to all three of the homicides after all.

For now they knew that the two latest victims, which had included the one from three months prior in which a seventy-two year old female named Sarah Gibbons had been bludgeoned to death with a blunt object, and the more recent death of a seventy-nine year old female named Martha Paris who'd been strangled to death with a lamp cord, were actually part of a small group of residents who'd had a minor run-in with the maintenance man, Gary Phillips.

So in the minds of the two detectives, it was beginning to look as if the maintenance man might just be good for all three of the murders. Or at the very least, they were beginning to believe that there might be enough motive to warrant them to bring him in to the main police headquarters for some additional questioning. Of course when asked Gary most readily agreed to submit to a polygraph test, which he said, would complete exonerate him of any wrongdoing; and so it did. For as a matter of fact Gary passed the lie detector test with flying colors.

Then back to square one, detectives Engle and Murray were forced to start all over again in their quest for the person responsible for the deaths of the three elderly residents. Yet when looking at the facts with a fresh mind, the detectives couldn't seem to find one single common denominator that would point directly to the guilty party; excepting, that is, for their own gut feelings that the killer had to be one of the current residents.

Of course a belief of that sort was somewhat fueled by the fact that access to the building was only possible through a communal front door which was located in the foyer of the building. Moreover, in order for a person to gain entrance through the locked front door without a passkey meant that they would have to be buzzed in after the apartment dweller had first viewed the person standing in the foyer via the closed-circuit television system that was installed in each apartment.

Then too, just knowing that the killer could be any one of the inhabitants that participates in the numerous activities which are held on the campus made the two detectives feel uneasy. Therefore, they decided that their presence during the noontime meal and the twice weekly bingo games might be enough to cause the guilty party to either move out of the building, or else to make a major mistake.

"So just what does a killer look like?" the detectives had asked themselves many times over; yet while they were sitting in the cafeteria along with several dozen of the residents as they ate their lunch had forced the detectives to reexamine the feelings about some of the more interesting characters they'd met while investigating the three homicides. Then given the time, the two detectives had come to the same conclusion that the ones who try to come off as being more grumpy than they actually are could most likely be removed from the list of probable suspects.

For in their opinion it was usually the quiet ones that you had to worry about. So as a rule, they were the ones that least wanted to get caught; and therefore, the quiet ones would more often than not subscribe to the theory that if you tell all your business, then you won't have any business of your own.

But be that as it may, a policeman cannot arrest a person based solely on their feelings and opinions; they need cold hard facts. So as a result, detectives Engle and Murray latest plan of action would be a sting operation in the hopes that the guilty party would take the bait. It would work something like this: the detectives would ask everybody involved in the operation of the apartment complex to pass the word along that the police were rapidly closing in on the killer; and also that they expected to make an arrest with the next twenty-fours.

Then not so surprisingly, the complex was suddenly abuzz with all sorts of rumors; and if the building had been a sinking ship instead of an apartment complex a person would have been able to watch the rats as they quickly deserted the ship.

Nonetheless, no one in a thousand years could have ever predicted that the sixty-five year old woman who was caught loading her personal items into a van around the midnight hour was the type of person that would ever harm another human being.

Yet when the detectives had Emily Pearson safely ensconced in an interrogation room at the main police headquarters, they were amazed by the amount of information that they'd received from all the various law enforcement organizations from across the country. For according to the information that they'd gleaned from an F. B. I. fingerprinting system named AFIS, and then also from the National Crime Information Center which was better known as (NCIC), the resident who was formally known as Emily Pearson was actually a woman named Naomi Brown who was wanted for questioning in another Midwestern state on a charge of homicide.

The Un-Crèche Trio

Never before in the ninety-seven years of its glorious existence had the caretakers of the Qualkenbush day nursery and orphanage of Exeter, England ever received such a set of triplets as the two boys and the one girl who'd just recently been turned over to their care. Of course just prior their family's most horrific and personal tragedy, the three children had resided with their parents, James D. and Janet P. Millard, in the Southwestern English community of Plymouth, Devon.

Melanie appeared to be the unquestioned leader of the trio which included her two younger brothers, William and Michael, both of which were also ten years of age but had actually been born a few minutes later than their older sister Melanie.

The trios' desire to disrupt anything and everything that was within their power to do so, could of course, be partially blamed on the unfortunate circumstances which had landed them in the orphanage in the first place. However, the stern and sometimes unforgiving headmaster of the highly distinguished school, a certain Mr. Phillip J. Westwood, had his own opinion as to why the three children were so inclined to be so completely at odds with the world.

In fact, Master Westwood was of the unshakeable opinion that a fairly sizeable percentage of the children of the world were just simply bad seeds. And for some unexplainable reason he sincerely believed that those dysfunctional types of children had failed miserably to develop into what he considered to be the normal twenty-first century proper English children and students. So for that reason, he was somewhat tempted to agree with a few of the more obscure and less famous of the modern-day genome scientists who were prone to state that the actions of those unfortunate types children were most likely pre-determined by their family's DNA.

And as unfortunate as it might have been for the faculty at such a distinguished school and orphanage, Master Westwood never saw the ending coming. Still, the situation was just as unfortunate for the three Millard children since quite a few of the numerous incidents which had taken place at the orphanage had been unfairly blamed on the trio whether they were guilty of the infractions or not; for it appeared to be a case of your reputation has preceded you.

As a matter of fact, one of the most notable of the more recent incidents to befall the prestigious school had come to light during the last week of May as all twenty-three of the fourth grade students were being primed to be promoted up to the fifth grade. This then, would just naturally include all three of the members of the Millard brood: Melanie, William, and Michael.

Then again, it wasn't so much that the so-called Un-Crèche Trio had earned extremely bad marks in their studies at the school during that particular year, for they had not; Melanie had seen to that. Instead, it was their deportment away from the classroom that left much to be desired.

So regardless of the pretentious claims of love and tolerance that Master Westwood had always publically expressed for the children in his care, he was solely intent upon on finding a way to expedite what he hoped would be the ultimate expulsion of that particular trio of overly imaginative and rambunctious ten year olds from his beloved school and orphanage. And to that end, he considered his goal to rid the school of the worrisome triplets to be especially urgent upon the heels of one of the trio's most diabolical escapades for which they were suspected of printing and then passing out a large number of handbills which expressly stated that summer school would be mandatory for every fourth grader who'd failed to carry an A average during the course of the regular school year.

Though needless to say, practically every one of the students at the academy would most likely be required to attend summer school anyway since they couldn't legally move away from the campus until they'd reached their fifteenth birthday. That said, it was a bitter pill for Master Westwood to swallow when the newly elected board of directors at the Qualkenbush Academy failed to back him on his third and latest attempt to evict what he considered to be the most troublesome trio of children that he'd ever had the displeasure to meet in his thirty-one years of service at the prestigious school and orphanage.

In the meantime, however, Master Westwood's latest thinking was that that he might have to resign himself to the unpleasant fact that he would most likely have to tolerate the Un-Crèche Trio for another five years; that is, of course, unless he decided to take an early retirement from the position that he most truly loved.

Eventually, though, the old proverbial straw that broke the camel's back just happened to come about during the last physical education class that Melanie and the rest of the fourth graders would have to participate in during that particular school year.

The major indiscretion which had supposedly been perpetrated by the now famous trio of the Millard clan had come about during a soccer match that'd pitted Melanie's fourth graders against the older and much more experienced fifth graders in the school's annual grudge match that was played at the end of the regular school year.

At first, everything appeared to be going normally, until, that is, when during the last period of the match the fifth graders had managed to go ahead by a score of two to one. Of course this infuriated Melanie to no end, and for that reason she was determined to do something about it. Then true to nature, her instincts told her that it would be extremely helpful if she could somehow manage to gravely injure the enemy's goalkeeper; but with the entire faculty present and accounted for, Melanie decided to settle for something a little less obvious and destructive.

But then as she was trying to find a way out of their jam, she decided that she might simply lay down a brand-new white line in the front of her own team's goal and which then would drastically alter the distance from whence an opposing player would have to kick the soccer ball in an effort to score a goal. So with a small plastic bag full of white chalk hidden in her uniform blouse, Melanie was all set to change the location of the goal lines when her brother William was able to not only assist his brother Michael in a takeaway, but while standing with his back toward the goal he was somehow able to use a bicycle-kick for the score.

Thus as a result of her brother's extreme effort, Melanie's team had found itself tied with the fifth grade team at a score of two and two. Then somewhat surprisingly, her team was able to score twice more in a row which had basically eliminated the need for her to cheat.

It was, however, quite possible that there would still be a mighty stiff price to pay for her high-minded intentions when just shortly thereafter a female staff member discovered a baggie full of crushed white chalk in Melanie's blouse while she was in the shower. So naturally, Melanie was called in to Master Westwood's office to answer the possibility of a conspiracy to cheat charge.

"Well just exactly what do you have to say for yourself?" Master Westwood said.

"In all honesty Master Westwood I was more expecting to be complimented for my desire to maintain the dignity of the out of bounds lines by refreshing them during our breaks than to be called on the carpet for my good intentions," Melanie said.

"Horse feathers: and if the truth be known neither you nor your brothers have ever appreciated what the Qualkenbush Academy has done for you and your little family; now have you?" Master Westwood said.

"Oh! Master Westwood, how can you say such a thing: my brothers and I dearly love both you and your school. Why just this morning I was telling Michael and William how fortunate we are to be associated with such a loving and caring staff of professionals as we have at this school; and that's not even counting the dozens of friends that we've made while during our sojourn at this wonderful institution," Melanie said.

"We'll see: in the meantime, however, I strongly suggest that you and brothers watch your step very carefully because I am definitely going to keep an eye on the three of you. You are now dismissed," Master Westwood said.

Glad to be out from under his clutches, Melanie very quickly then made her way over to the school's cafeteria where she hoped that she would be able to meet up with her two brothers, who at that very instant, were busily concocting the trio's next assault on society.

Then as shocking as it may be, the trios' newest plan of attack was fairly simple in its nature. The three Millard children would organize a secret society which in their immature minds would rival any of the finest intelligence agencies in the world; and in their opinion it might even be superior to America's very own C. I. A.

But then not to be outdone by some children, Master Westwood had resolved to attend the school's next board meeting which had been designated as an emergency meeting in order to celebrate the arrival of a new board member from London, England who'd just recently relocated to the southwestern English city of Exeter.

The school's newest board member, a certain Dr. Filmont J. Fowler, was a distinguished educator and a very highly regarded author of many of England's current school textbooks. It'd also been reported that he was looking forward to be in attendance at his first ever executive board meeting at the Qualkenbush School and Orphanage since moving back to his hometown of Exeter, England. Then without a doubt, the doctor's return could have easily been called a homecoming since he actually was an alumnus of the famous school.

In fact, Doctor Fowler's storybook life was familiar to every member of the faculty at Qualkenbush since he'd previously been in charge of one of the Queen Mother's favorite passions, the education of Great Britain's children. And in addition to that great honor, he was known as one of Queen Elizabeth's most favorite persons in the whole of Great Britain.

So at Doctor Fowler's very fist board meeting, the lists of charges against the trio that were being presented to the board by Master Westwood would have been very impressive indeed, had they been true. But when Master Westwood was being questioned by the board's newest member, about the children's surname, which was Millard of course, Doctor Fowler told the board that not only had he heard of the tragic case of the Millard family, but that he and the Queen Mother had determined to rescue the three children just as soon as they could be located.

As it turned out, the three Millard children, AKA the Un-Crèche Trio, were directly related to the queen of England and they would therefore be invited to live with the Queen and her family in Windsor Castle. At times, life can be stranger than fiction.

Cross-Words

For more years than he cared to remember, Joseph W. Martin had labored long and lovingly over the tens of thousands of crossword puzzles that he'd worked and saved for posterity. It was his life's greatest passion. Ultimately, though, the love of his life would end up destroying him.

Yet even after acknowledging that he might just possibly have an addictive personality, Joseph had unwittingly allowed this seemingly innocent and harmless looking hobby of working crossword puzzles to manifest itself into a situation that might have caused him to become even more mentally unbalanced than he already was. For to Joseph, the solving of the crossword puzzles was the most important thing on his mind during every waking moment of every single day; and at times, he'd even found himself dreaming about the "beautiful words" that he might learn on any given day.

Moreover, the greatest thrill that Joseph had ever found in his solitary way of life was simply the act of looking up his brand-new and "beautiful words" in an online dictionary just so he would not only know the meaning of the new word, but that he would also be aware of the proper pronunciation.

Yet all throughout the last few months of his life, Joseph had tried valiantly to learn how to cope with that overpowering obsession of his which was to constantly be working crossword puzzles. Unfortunately, however, his addiction had progressed to the point of overshadowing practically every other facet of his self-induced life of solitude. His addiction, the likes of which had caused him to continually move his lips and even mumble to himself whilst he was trying to remember the exact meaning and the proper pronunciation of the latest word that he'd just learned.

So it goes without saying that this peculiar practice would not necessarily be considered an attractive habit for a person to be practicing, and particularly when one is out and about in public places.

For as a matter of fact, some of the employees at the local neighborhood stores and malls where Joseph did most of his shopping had begun to point and snicker at him any time that he happened to enter their establishments. Then too, it would have been practically impossible for the other shoppers to miss the constant mumbling and the moving of the lips when Joseph either passed them by in the store aisles or when they were standing next to them at the checkouts.

"He's just a little crazy but hopefully he's harmless," was the general attitude taken by the majority of the local people. "For after all, his addiction could have been a lot worse," some said. "And besides, it's not as if he is actually harming anybody, and it's certainly a lot safer than texting while driving a car," said a few others who just happened to know that he was addicted to the working of crossword puzzles.

Joseph had apparently heard the whispers of discontent coming from his fellow shoppers in the small community where he resided; and yet, he still continued to act as if he were impervious to the outside influences of his own little world. It wasn't so much that Joseph was completely antisocial, he did, however, feel extremely blessed that he was able to work the nightshift at the local power plant where he was afforded only the barest amount of interaction with his fellow employees; and so naturally, his social skills were sorely lacking.

But then even after having been branded as a local pariah whose house was well-known, and even somewhat feared by the neighborhood children, that particular label suited Joseph just fine; for as he'd said many times over "he wasn't taking on any new friends."

Unfortunately, though, it was beginning to appear as if Joseph might have a problem of an unimaginable magnitude.

For in an unlikely turn of events, a sketch by a local police artist was being continually aired over the local television stations. It seems that for months on end a serial rapist had been running rampant all throughout Joseph's neighborhood; and reportedly, the rapist had just recently committed a brazen daytime home invasion where he'd raped a woman who lived in the adjoining block. The problem was, however, Joseph could have easily posed for the police artist who'd created the composite sketch of the rapist for in fact, the two faces really were that similar in appearance.

Yet for his own peace of mind Joseph knew full well that all he would have to do would be to allow the police investigators to enter his home where they would very quickly determine that the person who'd hoarded all of those previously worked crossword puzzles that were stacked neatly from the floor to the ceiling in each and every room of his fairly modern three bedroom ranch home could not possibly have had the inclination, or even the time, to commit the recent string of the home burglaries and the rapes of several different women in his neighborhood.

All the same, a few members of a local neighborhood watch committee were beginning to form their own opinion as to the guilt or innocence of their strange and somewhat elusive neighbor, Joseph W. Martin.

So with the planning already in progress on how best to celebrate during the upcoming holiday weekend, a few of the local children had made some secret Halloween plans of their own as a way to show their disapproval, and even their growing fear, of the mumbling and the terribly unkempt man who'd unwittingly become the target of their jokes.

Of course the super extravagant Halloween trick that the local children had rather foolishly decided upon in order to perpetrate a truly memorable joke against their newly named nemeses would normally be considered a far too dangerous of an event to levy against a person's vilest enemy.

Their plan was simple and straightforward. A chosen group of the neighborhood boys would gather up several paper bags full of their family's dog manure which would then be placed at both the front and rear doors of the mumbling man's home. Then after simultaneously knocking on both of the doors, the children would set the paper bags on fire.

The joke, if there ever was one to be had, would be to watch the hapless homeowner as he feverously stomped the burning paper sacks in an effort to extinguish the fire. Of course when the target of the ill-thought out prank attempted to put out the fire, he would just naturally end up with the dog's stool all over his shoes and his front porch.

Unfortunately, however, the children had interrupted Joseph while he was in the midst of stripping and refinishing an antique piece of furniture that he'd just recently purchased at an estate sale. And also just as regrettably, he just happened to be holding a freshly opened can of paint thinner which ended up being splayed generously on both the front porch floor and the interior of the front of the house as Joseph valiantly continued on with his vain attempt to stomp out the fire.

In the meantime, the interior of the front of the house had become so fully engulfed in the flames that Joseph had no option then but to hurriedly race to the rear of the house where the same exact scenario was about to take place. Thus with both ends of the house ablaze, and also with thousands of newspaper crossword puzzles stacked to the ceiling in each and every room of the house, Joseph was trapped; and as unfortunate as it may be he would perish in the flames.

The Grain Committee

pproximately one year after his death, a journal was discovered in Martin Balearic's upstate New York mansion. And hopefully, the following information will help to corroborate the authenticity of that almost unbelievable chapter of history. It reads as follows.

After arriving at The Hague in the Netherlands, I was hurriedly chauffeured over to the Ministry of Public Health, Welfare and Sports building where I'd been invited to attend a "Top-Secret" meeting of a very select group of some the world's most powerful leaders.

The reason given for this highly secretive meeting, which consisted of only a few select members of the United Nations Security Council, was for us to try to find a way to feed the burgeoning generations of the ever expanding population of the global world. So without a doubt, "The Grain Committee," as it was unofficially known, would inevitably become one of the most stringent regulatory commissions to have ever come out of the United Nations; and since I'd previously served as the Secretary General of the United Nations I'd been asked to write an ultra secretive and innocuous sounding white paper of which the contents had almost grudgingly been agreed upon by only a select few members of the Security Council.

Though at first glance, an outsider would have readily noticed that the ethnicity of the "special committee," as it was called, was made up entirely of protestant and catholic old white men who hailed primarily from North America and the middle European countries; and so basically, the committee was nothing more than a good ole boy's club. Although I'm quite sure that none of our members would have dared to admit publicly to that type of ethnic stereotyping. Even so, the very essence of that highly prejudice white paper had spelled out in no uncertain terms that no other types of people should even bother to apply.

Though by that point in time, the situation in the world had become increasingly intolerable; and of course that was due mainly to the fact that the world's population had begun to exceed the estimated number of people that could adequately be fed by the amount of tillable acreage and the technology that existed at the time. What's more, even the mostly peaceful protests around the world had not only started to turn violent, but more importantly, the demonstrations had begun to spread across the entire face of the globe.

In those days it was fairly common to read about the mass burials of tens of thousands of people who were dying of starvation and disease on a daily basis. Then in addition to those who were dying of starvation, there were untold numbers of street demonstrators who were continually being massacred by their own police and military units. Furthermore, the major food riots around the globe were projected to persist just as long as the starving and dying people of the world had the strength to resist

Yet to the representatives of those select countries who'd been invited to attend that top-secret Grain Committee meeting in the Netherlands, it was strongly recommended that the leaders of our native countries should seriously consider the use of both their vast financial resources and their superior military establishments to divert the bulk of the world's supply of grain, meat products, and produce to the ports of the Grain Committee members only.

This then meant, of course, that the members of our very select cartel would have to deploy numerous open sea blockades in and around the ports of the countries which had not been invited to become members of our special interest group.

Of course we were all terribly concerned about the responses from countries such as China and India; for after all, those two countries alone accounted for approximately one third of the world's total population; plus the fact, we were also well aware of the fact that both of those two countries were in possession of nuclear weaponry.

In the end, however, the panel decided that there was no other alternative available to us but to continue on down our path which would be to risk the possibility of having to go to war with those two giants. Nevertheless, the members of the committee eventually came to the conclusion that since China and India shared a common border, then they would most likely end up destroying each other anyway.

Indeed, the future looked bleak: for without the likes of a great scientist and agronomist such as, Norman Borlaug, who unfortunately had passed away back in the year of two thousand and nine, it's doubtful that the farmers of the future will be able to feed an estimated population of 9,352,458,484 human beings when the year 2050 rolls around. For during his lifetime, the 1970 Nobel Prize winning agronomist Norman Borlaug had not only been recognized for starting the Green Revolution, but he'd also been credited with saving over a billion people from starvation by developing a disease resistant type of wheat.

So without a doubt, the agronomists of the future will definitely have an enormous problem on their hands; and that's just simply because of the fact that our experts have deduced that our wheat production has already reached its "peak". This means, of course, that try as we might it's doubtful that we will ever be able to produce any more bushels of wheat per acre than we presently produce. However, we humans are also extremely busy in clearing the rain forest in South America in order to plant more crops. So as a result, that type of procedure will almost definitely add to the already dangerous global warming problem.

Thus after having laid out all of the necessary reasons for us to have to impose such draconian measures upon certain regions of the world in order for the citizens of the wealthier countries to be able to survive, the Secretary of Agriculture of one of the Scandinavian counties decided to very abruptly exit the meeting; and while at the same time stating that as long as he lived he could never in good conscience vote for such an elitist type of program.

Unfortunately, though, before that particular gentleman could safely exit the building, or even to make a phone call, he was kidnapped and then executed by two of the undercover Interpol Policemen who'd been placed there to provide security.

It was beginning to look as if the world was about to be divided into two distinct groups of people. If so, then the new world order would consist of the countries already in possession of the military establishments that would be capable of controlling both the shipping lanes on the high seas, and the air space above. In reality, however, this kind thinking is nothing new: for if a person of today were to venture back in history then they would see that the ancient Greeks and the Romans did precisely the very same thing; they used their military power to rule the world.

All the same, it certainly wouldn't be an easy matter for a select number of supposedly God-fearing people to allow billions of their fellow men to starve to death. Therefore, it was significantly important for me to make it abundantly clear to everyone else on the committee that some sort of a propaganda program would have to be instituted in order for the nations with the most sophisticated and powerful navies and air forces to feel justified in using force.

A hook or a wild card, such as the types that the writers of detective stories so cleverly impose upon their readers would definitely do the trick, we thought.

In other words, the inevitable subjects of starvation must be made to appear to be the aggressors. Moreover, we would need another country to blame for our troubles in as much the same way that we turned the sinking of the USS

Maine in Havana Harbor into a reason to begin the Spanish, American War.

Or perhaps it could be a situation similar to the sinking of the RMS Lusitania which helped to stampede the U. S. into entering WWI. Of course there was also the incidence of Pearl Harbor, Hawaii which had helped to push the U. S. into entering WWII. Then later on, the Gulf of Tonkin Resolution granted the then U. S. President, Lyndon Johnson the authority to stop the communist aggression in Southeast Asia. Then finally, there was the terrible 9/11 incident which eventually led the U. S. into a ten year plus war in the Middle East.

Anything is possible, we thought, and since somebody at the meeting had mentioned the phrase of bio-terrorism it was decided that a few nationals from each country on the list of nations that we intended to blockade would be kidnapped and then arrested on some trumped-up terrorism charges. It was honestly believed by the majority of us that once our countries had done a Machiavellian job of propagandizing some of the committee's fictitious terroristic types of exploits on those so-called rogue nations, then the citizens of our respective homelands would feel justified in demanding some type of retribution.

Another one of our committee members stated that it would actually be more humane for us to discontinue the exporting all types of edible goods to the countries that we no longer wished to trade with than it would be for us to use the more conventional and drastic measures such as the use of napalm or nuclear bombs.

Next, another panel member suggested that perhaps we should simply employ a propaganda type of strategy which would be comparable to the program that the Nazi Party of Germany had used prior to WWII. That is, we would debase and disparage the populace of the countries which the members of the grain committee were willing to let starve to death.

Then finally, one of our members just happened to envision one of the most ingenious and devious plans of all time. The members of our grain committee would publicly accuse the countries on our embargo list of harboring and exporting a new type of bird flu which had the potential to be even more deadly than strain of the 1918 bird flu which had killed an estimated 50,000,000 to a 130,000,000 million people worldwide.

Unfortunately, however, the story in the journal ended there; but what was not written in the journal, and never could have been included at the time that the journal was written, was the history that follows.

Author's Notes

In hindsight, one might say that justice has been served: for within only a short period of time following the planned starvation of approximately one third of the world's population, the authorities have since discovered that a scientist working at the laboratory where the 1918 Avian Influenza (Bird Flu) virus had not only been brought back to life, but that the rogue scientist had secretly removed the deadly virus from the lab with plans to personally avenge the deaths of the billions of people who would have starved to death as the direct result of the actions that were about to be taken by the grain committee.

It has now become perfectly clear to the modern-day investigators that a Kenyan National by the name of Dr. Adin Mila was the person most responsible for the unleashing of that particular live virus upon the world. It seems that Dr. Mila was so terribly distraught by the fact that his homeland in East Africa had been utterly devastated by the blockade which had prevented the lifesaving food supplies from reaching the drought and war stricken country of his ancestors.

At last count, NATO has estimated that the world's total population has now dropped below the four billion mark. Thankfully, though, the experts have said that the pandemic seems to have reached its peak. Then too, Dr. Mila and his supervisor, and then along with all of the rest of the scientist who'd worked at the laboratory where the 1918 Swine/Bird Flu virus had been revived and then unleashed have all been found guilty in an international court of law where they were summarily sentenced to death.

The Lorraine Park Mystery

Chapter One

During the past several decades, the Lorraine Park swimming pool had somehow managed to outlast a plethora of city administrations that seemed hell-bent on slashing the city budget to such a degree as to cause the pool to be shut down. Then too, the neighborhood pool had to also survive the Aids scare of the early nineteen eighties which had prompted more than a few communities around the country to shutter their pools for fear of contamination.

So when the longtime city parks and recreations department employee, Winfield Cousins, showed up for work at seven o'clock a. m. on that seemingly average Sunday which just happened to be the 2nd day August, it wasn't so much the threat of contamination that was on his mind, but rather it was the acrid smoke that could be seen billowing from the rooftop of a house that was barely a half block away from his vantage point at the pool.

Yet after only another few minutes Cousins was able to observe a lone male figure who was not only standing in the front yard of the burning residence, but the man appeared to be talking on a walkie-talkie as he was apparently waiting for the first fire trucks to arrive on the scene.

But then as soon as the house fire had been properly extinguished by the city's fire department, Cousins was more than a little amazed by the large numbers of police and fire officials that continued to enter and then exit that partially burned out residence. However, Cousins became a whole lot more interested in the goings on at the fire scene when he recognized that one of those officials was the county coroner.

This scenario most likely meant that there'd been a fatality in the house fire.

Chapter Two

Jeremy Blackford had honorably served on the River City Police Department for a period of several years before being become acquainted with an attractive and seemingly unattached brand-new civilian jailor at the River City Detention Center. Now whether Jeremy had initially been enthralled by Kathy Moore's sparkling personality and her lively presence, no one could say; but as far as Jeremy was concerned it was love at first sight. Nevertheless, there remained one very large obstacle in the two lover's path; Jeremy was already married to a wonderful woman who was doing an excellent job of raising their children.

Regrettably, though, those types of love triangles are certainly nothing new to this old world of ours; and generally speaking a situation of that type is most generally initiated by the male counterpart who then valiantly attempts to pull both ends of the relationship so tightly together so as to cause it to be completely unraveled. And in a number of these types of love and hate relationships it's almost commonplace for push to come to shove. Though more often than not, it's usually the male partner that feels obligated to make promises to the female counterpart that he's not always in a position to keep.

Then too, it could also be said that Kathy Moore was caught up in a dilemma of her own making; for at twenty-four years of age she was a woman that was certainly not getting any younger. And since she was still childless she would have had to very honestly weigh her future outlook on the relationship; and especially since she might just end up investing several years of her life with a married man. That is, of course, if having children was something that she might have wished for. Of course there was another side of Kathy's personal life that not everybody in River City was fully aware of; and that was simply the fact that on different occasions she'd been known to frequent gay bars.

Although some of the people that knew Kathy have said that she might have been prompted to search out the company of a few of her gay acquaintances on those particularly lonely evenings when Jeremy was forced to spend some time at home with his wife and children. Accordingly, then, it was supposedly during one of those times when Kathy was out on the town that she'd bumped into a coworker at a downtown nightclub which had resulted in her ending up in a most discreet relationship with yet another married man.

That particular relationship, if there ever really was one, would prove to be exceptionally short-lived when shortly thereafter Kathy was forced to file a complaint with her supervisor which included a sexual harassment charge, and then along with the allegation that that very same coworker had allegedly been seen abusing some of the prisoners that they were both accountable for.

In the end, however, it was Kathy's testimony against her former coworker which had proved to be the death knell of his existence at the county jail; and as a result, her complaint was one of the primary reasons for his dismissal. So naturally, this would have certainly accounted for the personal threats that the distraught and very angry man had allegedly made towards Kathy. In fact it was purported that he'd vowed to get even with her if it was the last thing that he ever did? Of course those types of thoughtless ravings and threats of violence by a former employee are pretty well commonplace nowadays; but if the object of the threats just happens to end up dead, then perhaps that person's threats should have been taken a little more seriously.

Chapter Three

During the entire timeframe of the Lorraine Park Mystery, which included both a case of arson and an act of homicide, the date of August the 1st just happened to fall on a Saturday. And it also so just happened that a River City Police Officer, a patrolman by the name of Jeremy Blackford, was scheduled to work the third shift on that very same evening. Jeremy didn't consider himself any different from the rest of the mostly young and energetic police patrol officers who were employed by the River City Police Department in as much as, he too, preferred working the second and third shifts. For as a rule, nighttime is when the players usually come out of their lairs and dens; and therefore, it's up to a special breed of proactive police officers to keep the unsavory types of citizens in line.

Though just prior to his appearance at that particular third shift roll call, which took place at the River City Police Department's main headquarters, Jeremy had stopped by Kathy Moore's house for a brief visit. Then immediately following his attendance at the roll call he'd proceeded to top off his patrol car's gas tank before advising dispatch that not only was he in the proper sector of the city, but that he was also available to start receiving radio calls. More importantly, though, it was at that particular time when Jeremy was performing those menial but necessary tasks that Kathy Moore was having a telephone conversation with a relative which had ended just shortly before 11:00 p m on the 1st of August. This then meant, of course, that Kathy was still alive and well when Jeremy began his 11:00 o'clock p.m. to 7:00 o'clock a.m. shift.

According to the River City Police Department's official dispatch records for that particular Saturday evening, and then on into the following Sunday morning, Jeremy's shift was unusually busy. For as a matter of fact the only time that his whereabouts couldn't be verified by dispatch was a period of sixty some-odd minutes which had ranged from 11:00 o'clock p.m. Saturday until a little past midnight on the following Sunday morning. This period of time would be the "window of opportunity" that the prosecution would seize upon in order to try to prove that Jeremy had had the necessary amount of time that it would have taken for him to return to Kathy Moore's house in order to commit the horrendous crime that he was about to be charged with.

In all actuality, however, the prosecution's proposed window of opportunity of sixty some-odd minutes in which Jeremy's time was unaccounted for was not entirely correct; for at one point during that critical period of time when Jeremy's exact whereabouts couldn't be confirmed, Jeremy had contacted dispatch in order to see if there were any outstanding warrants on a well-known drug dealer that he'd observed while driving through his district. Then after learning that there were no open warrants against the drug dealing man that he'd arrested in the past, Jeremy knew that he didn't have any probable cause to pull him over; and so naturally he had to give the man a pass.

Also during that same period of time on that fateful Saturday evening which the prosecution was fond of calling a grand window of opportunity, two impartial witnesses had reported seeing Jeremy driving his patrol car past a tavern which just happened to be located several miles from the house where Kathy Moore was murdered. Moreover, the prosecutor's "window of opportunity" was about to shrink even further when Jeremy recalled that while on patrol that evening he'd come across an unusual automobile accident which had taken place several miles from the arson and homicide crime scene. Then later on, Jeremy was able to make an exact drawing of the accident which he and his attorney would then ultimately present to the prosecution as part of his detailed and official alibi package for that particular Saturday evening.

Unbeknownst to Jeremy, however, a person who'd witnessed the very same accident that Jeremy had so accurately described in his alibi statement had not only been located, but the witness had positively identified Jeremy Blackford as one of the police officers he'd seen at the scene of the aforementioned accident. Yet for reasons known only to the authorities, that person's identity was never made known to either Jeremy or his defense attorney as the law requires.

Nonetheless, the prosecution's supposed "window of opportunity" would once again come under even more scrutiny when just shortly after midnight on the morning of August the 2^{nd,} Jeremy was dispatched to transport a suspect to the lockup. And interestingly enough, that very same suspect would testify in court that Jeremy had appeared to be both calm and composed and even a lot friendlier towards him than all of the other police officers that he'd previously been in contact with.

Chapter Four

So with his third shift of duty officially behind him, and also since it was his usual custom to do so, Jeremy drove over to Kathy's house before heading on home. On that particular Sunday morning, however, a camera just happened to take a photograph of him as he drove his personal car past a bank that not only was located on the same street where Kathy lived, but the bank was located only about a block away from her residence.

Those precious few seconds which had elapsed after the bank's camera had taken Jeremy's photograph, and then also including the time that it would take for a person to enter and then exit the burning house, would then ultimately end up being very crucial to Jeremy's defense. For during the subsequent trial, Detective Corporal Cliff Spence of the River City Police Department, who'd been assigned as the lead detective on the Kathy Moore arson and homicide case, would testify in court that there was a time span of some sixty some odd seconds from the time that Jeremy had driven past the bank and the time that he'd contacted dispatch to report the fire at Kathy's residence.

This then meant, of course, that Jeremy would have had to have driven the distance between the bank and Kathy's residence and then hurriedly enter her house where he was alleged to have started the fire. Yet when Jeremy testified at his own trial he swore under oath that upon entering the burning house he'd just barely had enough time to peer through a partially opened bedroom door where he'd observed Kathy's body lying on top of the burning bed before the intense heat from the fire chased him from the smoke filled residence.

Then immediately following that most awful disaster of having just witnessed the person that he supposedly loved being consumed by fire, Jeremy was ordered to return to the main police headquarters where he voluntarily gave a statement to the lead detective; and where he also willingly surrendered the police uniform that he'd worn during the previous evening. As per protocol, the uniform was then sent off to the state police lab where it could be checked for traces of accelerants and human blood. But then eventually, Jeremy's uniform would also be sent to the F. B. I. Lab in Washington, D. C. for further testing.

And so it goes without saying that Jeremy's total cooperation with the lead detective on that particular case could be called commendable; but since he'd taken these actions without the benefit of a Police Union Representative, or even his own personal attorney, his actions could have also been called foolhardy. Then again, that's usually the way that innocent people think for in their hearts they sincerely believe that since they have nothing to hide, the truth will set them free.

Chapter Five

Then further on down the road the fact ultimately emerged that the lead detective in charge of the Lorraine Park Mystery arson and homicide case had been Jeremy's FTO, or field training officer when Jeremy was still a probationary police officer. And according to most accounts the two of them had remained fairly good friends throughout the remaining years that Jeremy Blackford had served on the force.

Nevertheless, when an investigator is prone to leaping to conclusions as to the guilt or innocence of a fellow officer, one can only wonder if there might have been a well hidden and deep-seated resentment, or even possibly a personal dislike beneath the imitation of a true friendship which had supposedly been there all along. Yet at other times, a situation can occur when two men are attracted to the same woman. Of course speculations of that type can never be substantiated by mere assumptions for a state of affairs of that nature could have easily been a career buster for either one of the police officers.

Having said that, Jeremy was the one that was on trial for his life and not the lead investigator Detective Corporal Clifford Spence. So therefore, it would be up to Jeremy and his defense attorney to come up with an alternative and plausible person of interest for the police to investigate further.

Nonetheless, a tack of that nature would be extremely important for the defense team; and particularly being that the lead detective and his partner had spent very little of their time and energy investigating any of the other possible suspects that could be linked to "The Lorraine Park Mystery Case." Of course one of the most notable potential suspects was Kathy's former co-worker, Linus Enfield, who just prior to the arson and homicide case had not only been fired from his job at the jail, but had also been known to have made threats against Kathy; and consequently, he could have easily been considered a person of interest.

Chapter Six

As a former criminal defense attorney, Gregory Splittorf, had earned the reputation of being one of the most feared legal adversaries in the entire River City Metropolitan area; and consequently, he was well known throughout the entire Midwest as a complex man who could win a very difficult case. For in those days, the rumor was if you wanted to get away with murder in River City then you should hire Greg Splittorf.

Without a doubt, Mr. Splittorf could be a very difficult person to get along with. And being that River City was home to a sizable number of individuals who were directly related to some of the city's first inhabitants who'd emigrated to the U. S. from Germany, it seemed only natural that the locals would have attributed Greg's fierce determination and commitment to the fact that during World War I his grandfather had served as a Captain in the German Army.

What was truly amazingly, however, was the fact that Mr. Splittorf had decided to switch sides; and as unlikely as it might have seemed to the local members of the bar, Greg was elected to the office of prosecuting attorney. So naturally, this new state of affairs was especially vexing to the local criminal defense attorneys, who from then on, would have to accept the fact that their newly elected district attorney had already used up all of the tricks of the trade, legal or otherwise; and therefore, it was surmised by all that River City's new prosecuting attorney would never tolerate any of the types of courtroom shenanigans which he'd perfected while representing his former clients who primarily had been big-time drug dealers and murderers.

Even so, not everybody in the community was convinced that Mr. Splittorf would even hang around long enough to complete his first term in office; for since he was such a virile and healthy looking young man it was widely believed that the handsome and intelligent prosecutor was simply using his newfound political office as a stepping stone on the way to the mansion at the state capital. But then according to one of Greg's former associates, he'd once stated that the governorship was only a stone's throw away from the White House in Washington, D. C.

So when speaking of someone with personal ambitions of that magnitude it could easily be said that Greg Splittorf was the type of person that wouldn't hesitate to prosecute his own mother; and more than likely than not, he would seek the maximum sentence if he thought that it would better his chances of climbing up the social and political ladder.

Furthermore, one had only to research a few of the cases that Mr. Splittorf had won in the local court systems in order to gain some insight into just exactly what the trial lawyers could expect in the future. For as its plainly stated in the law text books; "in jurisprudence, prosecutorial misconduct is a procedural defense in which, a defendant may argue that they should not be held criminally liable for actions which may have broken the law because the prosecution acted in an "inappropriate" or unfair manner."

This type of defense is similar to selective prosecution and was one of Greg Splittorf's favorite courtroom and political maneuverings before being elected to the office of district attorney. For as a local newspaper journalist had so aptly defined the present climate in the various local county and city courtrooms: "the party in River City is definitely over, there will be no more easy victories for trial attorneys."

Chapter Seven

Now that Greg Splittorf would no longer be available to defend the less fortunate of the River City residents who found themselves in need of a good criminal attorney, the replacing of the reigning champion of the local courtrooms had proved to be more of a challenge than anyone had figured.

Yet after interviewing practically every single one of the three hundred or so attorneys that practiced law in River City it was mutually agreed upon that Greg's likely successor would be none other than the hard drinking, and the hard charging criminal attorney, Wes Fortune, who was the byproduct of the marriage between his English grandmother and his Italian American grandfather, Geno Fortunato, who'd been wounded in France during the Second World War. Then immediately following the war, his grandparent's had relocated to the United States of America where his grandfather had Americanized his surname by changing it to Fortune.

In short, Wes Fortune was especially well-known for his volatile temper and vulgar mouth; and it'd been wildly rumored that while awaiting a verdict in a courtroom hallway he'd actually struck another attorney in the face as they argued bitterly over the merits of a case. To their credit, however, the local leaders of the A. B. A. had managed to look under the exact and proper slippery rock in order to come up with a prospect of their liking. Yet with all of the bad press that Mr. Wes Fortune had brought to the bargaining table, his percentage of courtroom successes was literally unsurpassed in the local annals of River City's courtroom history. Indeed, Wes Fortune was legend in his own right.

Chapter Eight

So with Greg Splittorf now sitting in the District Attorney's office, Jeremy Blackford had no other alternative then but to hire Wes Fortune to represent him in the upcoming arson and murder trial. Of course the first thing that Wes had tried to accomplish was to have the trial moved to different county. He was, of course, fully aware of the fact that anytime that a former law enforcement officer is forced to face a jury of his peers in his own hometown, the officer will almost surely lose.

As a case in point, one prospective juror in the upcoming arson and murder trial had to be excused from serving because he'd very unwisely told a local television reporter that even if Jeremy Blackford weren't guilty of the crime that he was being accused of, he was most assuredly guilty of harming other individuals while wearing a River City Police Officer's uniform. Then again, a person needs to take into consideration the mood of the nation during that particular period of time in America. For as difficult as it might have been for the former policeman and his team of lawyers to put on a good defense, one must remember that the August 1991 murder of Kathy Moore had occurred just a few months after the terrible beating of Rodney King by members of the LAPD which had taken place on March 3, 1991.

So given the mood of the country, justice for any law enforcement officer who stood accused of committing an act of violence would have been terribly difficult to come by; and particularly when one considers that one of the most important mitigating circumstances of the Kathy Moore murder and arson case revolved around a married man who'd gone astray. So naturally, it would have been a huge obstacle for Wes Fortune, or any other criminal attorney to overcome, if it hadn't been for one very important principal; Wes sincerely believed that his client was innocent.

Chapter Nine

Meanwhile, after having been denied a change of venue to another county, Wes Fortune decided that he could best serve his client by practicing some of the very same tactics that his worthy adversary, the current prosecuting attorney Gregory Splittorf, had so successfully used for a great number of years. He would attack the case by challenging the testimony of both the lead detective and the fire department's chief arson investigator, who, by his own testimony, had practically predetermined the outcome of the case. As a matter of fact it was beginning to look as if the outcome of the case would rest entirely upon the testimony of the arson experts, and not the sum total of the circumstantial evidence that the prosecutor was planning on presenting to the jury.

To Wes, practically all of the evidence that he'd seen so far appeared to be mostly circumstantial. So hopefully, that could that end up being a blessing for the defense; and especially since the state police lab technicians hadn't found any traces of blood or accelerants anywhere on Jeremy Blackford's police uniform. Even so, the prosecution could always say that Jeremy would have had ample time to change his uniform during the previous evening. Though whether the act of committing the murder and then the changing his uniform could have been pulled off within the time frame of the sixty some odd minutes for which his whereabouts were unaccounted for would be another story; for as any police officer will tell you, it can take a great deal of time to just pin on the various I. D. tags, the badge, and the multitude of other accessories which normally appear on a police officer's uniform.

Seemingly, Jeremy's ace criminal defense attorney would be faced with making the only proper decision that was left open to him: he would have to find a way to lay the responsibility of Kathy's murder on somebody's else's doorstep, and not his client's. Thusly, it was decided that the defense team would hire a few of the River City's former policemen who're willing to ply their immeasurable expertise and experience to dig around a little more thoroughly into Kathy Moore's past.

So when the privately hired sleuths began to uncover some of the more unsavory bits and pieces of Kathy's past, it was assumed that the most personal details of her private life had not come as a total surprise to her closet friends and family members who already knew that not only did she seem to enjoy frequenting gay bars, but that she might have had an intimate relationship with several different individuals.

Then not so unexpectedly, the investigators on both sides of the Kathy Moore arson and homicide case had all come to the same conclusion; Kathy had been murdered by a person who'd been driven to great extremes by either the pangs of passion, such as a jilted lover might experience, or even perhaps by a person that was operating under another form of extreme duress, such as a desperate need for revenge.

Hence, the two most logical suspects in the Lorraine Park Mystery case of arson and homicide would have almost certainly been Kathy's lover, police officer Jeremy Blackford, or the former coworker, Linus Enfield, who'd been fired from his job at the jail because of the statements that Kathy had made to their supervisor. Then again, there was always the possibility that there was another person in Kathy's past who might have had a reason to do her harm. However, it seemed as if the River City Police Department in general, and the lead detective on the murder and arson case in particular, had decided to focus their attention almost entirely on Jeremy Blackford.

Chapter Ten

Now for the first time in his professional life, Greg Splittorf was forced to play entirely by the rule of law; and if he were to be completely honest with himself, then he didn't necessarily enjoy the position which he'd allowed himself to be placed in. But since he was the duly elected prosecuting attorney for the metropolitan area which included River City, he would try his best to comply with the majority of the evidentiary rules of law, such as handing over to the defense a goodly portion of the evidence that his office had collected against Jeremy Blackford. On the other hand, though, he certainly didn't feel the need to go overboard on any of the so-called rules of law; and so naturally, he'd made the decision not to share a few choice pieces of evidence with the defense until the latter parts of the trial. Even then, however, he would be extremely careful not to reveal any more evidence to the defense than was absolutely necessary.

Chapter Eleven

So to Wes Fortune and his client, the former police officer Jeremy Blackford, it must have seemed as if the deck had been stacked against them. For without a doubt Wes was beginning to believe that it would take some type of divine intervention for him to win a "not guilty verdict" for his client. As a matter of fact, he had to admit that not only was his case was a total mess, but that many of the facts were in complete disarray.

"Never before in all the years that he'd been practicing law had he ever seen such sloppy police work," Wes thought. In fact, he knew that this case of arson and homicide could have just as easily ended up being tried as a capital murder case. And if the possible mismanagement of the case by the police department weren't enough, Wes had to tolerate the unpredictable edicts that were being issued almost daily from the prosecutor's office which was under the sole directorship of the newly elected Greg Splittorf who'd made it a point of personal pride to fight tooth and nail over every single little bit of evidence that his office was in possession of.

Yet luckily for Wes and his dedicated group of defense lawyers, he'd heard a few softly whispered rumors which had supposedly come from a retired police officer who'd just recently become a private investigator.

The rumors flying around through the corridors of the courthouse had hinted strongly that a few members of the River City Police Department were not necessarily in total agreement with the way that the lead detective was handling the Lorraine Park arson and homicide case. And in a surprising turn of events, the River City Police Department's very own chief of detectives, Inspector Farleigh Erickson had been heard to say that, "his department was looking into the possibility that several other persons might have had a reason to harm Kathy Moore.

Then as a result of the latest courthouse gossip, Wes Fortune was beginning to hope that the latest rift in the "Long Blue Line" might just possibly force a crack in the solid wall at police headquarters that would somehow help him and his client to overcome what he considered to be a case of overzealous prosecution by his worthy opponent, Greg Splittorf.

Wes also was beginning to think that the more theories and possibilities that the potential jurors could garner from their local newspaper and T. V. journalist would help his defense team immensely. So naturally, those lingering questions in the minds of a few of the local law enforcement officers might just become even more important to his case if only he could find a way to raise additional doubts about his client's innocence by trying the case in the local media and not in the courtroom.

Chapter Twelve

So at that point in time it was beginning to look as if the River City Police Department's Chief of Detectives, Inspector Farleigh Erickson, might just possibly become one of Wes Fortune's best allies. Of course Wes was also aware of the fact that the inspector wore the same blue serge uniform as his officers. Still, Wes thought that it might be worth taking the risk. So therefore, Wes asked for, and was granted, an appointment with the chief of detectives.

"Have a seat and I'll be with you shortly," Chief Erickson said to Wes Fortune as he was hanging up the telephone.

"Thank you chief," Wes said.

"I don't suppose we've had a chance to visit since the time that you so magnificently handled my daughter's divorce case," the chief said.

"I believe that's correct sir; and thank you for the compliment," Wes said.

"So what brings you down to the innermost workings of our fair city's pulse?" the chief said.

"Well chief, I'm sure that you're aware of the fact that I'm the defense attorney on record for the Kathy Moore arson and homicide case," Wes said.

"Yes I have heard that you're representing Jeremy Blackford; and as you well know it's always a darn shame when one of our own is accused of malfeasance; and especially when it's a felony case," the chief said.

"Wes you might not remember but I was in the police academy with Jeremy's father, and then later on, I not only worked with Jeremy's father, but I also served on the force with his uncle, Frank Blackford," the chief said.

"Well chief, to be completely honest with you the main reason I'm here today is simply to relate to you some of goings on in the prosecutor's office; and then to also ask you to clear up a few particulars about the way that my defense team has been treated by the detective division on this case," Wes said.

"Of course you'll have to first appreciate how most police departments work; and by that statement I mean that since the case is still open there's really not a whole lot that I can talk about," the chief said.

"Naturally I wouldn't expect you to divulge any more information about the prosecuting attorney than you would want to, so I'm really just asking your opinion on how best I should proceed if I ever do decide to file a formal complaint against the detectives who're investigating this case," Wes said.

"Well Wes, I really can't give you any advice on just exactly to handle your complaint, it just wouldn't be prudent, but if I were you I would drop by Lieutenant Miller's office on the way out; for as you probably already know he is our Internal Affairs Officer. And consequently, it would be his job to field any complaints from the citizenry on how our officers are serving the public," the chief said.

But then while Wes was still roaming the hallways of the River City Police Department, and also since he now had a fresh piece of sage advice tucked safely under his belt, he decided to go ahead and file a complaint with Internal Affairs in the hopes of learning the whereabouts of a few pieces of evidence that the police investigators on the Lorraine Park homicide and arson case had allegedly misplaced.

Even so, Wes was still somewhat skeptical that any assistance would be forthcoming from the River City Police Department. Then again, he knew that he could always play his trump card by paying a visit to the local F. B. I. office which was conveniently located in the downtown business district. Then also luckily for Wes, the Bureau Chief for the F. B. I.'s Midwest Regional District Office in River City just happened to be an old card playing and drinking buddy of his who didn't necessarily trust any of the local authorities to do the right thing; in fact, he was quite fond of saying that he'd read too many of John Grisham's books to take anything that a policeman or an attorney said as gospel.

So in the end, Wes felt that he finally had all of his ducks in-a-row, and so naturally he couldn't wait to address his hand-picked jury with his famous stock-in-trade final argument which he believed would correctly describe the sum total of his client's life. He also couldn't wait to convey to the jury that his assessment of Jeremy's morals and virtues was unshakable regardless of the fact that the jury would eventually decide whether his client was to be declared either innocent or guilty. For in his heart, Wes still fervently believed that without hope and justice we're all left with only a lifetime of remembrances for the victims and the accused.

On the other hand, though, the newly elected prosecuting attorney, Greg Splittorf, had his own personal ways of winning over a jury; and one of the assets that he possessed was the fact that he always tried to make the female members of the jury feel pretty. Of course no sane person would ever wish to admit that they might vote for a candidate simply because of their good looks and sex-appeal, but if we were to be totally honest with ourselves, then it might just happen.

Chapter Thirteen

Ultimately, however, there would be ample time for both sides of the case to map out their final strategy for the upcoming battle; and particularly since the trial wasn't set to begin until the following summer. Yet for Wes Fortune and his entire defense team, it'd been decided early on that their main objective would be for them to concentrate on finding the guilty party.

But then after having been handed what he considered to be one of the worst defeats in his entire professional career, Wes Fortune considered the guilty verdict in the Lorrain Park Mystery case to be the beginning and not the end. For there would definitely be an appeal in his client's future.

Epilogue

The years passed and it wasn't until some six years after Jeremy Blackford had been convicted of murder and arson when a survivor of a vicious attack in the state of Kentucky lived to tell her amazing story. According to the official police reports her male friend had been killed in an attack which had left her both mentally and physically scarred for life.

It seems that while her attacker was in the act of raping her, he told her that she reminded him of a girl named Kathy whom he'd murdered some years in the past. Ultimately, that same attacker would come to be known as the Railroad Killer. Thankfully, however, he would eventually be caught and put to death. Unfortunately, though, in the course of his killing spree he was said to have raped and murdered over a dozen women.

Even or Even Worse
The Gambler

Nota bene=note well; take notice; gambling is a terrible addiction.

A while back, my friend Monte confided in me that for the past several years the urge to jump off a very tall bridge had consumed his every waking thought; and also that it'd taken every survival instinct in his being for him to get back into his car and then drive away from what would have almost surely been his death. Even so, that was only one of many close brushes with death that Monte had faced in his life.

Yet before his gambling addiction had landed him in hot water, Monte had only had a nodding acquaintance with trouble. Nowadays, however, it seemed as if Monte was facing a new and serious problem almost every single day. If it wasn't one thing then it was another, such as, when the repo man began to actively scour Monte's favorite haunts while searching for the fairly new set of wheels that Mark was so desperately behind on payments.

One of the latest exigencies which had just recently begun to crop up in his somewhat troubled life could have come from any one of the scores of his former friends and associates from whom he'd borrowed some money but were now threatening him with the possibility of legal recourse or even physical harm unless he was willing to make an immediate and full restitution.

It wasn't as if Monte hadn't tried to prevail over his gambling addiction. For in the past, hadn't he voluntarily committed himself to one of those long-term, in-house, rehabilitation centers where he would have been surrounded by people with a similar problem? Thus while in rehab, Monte, and all of the rest of the clients in that particular hospital, had been warned by the councilors that out all of the various twelve step programs which are currently available to the millions of addicted people in the United States, it was the ones with the gambling addictions that were most likely to take their own lives.

Unfortunately for Monte, however, he was also plagued with at least two of the other addictions that we humans are prone to succumb to; such as drug addiction and alcoholism, both, of which Mark had been fairly successful in his attempt to stay clean and sober. Nevertheless, unless a person has been diagnosed as being compulsive, as many of the gambling addicts like to refer to themselves, then the so-called normal people would find it very difficult to understand just exactly what drives a gambler to the point of no return.

This then reminds me of another inveterate compulsive gambler that I just happen to know personally. That particular gentleman once told me that it would be fairly easy for him to spot an alcoholic or a drug addict when they are in the throes of their active addictions by just simply observing their outward appearance. On the other hand, though, he said that a gambler like himself could walk into an office on a Monday morning after having just gambled away a brand new two hundred and fifty thousand house in the suburbs and nobody in the office would be any the wiser; that is, of course, unless the gambler decided to openly confess his latest dalliance into the world of momentary insanity. Also just as regrettably, that same man's gambling addiction would ultimately destroy his longtime marriage.

Then again, there's another friend of mine who might have been speaking metaphorically as he shared a poignant gambling story with me. He said, "that if he ever hit the mother lode, that is, if he ever won a great deal of money in one sitting, he would immediately retire from all of his regular gambling haunts and then write a book which would be titled; "Even or

Even Worse." Unfortunately, however, I don't suppose that we'll ever know for sure if the gentleman ever made good on that boast since he passed away while having dinner on a cruise ship after he'd just finished gambling for the day.

They say that moderation in everything is the best medicine; then again, if we do decide to take that advice then we will never have to win big just to break even.

Only the Horses Survived

As the American Civil War progressed towards its inevitable climax, the state of Virginia had become both literally and philosophically torn apart. No other group of people in the South had expressed more loyalty to the Southern Cause than those who lived in the Shenandoah Valley which lies just to the east of the Shenandoah Mountains.

And being that the Shenandoah Valley was widely known for producing enormous amounts of agricultural products and then along with the raising of livestock, the area was highly prized by both sides during the conflict. As a result, the entire valley was bitterly contested by the armies of the Southern Confederacy and the Union Army of the Potomac which had come down from the North. But for the thousands of non-combatants who lived and farmed in the Shenandoah Valley, the constraints of having to live in a virtual war zone must have been terribly devastating.

This then meant, of course, that the local farmers would have had no choice then but to devise some very clever ways in which to survive amidst the ever-growing numbers of starving soldiers that continually traversed the trails and the roads of their once peaceful valley. As an example, one of the most ingenious ways that the inhabitants of the valley had of insuring that a constant supply of food would be available for their own families was to hide their chickens and their livestock in the neighboring forest anytime that they were fortunate enough to receive an advanced warning of an approaching army; whether it be friend or foe.

Thus it was during one of those mornings in the fall of eighteen hundred and sixty-four when twelve-year old Josh Walker was preparing to move his family's livestock from the forest where they'd been tethered during the previous evening over to a adjacent meadow where they would hopefully be able graze peaceably without the Walker family having to worry about them being commandeered by a foraging military patrol. Yet just as young Josh was preparing to move the family's livestock out of the woods, he heard the distinct sound of horses walking across the dry leaves on the nearby forest floor from whence just moments later he would observe the five mounted Yankee cavalrymen who were emerging from a small copse of woods that lay off to the west of where the livestock were hidden.

And even though young Josh was somewhat taken aback by the sudden turn of events, the situation had further steeled his firm resolve to move his families' livestock even deeper into the surrounding forest where he hoped that they would be safe. However, Josh was about to once again be surprised when an additional five mounted troopers came charging out of the forest on the eastern side of the meadow. Though luckily for Josh and his family's livestock, that particular squad of troopers appeared to be members of the 1st. Virginia Volunteer Cavalry Regiment.

Then without a moment of hesitation, the ten mounted cavalrymen proceeded to charge directly towards one another with such an amazing burst of speed that they couldn't help but to collide headlong into one another at the center of the meadow where the slashing of their sabers and the smoke from their carbines and pistols became partially hidden by the dust that was being kicked up by the hooves of the ten warhorses.

Regrettably, though, within only another few minutes, all ten of the brave cavalrymen lay dead upon the bloody ground of yet one more battlefield. So the only thing that remained for young Joshua to do was to round up and then hobble the dead cavalrymen's horse's before then heading on back home where he hoped to be able to find enough friends and relatives with strong backs that could help him bury the dead soldiers.

There was another distinct possibility that Josh had not fully counted on, and that was simply the fact that the entire area might have also become infested with deserters, partisans, and even possibly some members of the Home Guard, who as a rule, were more than happy to kill the deserters and the stray soldiers from both sides of the conflict.

Yet luckily for the Walker family, the situation in northern Virginia had not deteriorated to the extinct that it had in the mountainous regions of the Carolinas. That said, it'd been rumored that at least a goodly portion of the confiscated and missing livestock from around the immediate area could be attributed to the injured and the furloughed soldiers from the Southern armies who seemed determined to claim whatever spoils of war they could get their hands on in order to replace what was being lost to the rampaging armies from the North that were beginning to march through the Shenandoah Valley in what could only be called a "Scorched Earth" policy of the type which would later be exemplified more fully during General Sherman's "March to the Sea" campaign in the Southern States of Georgia and the Carolinas.

Of course the first thing that Josh would have had to contend with on that particular morning was to immediately corral all ten of the warhorses. This chore was accomplished primarily by using the lariats and the other ropes which he'd used to tether his own livestock with during the previous evening.

Thankfully for young Josh, he was able to round up enough of his family members and neighbors to help him with the burying of the ten dead cavalry troopers. The soldier's weapons, however, were to be equally divided amongst the neighboring farmers who were extremely fearful that they might just end up fighting with the ragtag groups of misfits and the ex-soldiers that were already beginning to travel the roads and the trails of their beautiful Shenandoah Valley.

The Yellow House

At first, it was somewhat difficult for me to believe that it'd been twenty-five years since I'd last paid a visit to the grand old two-story yellow frame house that sits so majestically on the southern bank of the Tradewater River.

That fact alone seemed quite curious to me, and especially since many of my fondest childhood memories spring from the formative years that I'd spent in the Western Kentucky area; and even though many of those far distant memories seem to be well hidden in the past, they're certainly not lost and gone forever

At one time in the past my paternal grandparents had owned the old yellow house and not only have they both been gone from that residence for a very long time, but they've also been gone from this earthly world for a good number of years

Then just as I'd expected, more than a few of those old memories came rushing to the forefront of my mind as I slowly pulled into the driveway of that once beautiful old edifice; unfortunately, though, the old yellow house was beginning to show signs of extreme neglect

Though at that point in time the residence appeared to be uninhabited. But then as I slowly turned the knob on the front door I was pleased to discover that it was unlocked; and from the looks of things the house had been unoccupied for an indeterminate amount of time.

Of course to me, the grand old house still held a certain degree of charm and elegance, and so naturally it wasn't long before those recollections of a more innocent time began to flood into my consciousness with memories of those Sunday afternoons which I'd enjoyed in the company of my large and rather colorful family

Also just as interestingly, the sometimes narrow but relatively deep Tradewater River flows but a mere seventy-five paces from the rear of the house that my paternal grandparents had once called home. But then after standing on the river bank for only another moment or so, the memories of yesteryear began to invoke in me a feeling of melancholy which caused me to vividly remember one of my last visits.

If memory serves, it was a very hot and humid summer day when I'd last stopped by the old house to visit with my grandparents and extended family. And as I recall, the reason for the get-together was two-fold. First, everyone who planned to attend was in full agreement that we should celebrate the 4th of July by holding a family reunion and picnic. Secondly, it was agreed upon by the men of the family that it would also be a fine day for us to go for a swim in the river

Of course at this point in the story I must give full credit to the majority of the members of my family who've always fervently believed that no amount of energy should ever be wasted without realizing some fruits for your labor; and therefore, it was agreed upon by all that the day would be best served if we indulged in a water sport called (hogging), which is a custom that's more commonly known as (noodling) in some of the northern states.

While practicing that age-old art of hogging a person simply has to dive below the surface of the river water in search of a hollowed out area around the roots of one of the large trees that happens to line the riverbank. Of course the main objective of the sport is to reach into the empty space beneath the tree just as far as you possibly can; and if you're real lucky, you might just find a nice sized catfish that's just lying-in-wait for one of the smaller fish to swim by

Although from time to time, a person might also end up getting hold of a large turtle, or even a water snake, which might have positioned itself in the hollowed-out cavern beneath the base of the tree.

Then once the swimmers had dried off, and then also after everybody had eaten their fill of catfish steaks, it was off to the rear of the house where all of the folks would then hurriedly gather their favorite lawn chairs in a circle for that's when the real fun would begin

In due course, the air around the rear of the house would be filled with dense smoke; but the smoke wasn't necessarily from the men's pipes, or even from the barbeque pit, but more likely the smoke was coming from their colorful stories about the past

All of their stories were first-class, but some of my favorites were the ones about the American Civil War, of which there were aplenty. Of course the rest our nation's wars would also end up being discussed; and this was particularly true of the stories concerning World War II since several members of my family had served honorably in that terrible war

As a whole, my family appears to be a very patriotic group of people; and as such, there were always stories about how our ancestors had fought in just about every single one of our nation's wars

The war theme seemed to ring true at practically everyone of my family's get-togethers, for as a rule, my maternal uncle would almost always make it a point to share with us some of his personal accounts of the World War II battles in which he had participated in while serving in the Pacific Theater; more notably, the campaigns of New Guinea and the Philippines. Then too, another one of my favorite uncles would generally relate to us some of his wartime experiences while serving on the U. S. S. Enterprise

Then not wanting to be outdone, another one of our relatives would detail some of the experiences that he'd had during the World War II era while serving in the Civilian Conservation Corps, or C. C. C.; that particular man was very proud of having helped build Western Kentucky's very own Camp Breckenridge which of course has been closed for many years; but then at one point during World War II it was one of the largest of the U. S. Army's Boot Camps in the country.

Then too, the men of my family would almost always get around to listing the names of our family's deceased war veterans, and even the locations of their gravesites. And from what I understand, some of the graves were dated as far back as the American Civil War and the American Revolutionary War

Ultimately, though, it was inevitable that some of the more pleasant conversations would eventually crop up, such as, the current prices of corn and soybeans; but then every now and again a few of the men might even comment on the current price of a ton of coal

The Great American Depression was always a subject that almost never failed to be included in the lists of topics to be discussed; and every now and again the men might even get around to discussing religion

Nonetheless, the discussion of politics was always my favorite and from time to time the conversation could become quite heated; and this was particularly true when they discussed the politics of the nation

Most generally, though, the opinions held by the men of my large and quite vociferous family were almost always divided equally between the republicans and the democrats with the farmers representing the republicans and the coal miners lining up on the side of the democrats

Then after a rather lengthy period of reminiscing about those pleasant memories of the past I decided to venture upstairs to the attic where some of my grandparent's furniture, and even a few of the family's keepsakes, had been stored during the disastrous nineteen hundred and thirty-seven flood which had so completely inundated the entire Ohio River Valley.

During that terrible flood, some of my family members had lost a great many of their important personal papers such as their old photographs and even a few of their family's bibles;

and then along with, of course, a good many of their genealogical records. Up to that point in time the thirty-seven flood was said to have been the greatest known deluge of water to have ever ascended upon the Midwestern part of our country

In retrospect, however, it wasn't so much about the material things that our family members had once owned and lost, but rather, it was simply the fact that God and Mother Nature had once again proved that they were in charge and not a mere group of men and women

Robert R. Railey

The Undertaker

For the past several years, the people living in the extreme north-western parts of the River City metropolitan area had mistakenly blamed the terrible odor that sometimes wafted through their neighborhoods on the trash fires at the nearby sanitary landfill which seemed to burn almost continuously.

Of course the degree to which the stench might offend the average person's sensibilities would depend largely upon which way the wind was blowing. For example, if the wind just happened to be coming directly from the northwest, then a large number of people in that particular neighborhood could expect to experience an almost smog-like condition which would consist of a cloud of noxious foul odors and acrid smoke that could linger for long periods of time over certain parts of the city. Though for some unknown reason the odor was almost always worse on the weekends.

Yet when the River City Herald newspaper assigned an investigative reporter to look into the root cause of the foul air that seemed to permeate only specific areas of the northwestern part of town, it was determined that the people who lived in that part of town had been right on target when they'd first described the pungent odor as the smell of death. For as it turned out, one of the employees at one of the city's largest cemetery had metaphorically been burning the midnight oil by keeping the ovens in the crematorium running full blast for what had seemed like almost every evening during the weekends.

Of course that tidbit of information wasn't exactly the type of breaking news that a person would expect to take notice of while watching a local television newscast. But when that same reporter stated that his investigation had uncovered the fact that there were more cremations being performed at that particular cemetery than the management was aware of, then a report of that nature would indeed become big news.

So then naturally, one of the first persons that the River City Herald's newspaper reporter, Leon Goebbels, wished to speak with was a man by the name of Reggie Wallace who for the past several years had held a position at the cemetery where he was primarily responsible for the maintenance and the landscaping at the graveyard which included such duties as the mowing of the grass and the snow removal; however, Mr. Wallace had also been entrusted with the responsibility of maintaining the cemetery's crematorium.

At first glance, Reggie Wallace would appear to be a candidate for employee of the year, but then after carefully researching the man's previous employment records from several of his previous jobs which had included those back in the city of Milwaukee, Wisconsin, Leon the reporter discovered that Reggie had lied repeatedly on his job application when he'd first applied for the position of head maintenance man at the River City Cemetery. In fact, with the help of the River City Police Department, Leon had uncovered an old missing persons case in the city of Milwaukee in which Reggie Wallace had been listed as a person of interest.

Until recently, the majority of the staff writers at the River City Herald newspaper, and more specifically the people who lived in the vicinity of the cemetery, had attributed the foul air that occasionally drifted across the north-western most parts of city to the fact that the cemetery was located in close proximity to the city dump.

However, the newspaper's staff writer and columnist, Leon Goebbels, just happened to also be the crime reporter for the Herald which required of him to make the daily trip over to the main police headquarters in order to keep up with the goings on of the local thugs. So in view of the fact that Leon had become somewhat friendly with a good many of the city's policemen, it offered him a unique relationship with the local constabularies that would eventually pay off handsomely for him and his newspaper.

Moreover, after having had read the latest F. B. I.'s Annual Crime Report, Leon had begun to compile a series of essays for the River City Herald; and in one of those pieces he'd stated that River City was experiencing an inordinate number of cases of missing persons. In fact, he'd discovered that during the past year alone the metropolitan area had recorded more than ten times the number of unsolved missing person cases per capita than the national average. So with Leon's close working relationship with a few of the local homicide detectives, he was in a unique position to assess the local problem with the eyes of a detached person.

So as a result of his inquiries, Leon had begun to actively investigate what he believed to be the main reason behind River City's sudden increase in the number of missing persons. "Was it a matter of people simply running away from their families and their responsibilities?" Leon wondered. "Or just possibly, was it something a lot more sinister such as murder? Leon asked.

So as a result of his findings, Leon figured that the upcoming Saturday evening would be a perfect time for him to test one of his latest theories. He would once and for all try to prove his theory by camping out in a parking lot that was situated on a hill which was adjacent to the section of the River City Cemetery that housed the crematorium.

Then at precisely eight o'clock on that very next Saturday evening, Leon observed a dark colored panel van sitting at the cemetery's main entrance while at the same time he noticed that a man who was wearing white coveralls was unlocking the front gate. Then once clear of the entrance, the man relocked the gate and then proceeded to drive directly toward the crematorium where he parked his van in the rear of the concrete block building. Then after retrieving a gurney bed from the rear of the crematoria, the man in the white coveralls positioned the device directly under the bed of his van.

Thus with the zoom lens on his camcorder trained on the rear of the crematorium, Leon was able to record what appeared to be a lifeless human body wrapped in a body bag that was being transferred from the van onto the gurney and then ultimately on into the rear doors of the block building.

Fortunately for Leon he didn't have long to wait. For in just another few minutes he was able to observe some wisps of white/gray smoke that appeared to be billowing from the crematorium's chimney. Then after a period of time, Leon was able to observe the same dark colored van as it exited the front gate of the cemetery where it then disappeared into the darkness night by blending in with the normal Saturday evening traffic.

A Blank Page

Like many of his former coworkers, Special Agent Curtis Tedrow had planned on doing the twenty years and out when the Special Agent in charge of the F. B. I.s Midwest Regional Office at Indianapolis, Indiana assigned him to a brand new missing person case which had just been reported in River City which was located in the southwestern part of the state.

In his opinion, this particular missing person case was still a bit too fresh to merit a full-scale investigation by a Federal agency; and especially since the young woman in question had only been missing for a period of less than twenty-four hours which is generally considered to be the minimum amount of time that's required by the majority of the law enforcement agencies in the U. S.

Of course the length of time that determines when a person can officially be listed as missing can vary greatly from state to state; and sometimes it can even vary within the different jurisdictions within a state. But with a previously unblemished record of some twenty-odd years of service behind him, Curtis would most likely do as he had always done; and that would be to follow orders.

Though while he was driving south towards River City, another thought had entered his mind; and that was simply the fact that the twenty-two year old missing female was most likely connected to some very influential people in order to have warranted such an immediate interest in her case.

So after arriving in River City, then the first thing that Curtis and his partner Special Agent Ben Wilson had planned on doing was to visit the local F. B. I. office where Curtis would apologize to the local agent in charge for invading his territory. For not only would that be the right thing to do, but if that situation were to be handled in any other way then he and his partner might expect to receive a negative or even a violent response from a man who'd served undercover in the Middle East for over seven years.

Thus following that special act of in-house protocol and kindness, the two agents would then, of course, be obliged to pay a visit to the River City Police Department where the Missing Persons Bureau Division was so small that it'd just recently been merged with the Detective Division which also handled the majority of the robbery and homicide cases. Nevertheless, Curtis was greatly impressed by the work of Detective Sergeant Ronald Munson, who as the lone missing person investigator, had already conducted a very thorough and professional investigation into the disappearance of the twenty-two year old white female x-ray technician who'd been identified as Lori Miller of Mt. Auburn, Indiana which was a small town located just to the northwest of River City.

As a rule, the most experienced investigators will usually begin their quest of attempting to locate a missing person by simply working backwards from the facts that they have on hand; and which then almost always entails a trip to the missing person's residence. Though once again, Detective Sergeant Munson had made their job a lot easier by having already obtained a search warrant which would allow them to enter the missing woman's apartment. But since her telephone records had not as yet been made available to the police, Curtis was especially interested in what had been written in the oversized day-planner that lay open on a lamp table in the living room.

Of course the first thing that Special Agent Curtis Tedrow couldn't help but to notice about the woman's address book was that the page concerning the day that she'd supposedly gone missing was completely blank; however, after flipping the pages backwards he noticed among other things that Lori had scribbled a note in the margin of the previous page which read as follows; "(Friday at 5:30 PM: Meet Mike at Toni's.)"

Of course being that Curtis and his partner were newly arrived from out of town, they weren't all that familiar with the local businesses; with the exception, that is, of the national franchises which seemed so commonplace nowadays that practically every city in America had a shopping district which appeared to be a virtual carbon copy of all the other cities. Luckily, though, sergeant Munson was on hand to inform the two agents that Toni's Pizzeria was a local and very popular restaurant which was located on the North Side of River City.

So with several photographs of the missing woman in hand, and also with the knowledge that detective Munson had already confirmed that the pictures in question were in fact those of the missing x-ray technician, the two Federal Agents headed on up to Mt. Auburn in order to check out the pizza restaurant. Unfortunately, however, the trip to Toni's Pizza establishment didn't produce any additional information. And so, their next stop would be the hospital where the young woman was supposedly employed.

Then luckily for the investigators it seemed as if practically everybody that was even remotely connected with the radiology department at the hospital where Lori was employed seemed to know a little something about her personal life; excepting, that is, when it came to her love life for that's when the investigators came against a brick wall.

Special Agent Curtis Tedrow was also about to discover that not only had Lori been extremely dedicated to her demanding job at the hospital, but she'd also been taking some classes at the local state university in order to earn her master's degree in radiology. Thusly, the agents had only to assume that her busy schedule didn't leave her a whole lot of time for dating.

Generally speaking, a missing person's immediate family would more than likely be able to answer those types of personal questions. And that would certainly be true if the person in question had a family of her own. Yet as ill-fated as the present situation appeared to be it was widely believed that

Lori was an orphan who'd been adopted and then raised by an older and childless couple in Phoenix, Arizona who'd just recently passed away.

So naturally, this latest development would almost certainly throw a curve into the investigation. This then meant of course, that Special Agent Tedrow and his partner would have to interpret Lori's timetable as best they could in order to come up with an accurate assessment of her comings and goings. They were also hoping that her itinerary could be more positively verified with her coworkers at the hospital, her neighbors, and even possibly with her classmates at the university.

But then somewhat surprisingly, the next piece of information to reach the two Federal Agents in charge of the River City missing person's case was to be personally delivered by the commander of the local Indiana State Police Post who must have considered it his sacred duty to convey this latest, and quite possibly, one of the most important directives that the combined law enforcement agencies had received so far. The missing young woman was none other than the niece of the current governor of Indiana, the honorable Winfred H. Mallard.

Needless to say, that would certainly help to explain why the F. B. I. and the Indiana State Police had been asked to override the usual protocol of the local authorities by initiating their own full-blown investigation into a missing person's case that wasn't even two days old. This new development would also mean that more manpower would be available if needed;"so in the long run, the extra boots on the ground might just make huge a difference in their ability able to solve this particular case," Curtis thought.

Though in Curtis's mind, the locating of the mystery person that Lori had supposedly planned on meeting at the pizza restaurant on the day that she went missing would have be one of the most important pieces of the puzzle. And since that the team had already interviewed a good many of the employees, and even a few of the regular customers at Toni's Pizzeria, it was decided that they should also pay a visit to the state university where Lori was known to be studying for her master's degree.

Regrettably, though, except for the tremendous amount of praise that her fellow students and the faculty at the state college were eager to heap upon Lori for all of her achievements, not a single person at the state-run university could explain why an otherwise levelheaded person would suddenly end up missing; unless of course, she'd been forcefully abducted.

Thus with the names of Lori's professors and the types of classes that she'd attended in their possession, the agents decided to take the age-old tack of waiting outside one of the classrooms that Lori normally attended just so they could then speak with some of her classmates. And by chance, one of Lori's classmates, who just also happened to be an employee of the very same radiology department at the hospital where Lori worked, exited the lab classroom where she'd been studying.

And from the information supplied by one of Lori's classmates, the agents were to learn that Lori had purportedly been dating a twenty-four year old man by the name of Mike Gerhardt who was employed as a security guard at the same hospital where Lori worked.

Nonetheless, when the Federal Agents returned to the hospital they were told that Mike Gerhardt had called in sick that morning and had not been heard of since. Though as a rule, a situation of that type wouldn't be all that unusual, for people do become ill. But to seasoned investigators such as Curtis and Ben, just the act of not showing up for work after a friend had supposedly gone missing seemed to be more than a little unusual.

So then as a direct result of receiving that latest piece of information, the only logical thing left for the investigators to do would be for them to pay the security guard a little visit at his residence which just happened to be located fairly close by to the hospital where both he and Lori were employed.

At first, it appeared as if nobody was at home in the aluminum sided, two-story frame house which occupied a corner lot on a city block that was populated with very similar looking structures; but then by peering through the partially drawn drapes which hung in the picture window on the front of the house, Curtis and Ben could make out what appeared to be a human body that was lying face down on the living room floor.

But then with law enforcement's recognized obligation to protect and serve the public, it was soon agreed upon by all that one of River City's uniformed policemen should forcefully open the front door of the residence. Unfortunately, though, it was quickly determined that the corpse on the floor was none other than the missing security guard, Mike Gerhardt.

Then despite the fact that the Medical Examiner on the scene didn't particularly care to make an official pronouncement as to the cause of death until after the autopsy had been performed, the experienced investigators were inclined to believe that it was a case of suicide. Nevertheless, the lawmen had not made that determination based solely on the suicide note that had been left on the still running computer, for as they knew, almost anyone could have typed that note. Instead, they'd based their preliminary decision to accept the young man's tragic death as a suicide because of the email that Mike Gerhardt had apparently been replying to when he took his own life.

Curiously enough, however, the email in question had been electronically mailed to Mike Gerhardt a full two days earlier; and also just as peculiar, the email had ostensibly been written by none other than Lori Miller who was apparently still alive and well at the time the message had been compiled and then emailed to Mike Gerhardt.

In essence, the message on the computer was basically a Dear John letter from Lori Miller to Mike Gerhardt. So to the investigators, it was beginning to appear as if Mike might have taken his own life while he was in the act of replying to the missing woman's Dear John letter. Then again, both Curtis and Ben knew from past experience that the kind of situation which they were being asked to accept as gospel was seldom as it seemed. And for that reason, the agents knew from past experiences that there are usually some underlying currents that must be more thoroughly investigated.

Naturally, the most important item on the agent's agenda that day would be to locate the x-ray technician who'd gone missing. By then, however, the two investigators were beginning to wonder if perhaps the missing young woman had purposely decided to remain unavailable to the authorities. Even so, when seasoned investigators are working a death, be it a homicide or a suicide, they understand that a case can often be made against the person who was closest to the deceased; and in a case such as this one the usual suspect would be no other than the missing girlfriend, Lori Miller.

Yet somewhat surprisingly, the assistance that the Federal Agents so desperately needed would come from an unsuspecting source when the Mt. Auburn Town Marshall pulled Lori Miller over for a routine traffic violation. And since her name had already been entered into a Federal database known as the National Crime Information Center, or NCIC, as a person of interest, she was detained and then transported to the River City Police Department where she would be held without bond until she could be interviewed by the two F. B. I. men.

Of course once the River City Policemen had full access to their person of interest in the murder/suicide case of Mike Gerhardt, Lori Miller was processed as if she were a viable suspect. This then meant, of course, that her hands would have been swabbed for traces of a nitrate compound which is commonly found in gunshot residue.

Then later on, but only after a jury had convicted her of first-degree murder, did Lori Miller finally decide to speak up.

By then, however, it was fairly obvious to everybody involved in the case that she was presently with child. So then all throughout her well rehearsed discourse, which took place during the sentencing phase of the trial, she tried very desperately to lay the blame at the feet of her deceased ex-lover, Mike Gerhardt, for his not wanting to marry her after she'd told him about her pregnancy.

Still, it was fairly easy to tell that not a single person in the courtroom was buying her sad story. So at the end of her rather lengthy and mostly self-serving testimony, she was sentenced from thirty to sixty-five years in prison. Yet later on that same day when a River City Herald newspaper reporter was able to corner the prosecutor in one of the hallways outside of the courtroom, the reporter then very bluntly asked the prosecutor as to why the court had felt the need to hand down such a severe sentence; and especially since the defendant appeared to be pregnant.

Then somewhat remarkably, the prosecutor's response to the reporter's rather pointed question as to the reasoning behind the logic of having asked for such a severe sentence would end up shocking almost anyone who'd been following the case. And from that moment on, the defense attorneys had to feel mightily confident that they would be on solid ground whenever they got around to appealing what they thought was an extremely harsh sentence.

It seems that both the judge and the prosecutor were equally disturbed by the fact that the defendant had used cyberspace technology to write the aforementioned Dear John email letter. Then too, there was the question of the authenticity of the possibly bogus suicide note which had been left on the victim's own personal computer for everybody to see. For it was widely known that both the judge and the prosecutor had publically expressed their aversion to the type of cyber bullying which had previously been noted in a notorious case involving the mother of a teenage cheerleader who'd allegedly driven a young girl to commit suicide.

Dust Pans & Brooms
vs the Blowers

By day, Bushrod Feller was known by his friends and neighbors as a mild-mannered person who generally kept the front and rear lawns of his neat little bungalow in perfect condition; and of course, he most assuredly preferred to use an old-fashioned broom when sweeping his side of the street. For as a matter of fact Bushrod was so adamantly against the use of the electric and gas-powered leaf-blowers that he'd become somewhat of a raving lunatic type of an activist whose main goal in life was to obtain an injunction from the courts that would permanently outlaw the use of the very popular leaf-blowers.

In fact, Bushrod thought surely that the extremely menacing words he'd used in his latest letter to the local newspaper's editor should have easily been enough to dissuade the majority of the River City's residents to cease and desist in the use of all types of leaf blowers; whether they were the gas-powered or the electric types of machines.

But then one day as Bushrod was walking home from the neighborhood grocery he was somewhat surprised, and even a little dismayed, to see a young man still using one of those horribly inefficient leaf-blowers in order to clear away some fresh grass clippings and the recently fallen leaves from the sidewalk in the front of his house. Moreover, it appeared to Bushrod that the young man intended to use his evil, and very powerful machine, in order to purposely relocate every single piece of the lawn material that wasn't nailed down all the way over to the next street.

To Bushrod, the all too apparent leaf-blower conspiracy which seemed to be taking place across America would go something like this; the do-gooders and the leaf-blowing enthusiast that lived on the westernmost side of the Rocky Mountains would have to be the first ones to take up the challenge.

Then once all of the dust and the lawn clippings, and then along with all of other waste materials from the west coast had made its way up into the upper jet stream which normally travels across the U. S. from the west to the east coast; the weekend warriors who were all armed with their powerful machines with names like, Stihls, and Echos, and even the mainline Black and Decker super blowers, would then own the awesome responsibility of having to move that enormous dust cloud, city by city, until ultimately, that ungodly mess of debris reached the Mississippi River where a natural barrier might stop them; but only temporarily.

Of course the next step in this illogical operation would be for the leaf blowing co-conspirators who lived on the eastern side of the Mississippi River to add their own dust and grass clippings to that already huge cloud of dust which had originated in the west. Then, the people on the eastern half of the country would just naturally assume the responsibility of forwarding that god-awful mess in an easterly fashion until those horrible and nauseous clouds of nature's own fallout had reached its final and ultimate goal, the Atlantic Ocean.

Nonetheless, since Bushrod Feller was a zealot to the nth degree he'd always felt vindicated in what he believed to be a righteous cause by trying to outlaw every single leaf-blower in the United States. For according to the E. P. A.s own standards, the air in the Midwest had become so dirty and polluted that Bushrod was beginning to have grave concerns that some of the U. S. airports might have to actually be shut down for the passenger's safety.

Then lo and behold it wasn't long thereafter when some of the local meteorologists had discovered that the red loam and the topsoil that was hovering in the air over the Midwest had actually been caused by a natural phenomenon that was the direct result of a violent windstorm which had come roaring out of Mexico; and also that the menacing cloud of dust had travelled all throughout the majority of the Southwestern and the Midwestern U. S. states.

So in Bushrod's latest and most treasured letter to the editor, he posited for the reader's consideration what he believed to be the sanest argument of all when he suggested that we might want to trade all of the worthless and noisy leaf-blowers in on the old-fashioned brooms and dust pans. For as it was so clearly stated in his now famous manifesto, he suggested that we should, "just bag it and then send it to off the nearest landfill."

Robert R. Railey

The Home

"Civility cost nothing." Good manners and politeness cost us absolutely nothing; or so the old English Proverb goes. Nevertheless, patience was something that wasn't practiced regularly in the retirement-home where I once resided. For in that particular institution it seemed as if the daily goal of each resident was to irritate as many of the other residents as they possibly could; until evening time, that is, for that's usually when everybody in the building is just too darned exhausted to continue on with the fight.

Then again, I'm not suggesting that any of residents of that particular complex would actually participate in a physical altercation; although that was certainly a possibly if any one of them had a little too much to drink.

But then also just as unfortunately, the people living in that particular retirement home would most likely tell you that all of their money is tied up in bills; and therefore, the very act of moving into one of the more private retirement-villages, such as those assisted living establishments, wouldn't be a viable plan for the majority of those folks.

Consequently, then, those of us who were living at near or below the national poverty level would simply have to persevere, and then also to learn how to tolerate one another as best we could. Generally speaking, however, you could never meet a nicer group of people than what could be found living in that particular institution. Then too, the most interesting of all the people that we had living in our complex would be the ones that tend to volunteer to serve on the community-council board.

Now whether it was pre-planned or not, those beloved neighbors and fellow tenants of ours would almost always end up acting as if they were the ruling party in charge; and yet beneath their carefully hidden agenda our duly elected council members were mainly selected from the masses of tenants in order to be of assistance to the cadre of activists and revolutionaries in the front office who're supposedly there to enforce our building's constitution. Yet to give the devil its due, there were times when all of their rules actually made a little sense; such as, when they introduced into the system some very strict guidelines that would actually help to control our building's burgeoning pet population.

Still, after having been a member of several fraternal-organizations and various other civic fellowships in the past, I have personally seen how co-operation amongst a large group of people can sometimes pay very handsome rewards; that is, of course, if the ones who're being served are willing to compromise and then to also allow the democratic process to carry on forward.

For when it comes to governing a large group of people one of the most highly contested areas of contention is always the dreaded territorial disputes. This situation most normally occurs when a non-board member accidently steps on the toes of one of the elected board member's areas of responsibility. This, of course, can be particularly troubling if the non-board resident has the audacity to actually complain to the building's manager.

So then naturally, that's when the real fireworks begin. For all throughout history it seems as if the masses will only vote for change if they feel as though they're being treated unfairly. Yet on certain other occasions the citizens might actually choose to revolt and even dispose of the miserable tyrants in as much the same as we did when we severed our allegiance with our mother country England.

Of course there are other times when the best strategy is simply to sabotage the system from the inside out. Subsequently, this was exactly the type of insurrection that was chosen by a few of the more brazen senior citizens in the community where I formerly resided. Surprisingly enough, however, that particular act of sedition was accomplished without even the need of a mass meeting; and they didn't even to have to coordinate their ideas with their fellow rebels in order to integrate their wishes into their somewhat sloppily fabricated plans.

Also just as interestingly, there appeared to be an unspoken agreement amongst more than a few of the more courageous members of our little den of conspirators that conveyed a silent, and yet persistent determination, to totally dismantle the effectiveness of both the community board, and the institution's management. For in their zeal to make changes this particular group of people had committed just about every type of sabotage that could possibly be dreamed of. In fact, their manifesto had included their willingness to commit acts that fell just short of causing severe physical damage to the building.

Yet another amazing bit of clarity had surfaced when it was discovered that not one single person in our building had ever personally been asked to commit an act of rebellious behavior. Even so, the prevailing thought among even the most willing conspirators must have been that the "grand cause" would be more effectively accomplished if the individual guerillas were allowed to follow their own dictates; and which then meant, of course, that their own individual talents could more easily shine through if they were allowed to commit their own personalized types of subversion.

For instance, a woman whom we will call Mary would most willingly do her part by frequenting the community laundry room when it was unoccupied just so she could open the windows while the air-conditioning or the heat unit was turned on. It was apparent to everyone in the building that Mary immensely enjoyed participating in this type of rebellious behavior; and since there were no screens in the windows in the laundry room, it was a simple matter for the bugs to come indoors where they would just naturally find their way into the hallways and the resident's apartments.

Mary was extremely adept at practicing her chosen craft: I. E., the opening of the windows; but then one day after consuming a few too many alcoholic beverages she had a run-in with a three thousand pound automobile which left poor old Mary on a walker. It truly was a travesty, alright, and not only because Mary had been very adept at performing her own individual style of subversion, but the saddest part of the whole situation was that nobody else had the guts to step up and take her place.

There were, however, plenty of other areas where the unhappy residents could make a name for themselves. For instance, a woman named Nancy decided on her own initiative to aid and abet the "grand cause" by allowing her pet to urinate in the stairwell instead of bothering to take the poodle outside. Though for the record, and also in her own defense, we must state that Nancy wasn't very mobile; and therefore, we must give her credit by her continuing to support the effort by contributing in one of the few ways in which she able to help out.

Then again, some of the most fun times came about when the building manager, or else a member of the community board decided that a change in the rules was in order. Then shortly thereafter the first hint that another of our surviving freedoms was about to be attacked would be delivered to us in the guise of an important announcement which was printed on copying paper and then ever so stealthily slid under our apartment doors. By then, of course, the long-term residents could sense that the first murmurings of a brand-new frontal-attack were a brewing.

Yet what was truly amazing about the place that we called home was the fact that the axis of evil types of residents in our complex didn't have an in-house pipeline of propaganda machine, or even a news network system that could even come close to equaling what a character in the Butch Cassidy and the Sundance Kid film was able to accomplish. For in that movie the character named "News" was always in possession of a satchel-full of wanted-posters and newspaper clippings that greatly extolled the Hole in the Wall Gang's latest exploits.

Yet in our own little slice of heaven we were fortunate enough to have a few people that might just qualify for the movie role of Mr. or Mrs. News. For it seems as if their sole purpose on earth was simply to ensure us that if you ever missed out on any of the daily happenings, then one of our so-called in-house reporters would be more than happy to fill you in with all the gory details; then again, a person could always choose to sit outside in the rear of the building where they would almost assuredly hear all of the latest gossip.

Most probably, though, the community-room would be the likeliest place to catch up on all of the latest undertakings of our more extreme miscreants. For as a rule, the community room is the place where many of residents tend to migrate in order to finish off a previous squabble, or perhaps even to start a new one.

The community room is also where the catered lunch is served daily; and unfortunately for most people's digestive system, the mood during those lunchtimes is nothing less than controlled pandemonium. Most generally, though, the number one complaint from the residents is that the senior citizen's organization that prepares and delivers the food is just too darn adamant in its refusal to serve Buffalo Wings. Even though that particular disagreement is most likely only a minor sticking point for I'm not entirely sure that the residents actually want to eat those horrid things. To me personally, I'm more inclined to believe that the people in charge simply don't believe that the older residents should be eating that type of food in the first place; and so naturally, the group will continue to ask for them.

However, there're still plenty of other types of protest that tend to occur on an almost daily basis. Such as, if someone happened to be away from the building for most of the day, but then upon their return they might just find that the floors in the foyer and the hallways had all been covered with little pieces of torn up paper-litter. And when that situation occurs, you can take it to the bank that a very unpopular edict had been handed-down through the chain of command.

Though by and large one of the best ways to take the pulse of the natives is to count the numbers of cigarette butts which are lackadaisically discarded on the grounds of the campus; and at times, they might even get squashed out on the tile floors nearby to the elevators.

Of course that never happens when the security people are standing nearby; and speaking of security there were occasions in the past when a few of the residents had actually worked as security guards in their past lives; so naturally, those men tended to take on the roles of quasi-policemen. Nevertheless, hardly anyone ever paid any attention to them; they did, however, actually try their best to help police the grounds.

Our security was very important to us: and this was an especially obvious problem in our parking lot. For since we were located nearby to some churches, schools, and a few large business enterprises, the lack of parking spaces could sometimes be a problem for everybody. Therefore, it would take an extremely dedicated team of enthusiastic commando-styled residents just to keep the wannabe illegal-parkers from using our building's parking spaces.

Of course nowadays it's fair to say that a goodly number of our senior citizens take an enormous amount of prescribed medication; so welcome to the wonderful world of pharmacology. Unfortunately, though, some of our senior citizens, and even a portion of the general population, are silly enough before they even take any medication, but then when you add prescribed medications to a senior citizen's normal diet and daily regimen, a phenomenon occurs which can baffle those of us who supposedly have sound minds.

So then as a result of some of the residents having seriously over medicated themselves, they would either become extremely boisterous and confrontational, or else, they would become unusually shy and reticent. There seemed to be no middle of the road for the people who consume too much of their legally prescribed medication.

On another particular day, however, an example of extreme excess occurred when a normally mild-mannered tenant had taken so much of a prescribed medication that the man actually shot and killed his own microwave oven with a three fifty-seven magnum revolver as a direct result of having just experienced a drug induced psychosis. Of course there's always the possibility that the medication will affect a person's mind in many different ways; this then brings to mind the story of another one of our tenants who was nicknamed Bud.

That particular gentleman was similar to many of the other residents in the complex in as much as he greatly enjoyed embellishing his life's accomplishments prior to settling in the home. For without a doubt, Bud would try to convince everybody in the complex that at one time in the past he'd held one of the highest-ranking positions in the entire Civil Service Administration; for in his mind, he honestly believed that his job was more important than even the office of the President of the United States. So when thinking of Bud, an old saying would come to mind; it would be nice to buy him for what he's worth and then sell him for what he thinks he's worth.

That said, we might all strive to be more like a longtime friend of mine who tried his best to be the least pretentious man alive. Then again, what's the fun in that? For if we ever stop dreaming and pretending then our imagination might just slip down into that plane of existence that some people call the modicums.

But then after having personally known a few of the so-called extroverted types of people, who in my opinion are just as hollow as a spent Fourth of July rocket-shell, it has also been my pleasure to know a good many of the so-called down-to-earth people. One such person I knew was a supervisor on an assembly line in a factory; and not only did this man usually have a perpetual smile on his countenance, but he was also blessed with a terrific amount of common sense.

It was quite understandable that majority of the people who were acquainted with this man knew that he didn't really try to make a whole lot of sense. Nevertheless, his coworkers must have thoroughly appreciated his efforts for as they were prone to say, his attitude and style seemed to make the time pass. Does this then mean that we don't necessarily have to have the talents of a stand-up comic in order to help us endure our brief sojourn on Planet Earth? I would think not, for our relationships with one another will depend largely upon our willingness to compliment our fellows on their good points, and then also for us to have the decency to lie by omission about their character defects and shortcomings.

Besides, who wants to be around someone who is always so brutally honest? Give us good propaganda, I say, and please don't tell us to just eat cake or to just suck it up when we would much rather have you lie to us.

Nonetheless, one of the most interesting aspects of living in one of those types of retirement villages is the fact that the managers must keep the rooms full of paying clients. So as a result, the management must continually be bringing in new people to replace the ones that have either moved out, or else have passed away. This brings to mind a particular situation that occurred when a retired U. S. Army Special-Forces soldier was introduced to our little part of the world. And not so surprisingly, the first suggestion out of the former army sergeant's mouth was that majority of the lazy and out-of-shape residents at the home could benefit from a hearty exercise-regimen.

In this highly-decorated veterans' opinion, a heavy-duty workout system that entailed several different types of aerobics should most definitely be prescribed for the healthier clientele. Of course his military approach to an exercise program would just naturally exempt a good many of the residents who relied heavily on walkers and canes which they desperately needed in order to just get around.

Then too, after a more thorough investigation, the sergeant found that he would also have to excuse the ones who wore cervical-collars. And unbelievable, this unhealthy dose of torture had actually been considered by the community board until finally, the director stepped in and told them that any exercise program would have to be approved by the medical people.

We dodged the bullet that time: and then also luckily for us the ex military man in question just happened to be a raging alcoholic who shortly thereafter was shipped off to a V. A. hospital somewhere in the boonies where he could be dried-out.

Of course it's also true that some of the daily goings-on in our building can be quite serious; such as when we all too frequently had an ambulance parked out in the front of our building. Nonetheless, that's a type of situation that one should come to expect from a building full of elderly people; and besides, without that kind of excitement then the only other topic of conversation that we would have in common would be the weather.

We also had an entertainment committee who spent a great deal of their time and energy on trying to find some new and interesting ways to keep the residents happy and fulfilled. That particular feat normally is accomplished by recruiting as many volunteers from the home as possible. Then the remainder of the days and nights are filled with as much of the local talent from around the community as the budget will allow.

Hence, there are numerous functions slated for almost every day of the week. Then on Sundays, the non-denominational church-service that's offered in the morning is usually followed by an evening's worth of either movies or bingo. Thus from Monday through Saturday the activities might consist of something as bland as free Blood-Pressure checks, or even possibly an occasional Elvis Impersonator.

Of course when the weather's real nice the inhabitants are encouraged to attend the on campus Bar-B-Q which is sometimes spiced up with live musicians. Those parties can be extremely lively, and a few of the people at the complex have been heard to say that the entertainment in our building is almost as good as it is on a cruise-ship.

Though what's truly amazing is that the new people who're constantly moving into the building tend to have expectations of finding their own little personal Eden. Of course later on, they will ultimately discover that their illusion will most likely be shattered; and that's simply because of the fact that they'd failed to remember that they still had to deal with people, rather than just an institution. So generally speaking they're the ones that will usually withdraw from any further socializing while they continue to dream of greener pastures.

Yet another interestingly aspect concerning us human beings is that we never fail to surprise ourselves; for example, one of the more outrageous suggestions to have ever come out of the community council at the home where I formerly resided implied that some of the more well-adjusted and happy residents who're content to simply remain inside their apartments are somehow guilty of the most egregious sin of all. Apparently, a few of the council-members felt that if the so-called recluses would only come out of their apartments and join in the bedlam, then the entire community of oldsters would be more united under one common goal.

Their reasoning must have been: why should a few of the residents dare to be content with their lives when the majority of the residents are in total and constant disarray? Then later on, this theory of theirs would be well documented when a few of the council members were overheard describing some of the people whose names appeared on a secret list. Those well-known solitary types were thought to be part of a potentially subversive group of people which had been labeled as being too peaceable; and they were also accused of being too polite and reasonable.

So without a doubt, this proved to some of us that by simply minding our own business that it would ultimately result in our being unjustly labeled as odd ducks. For in that particular establishment it was readily apparent to almost everybody that a person must either join their fraternity of madness, or else they would be no rest.

On the other hand, though, I honestly feel that with a little effort almost anybody can behave as badly as some of those people in the home did; and it really wouldn't be that difficult of a task to perform. For in reality, all a person has to do is to speak very loudly and in the rudest way. Then too, a person must also insist on being right all of the time. But since I'd been a witness to their shenanigans for a period of several years, they'd prepped me for the course and they probably didn't even realize it.

Accordingly, then, I couldn't wait for the next council meeting to appear on the calendar just so I could show up with a legal pad full of notes and suggestions. My primary thoughts were that I might just be a big hit with the other residents. But with all three of us recluses in attendance at that particular council meeting, it must have been unsettling to the group of elected residents who'd been governing and bulling us around for quite some time.

So then immediately after the secretary had finished reading the minutes from the last meeting, the council president just couldn't help but to yak on and on for what seemed like eternity. Ultimately, though, the treasurer got around to giving a detailed, and a very lengthy-report, as to where every single penny had gone for what seemed to be the last four-hundred years. Eventually, then, but only after some additional monotonous ramblings from every single member of the council, the president stated that the floor was open for the discussion of new business.

So at the exact same time, all three of us so-called recluses raised our hands in unison; and for the next two-hours we virtually inundated the board members with one inane suggestion after another. It was somewhat comical to watch, but then every time that one of the council members tried to interrupt us, they were summarily then shouted down as we loudly decried our democratic right to be heard.

But then after about a week following our most outrageous behavior in the council meeting, we noticed that the number of fliers under our doors had slowed to a mere trickle. Then also luckily for everybody else at the home the atmosphere seemed to clear somewhat. It was almost as if the council members had finally come to realize just exactly what a few dissenting rebels were capable of. Thus as a result, they must have also realized what would happen if the entire populace were to ever rise-up and decide to impeach the whole lot of them.

So as far as the elected council members were concerned, it must have been a thoroughly sobering and terrifying time; but with the date of another council meeting rapidly approaching, the council members had finally realized that our elected officials can only govern us for as long we allow them to.

Small Steps and Large Rewards

There are days when even the accomplishment of a simple task can seem as important as having just achieved a great victory over one of our most reviled archenemies. And best of all, the feeling of satisfaction that comes from doing something well might just linger with us for the better part of that particular day. For as a famous singer and songwriter once said, after having just won the prestigious Gershwin Award for musical excellence, "when I write something good my brain receives a serotonin wash; and which then makes me want more of it because it's addictive."

For the most part, though, our days are usually filled with routine and rather dull task for which we receive very little or no recompense. Then again, there're those other types of days when the litany of falsehoods that are continuously being compiled against us will simply dissipate on their own accord; and if we're real lucky, we will once more be free of all of those negative thoughts.

The secret, we think, is for us to learn how to recapture those wonderful feelings of bliss on those not so perfect days; such as when we're unable to accomplish even the most trivial and mundane task without having to extend a tremendous amount of effort. So for that reason, we bravely posit the idea that in order for us to be more successful in managing our own time, we have only to break the day down into smaller and more manageable parts.

Therefore, our mornings might have to be sacrificed to the colossal world of extreme ennui by simply managing all of those inane, but necessary chores, which help us to live healthier and happier lives. So naturally, we will complete those chores even though they don't afford us any outwardly apparent rewards. Hopefully, then, our afternoons could be spent in the pursuit of creative excellence; that is, of course, if our creative juices are still flowing by the time we complete that inordinately long list of necessary task which help us to live more comfortably.

Then if possible, our evenings could be spent amidst the most luxurious trappings of creature comfort that we have the means to acquire. Conversely, though, solitaire isolation and/or extreme tranquility should never be mandatory as they are not necessarily conducive to turning an unproductive day into a five-star extravaganza type of day.

Yet in all our endeavors, we might just want to throw caution to the wind. For as we all know, baby steps are typically for beginners; and as such, they should be used only by the tyros of social pretenders and not the rest of us who've lived long enough to be able to function quite aptly in a real and grownup society. This then brings us to another point of contention for it seems as if the ones who don't always get their way when it comes to being eligible to receive certain kinds of entitlement programs, are the very same ones who will prate on about the need to replace our present government with a more socialistic type of system.

Conversely, though, those same people would be the first to complain if they ever had to live in a world which had truly run amok. And some of those very same people might also tend to forget that our freedom to whine and gripe about the current state of affairs is only made possible by our voluntarily commitment to personally follow the stringent rules that we as a society have set in place which helps to guard against certain types of civil disobedience. Yet if someone were to ever cast a stone at any of those self-proclaimed dissidents, then they would almost assuredly insist that the bully-boy gendarmes protect them and their property from any further harm.

"The rewards that we reap by contributing our labors to the common good of the people will always justify the means to an end." Or least so the well-known professor of theology, Thurmond Morton, who'd written numerous books on the subject of social science would have us to believe. Morton was always been a big hit amongst the psychology and political science majors at the university where he was employed; and so as a direct result of his immense popularity with the student body his classes were usually packed full with the eager young and men and women who wished to ascend to the top of the heap by learning how best to manipulate the common masses.

Though while he was working at home, Professor Morton was more often than not in need of more than a few shots of some very old scotch whiskey in order to be able to write the meaningless drivel which he so freely espoused during the social science lectures that he continued to deliver to his students. He knew better, of course, for at one time he'd attended one of the very best universities in the country. He'd also been formally trained as a clinical psychologist.

But then later on, both the dean of the political science department, and even the president of that prestigious university where he was employed, would most fervently deny having any prior qualms about the subject matter that Professor Morton had been teaching in his classes; after all, they said, "for all we knew the learned professor was teaching from the appropriate and previously approved college textbooks." In all actuality, however, the college administrators almost had to have known that a few of Professor Morton's lectures contained topics that were better left unsaid; and yet, Morton was allowed to continue to preach his nonsensical themes to what he considered to be the masses of gullible students.

In some ways, however, Professor Morton wasn't even a true hypocrite; for in his private life he considered himself to be a dyed-in-the-wool, ultra conservative Republican who honestly believed that the Social Democrats of America were trying to destroy the basic fabric of our great society. And in his way of thinking, our country would be better off if we simply eliminated the word "entitlement" from our collective vocabulary. For then not only would the U. S. Congress have the moral authority to greatly reduce the enormous amounts of tax money that's being spent on all of the various entitlement programs, but the requirements for admission onto the future welfare rolls would be so stringent in their nature that only the most deserving recipients need to apply.

Nevertheless, after having been embroiled in the Great Recession of the 21st Century, both the Federal and State Governments had found themselves facing such monumental shortfalls that the governments had no choice, then, but to drastically reduce the amount of money that would normally be available to the various departments of education. And even though history has proved that our government benefits financially by making loans and grants available to those who're interested in pursuing a degree in higher education, the die was cast; and therefore, the states had to either reduce the amount of money that would normally be allocated to their schools, or else the states would risk the very real possibility of going bankrupt.

So when the Federal and the state governments were forced to slash the departments of education budgets by hundreds of millions of dollars, the state colleges and many of the universities were forced to furlough literally thousands of professors from their payrolls. Then as unlikely and as unfair as it must have seemed, Professor Thurmond Morton was one of the teachers that had to be let go.

"What now?" Professor Morton, had asked himself as he slowly watched his lifesaving disappear while he searched desperately for any type of job that might let him retain the ownership of the somewhat quaint, but beautiful old Cape Cod style cottage which he'd called home for a number of years.

What's more, after a full ten years following the divorce from his ex-wife Shelly, the only other living creature that Professor Thurmond Morton had allowed into his very private life, excepting, that is, his Labrador retriever, Innu, was an associate professor female friend of his who'd also been furloughed from her job at the university where they'd both previously been employed. At thirty-six years of age, Janice Holder was about the same age of Thurmond Morton. However, their relationship could not be deemed as close; in fact, their preferred way of communicating with one another was by email.

So it goes without saying that both of their lives had been drastically changed by the furloughs. Nevertheless, on the Monday immediately following their termination from their former positions at the university, Thurmond and Janice decided to drive in to town together in order to sign up for their first ever unemployment check.

Thurmond's pride was still smarting from the realization that he was no longer a duly employed and well respected member of the academic world; but then during the previous Friday evening he'd made matters even worse by drinking to excess and then getting behind the wheel of his old station wagon while he was still legally drunk. Then fortunately or unfortunately, I suppose it depends on your own personal outlook on the subject, Thurmond was arrested for Driving while Intoxicated.

Then as if to add insult to injury, Thurmond was forced to sit in a holding cell until such time as the alcohol content in his blood had fallen below the legal limit. So naturally, a pride leveling experience of that extinct had to be extremely embarrassing for such an esteemed educator. Yet the worst of all were the words in the arresting officer's report which stated that the professor had allegedly said, "Do you know who I am?"

So not only had Thurmond been soundly embarrassed at the police station, but in his own mind he was still somewhat perturbed after having been forced to answer some rather personal questions from a person who was a mere civil servant of the state. For at thirty-six years of age, and with all of his many successes behind him, no one had ever spoken that way to Thurmond Morton. As a matter of fact, he felt as if he'd been treated as a common person; and this, of course, was something that he'd never considered himself to be.

Even so, the first thoughts of revenge and retaliation against the state government had not as yet begun to formulate in Thurmond's mind; or at very least, the thoughts had not become apparent until he began a job search on the internet. Then as he was submitting his resumes to the various universities and colleges around the country, he became painfully aware of some of the copycat shootings that were taking place across the entire United States. Most notably was one of the first of the modern-day incidents involving a college professor which had just recently taken place at the University of Alabama's, Huntsville campus.

From then on, a constant rumbling of discontent could be heard from the thousands of the recently unemployed educators from around the country. "How many copycat mass slayings would occur in the world of academia before the government would be forced to come to its senses and restore the lost jobs at the universities?" Thurmond wondered, as he was loading the thirty round clips that he'd just recently purchased for his newly acquired assault rifle.

Princess Purdy

Long, long ago, there was a beautiful young princess named Purdy who lived in a lovely green valley called Earthton.

Regrettably, though, Purdy's father, King Estes, had been killed while fighting the Vandals who were an extremely violent tribe of people that lived on the opposite side of the mountain where Purdy and the rest of the Purtans lived

Then immediately following the tragic death of Purdy's father, her mother, Queen Monacy, was forced to marry a man by the name of Theseus who claimed to be the new king of the Purtans.

Of course it was only natural for Purdy to be saddened by father's death; but now, she was being asked to accept the fact that her mother was about to marry another man when her husband the king had only been dead for a short period of time

Though when asked, Queen Monacy stated "that she was well aware of the fact that Purdy still missed her father," but then added that "she hoped that Purdy would come to understand that she'd married the new king in order to protect her from any possible harm."

So even though Purdy still missed her father terribly, she eventually came to accept the fact that her mother had indeed married the new king out of the love that she had for her own daughter

It was also around that same point in time when Purdy had begun to wonder how the Vandal Army could have sneaked up so easily on her father's soldiers: and especially since most of the trees in the valley had been cut down in order to make logs for their homes. This then meant, of course, that the guards who were on duty on the day of the surprise attack should have been able to see the approaching enemy long before they had a chance to attack her father's army. Thankfully, though, it wouldn't be too long before Purdy would have the answers to all her questions

Without a doubt, Purdy knew it would take a long time to get over her father's sudden death; but in the end she'd to decide that life must go on. Purdy also understood that in order for the Purtans to survive as a people that each and every one of them would have to take on some added responsibilities; and since Purdy loved the baby chicks so much, the council decided that it would be her job to feed and water the chickens. Additionally, she would also gather up the chicken's eggs on a daily basis

Purdy dearly loved caring for and protecting her baby chicks; she did, however, have one major concern and that situation was caused by a family of chicken hawks that lived about halfway up on the side of her mountain

Purdy was well aware of the fact that the chicken hawks had a long history of sweeping down from the sky and then carrying off her people's baby chicks; but what the chicken hawks couldn't know was that Purdy had just recently started carrying a slingshot along with some very smooth stones; and, that, she was also so proficient with her sling that she could put a hole in a watermelon from a distance of some forty paces, or even more

Unfortunately, though, it was during one of those unparticular afternoons when Purdy was being tutored by a teacher that one of the chicken hawks swept down from the sky and snatched up one of Purdy's favorite baby chicks

Purdy was angry, alright, and she'd vowed right then and there that she intended to put a stop to that evil practice. In fact, Purdy was so determined to get rid of the mean old chicken hawks that she was willing to climb halfway up on the mountain just so she could then try to scare away the hawks. So then later on that same day, but only after she had finished doing her chores, Purdy decided that she would get rid of the chicken hawks once and for all

She knew, of course, that it could be very dangerous for her to climb halfway up the mountain all by herself; but she also knew that she was a very strong young girl. And besides, she'd just about had enough of those darned old chicken hawks

Then somewhat surprisingly, the climb up the side of the mountain took Purdy less than an hour to complete; and then shortly thereafter she was standing about forty paces from the nest where the chicken hawks lived. The problem was, however, the nest was resting on a ledge which was right above a large bush that was growing out of the side of the mountain

Though at that point, Purdy wasn't about to let something as minor as a bush deter her, so she began to swing her sling above her head with all of her might; and just when she thought that her aim was perfect she released the stone from the sling

Crack, was the sound as the stone hit the nest and the rock ledge at the same exact instant Amazingly, though, when the nest and the two stunned adult chicken hawks came falling down on top of the bush, Purdy couldn't help but notice that there seemed to be a light coming from the interior of the mountain

"How can that be?" Purdy wondered; then again, there was nothing left for her to do but to inch her way on up over those last forty paces on the narrow stone ledge just so she could take a closer look at the light which appeared to be coming from behind the bush

Then upon a closer examination, Purdy decided that the light that was shining from the cave seemed to be coming from the opposite side of the mountain; and therefore, it would be a simple matter for her to make her way along the well-beaten path of the cave to the other side of the mountain.

Yet to her great amazement, Purdy was startled by what appeared to be some very scary looking pre-historic type of large birds as they flew nosily above her head before then exiting the cave on the opposite side of the mountain

Though by then, Purdy had traveled even deeper into the cave until she was eventually standing in the middle of a large room which had a stone chair placed directly beneath yet another mysterious ray of light which appeared to be coming from an opening in the top of the mountain.

At that point in time Purdy was surprised and even a little stunned to see what appeared to be an image of her supposedly dead father who was sitting majestically in a stone chair beneath that strange white light which was shinning down from above.

"Please don't be afraid of me for I have something of importance to say to you" her father's image said

"But how can this be? I thought you were dead", Purdy said, as she started walking slowly toward the ghost-like image of her father

"Please do not try to touch me", Purdy's father said, "For as you can see I am no longer of this world. I am of the world where the Purtans go after we leave this earth

"Well just exactly what is it that you wish to say to me," Purdy said, as she calmly sat down at the foot of her father's chair

"I've been allowed to visit Earth just so I can warn you and your mother about a serious and grave situation," Purdy's father said

"As you might have already guessed, King Theseus was responsible for my death. And I've also learned that he was the one who told the Vandals about this secret cave which allowed their army to surprise and then defeat our soldiers," Purdy's dad said

"So it was a stroke of good luck for our people that I decided to chase the chicken hawks away from the valley, wasn't it?" Purdy said

"It certainly was," King Estes said. "But the message that I have for you today is that King Theseus has vowed that he will marry the Queen of the Vandals. This of course means that he will forced to do away with both you and your mother, Queen Monacy," Purdy's dad said

"Yes, but since we Purtans now know about this secret cave, doesn't that mean that we might be able to surprise, and possibly even defeat the Vandal Army," Purdy said

Unfortunately for Purdy, however, however, her father's image began to slowly fade away. Though in due time her father's prophecy would help to save the day; for not only were Purdy and Queen Monacy's lives' spared, but all of the rest of the Purtans were allowed to live peaceably in their beautiful green valley.

By Candlelight

At that point in his life, a power failure was the very last thing that Christian Lanner would have ever wished for; and particularly since he was already running seriously behind in his work. For according to the deadline date on the contract with his publisher, Chris had only a short period of time left in which to finish the final draft of his latest mystery novel. But then because of the apparent brownout that his neighborhood was experiencing, it was beginning to look as if he might have to finish the rewriting of his manuscript by candlelight.

Yet as Chris was rummaging around in the utility room closet in search of candles and flashlights he heard what he believed to be a woman's scream for help. So after grabbing onto the first flashlight that he came upon, he very quickly headed for the hallway outside of his apartment where he thought that the sound had originated from. However, the pitch-black darkness in the hallway was so overwhelming to his senses that the only other time he remembered experiencing anything that close to total darkness was when he'd visited the Mammoth Cave National Park.

Though what followed next would chill Chris to his mortal being: and it wasn't just the horrible scream that he'd heard, although that was definitely unlike anything that he'd ever heard before. But by judging the awful smell which had suddenly permeated the entire hallway, something terrible and wicked had just pierced that exceptionally stormy evening.

What's more, that feeble ray of light which was emanating from his ancient flashlight had failed miserably to illuminate anything out of the ordinary in his part of the hallway. But since his apartment was located at the end of a long hallway which consisted of six units on either side beginning at the elevator which was located in the center of the hallway, he quickly realized that the scream he'd heard could have come from almost any one of the units on his floor.

So after being unable to detect the exact direction from whence the scream had originated, Chris closed, and then double-locked his own apartment door. Next, he attempted to use his landline telephone, but as luck would have it that system was down too. However, he was especially astonished when even his cell phone was dead. Apparently, the lightning had struck some of the communication towers which were scattered loosely all throughout the tri-state and had therefore caused literally tens of thousands of cell phone users to overwhelm the system to such a degree that the entire system had ceased to operate.

So the next question that Chris had to ask himself was one that mankind has been trying to fathom since ancient times; should a person risk life and limb for a another fellow human being, or is it sometimes wiser to think only of one's own self?

Yet at that very moment his thoughts were punctuated by a rapid succession of the most piercing and terrifyingly sounding screams that he'd ever heard; and which then left Chris with no other recourse but to retrieve a fully loaded twelve gauge pump shotgun from the bedroom closet and then hurriedly re-enter the hallway where the first thing that he noticed was that the terrible screaming has ceased.

Then with no other immediate plan of action in mind, Chris decided to knock on all the doors on the fourth floor of his building; or at least he would so until he found the person whose life was apparently in peril. But for the sake convenience, the first door he tried would be that of his neighbor who lived directly across the hall from him. Thus while knocking on the door he at the same time had turned the doorknob which allowed his neighbor's door to swing freely open towards the inside of the apartment. It was then that he realized that both the door and the floor were sopping wet with a liquid that appeared to be human blood.

At that moment, Chris was momentarily frozen in that ancient flight or fight stage when an unrecognizable figure came charging out of the darkness and then slammed into him with such force that he was knocked flat on the hallway floor where he was left to scramble back to his feet while at the same time trying to locate the flashlight that was no longer emitting light.

And even though Chris had not been seriously injured, he'd been spiritually wounded by the foul odor of the creature which had just knocked him senseless to the floor. Yet luckily for Chris, he eventually found the old flashlight, and then after carefully coaxing it back to life he was furnished with enough light to help him navigate his way back to his own apartment. The shotgun, however, was nowhere to be found.

Now, the screaming seemed to take on a more noticeable pattern which consisted of long intervals of quite but then were quickly followed by some extremely loud moans and groans that didn't sound anything like human noises. Though by then, the screams seemed to be coming primarily from the opposite wing of his apartment building. And so armed with both a workable flashlight and a very old 1913 Model, Army Colt 45 caliber semiautomatic pistol, Chris decided to more thoroughly explore the human carnage which he thought had been visited upon his apartment building.

Strangely enough, however, not a single soul answered the knock at any of the doors on his end of the building. So by then, Chris had rather bravely decided that it would be prudent for him to checkup on his neighbors who lived on the south wing of the building. Though without personally knowing any of those people, he had only to assume that the killer or killers could be hiding behind any one of the twelve apartment doors on the opposite end of the fourth floor; and consequently, he reluctantly decided to turn off his flashlight and then just feel his way along the railing in the hallway as he gripped his pistol ever more tightly before knocking on any more of his neighbor's doors.

Though somewhat surprisingly, nobody was answering his repeated knocks on any of the doors on the south wing of the fourth floor; until, this is, when he was at the end of the hallway when a person opened their door and dragged him inside.

"Please help me," the stranger said, but when Chris was finally able to shine his flashlight on the face of person who'd just grabbed him by the shoulders, he had only to wonder if he might be in the presence of a killer.

"Well madam, besides the fact that we are experiencing a power failure, do you happen to know what else is going on?" Chris said to the elderly woman.

"No sir, I don't: I'm just glad to have someone to talk to," the woman said as she introduced herself to Chris.

"Well Judy, as you might not be aware of, I live on down the other end of this hallway where at least one person has already been murdered," Chris said.

But then suddenly, Chris's attention was attracted by an extremely loud noise which seemed to be coming from the sidewalk which was four stories below. The piercing sound was so pervasive that it could have easily been heard over and above the sounds of the terrible storm that was still raging on the outside. Thus after assessing the situation below, Chris advised the woman that he knew only as Judy, to hurriedly gather her raingear and then follow him to the stairwell.

Then just moments later, after the two of them had very carefully crept down the three flights of stairs, both Chris and the elderly woman entered the front lobby of the apartment building, while at the same time, a series of extremely bright flashes of lightening had starkly illuminated the lobby with enough light for him to make out the figures of some of his neighbors from the fourth floor who'd bravely taken the initiative to distance themselves from the maddening screams and the possible killer that might still be lurking around upstairs. Of course, Chris had only to wonder if the killer might be one of the people who'd bunched up around the plate glass windows in the front of the lobby.

So with that thought in mind, Chris covered up his pistol with the lightweight jacket that he'd thrown on before venturing out of his apartment; he also noticed that in his haste to determine the source of the screams that he must have retrieved a razor sharp hunting knife from the top shelf of his bedroom closet when he was grappling for his pistol. Luckily, though, the people who'd gathered at the front of the lobby of his apartment building appeared to be just as nervous and afraid as he and Judy were. The question was, then, where was the killer? But with what appeared to be a chaotic situation in the streets outside, Chris decided that it would behoove him and the rest of the tenants to remain indoors.

Eventually, though, the lightning strikes became so frequent and intense that Chris couldn't help but notice that his whole being was literally soaked with appeared to be human blood. It was also at that point in time that Chris was able to vaguely recall the last scene in the novel that he'd been writing wherein he'd described in graphic detail just exactly how the central character in his story had butchered a number of people on the fourth floor of his own apartment building.

The Bronze Bust Caper

At the time, it seemed as if Jonathon and Marilee Bracket of Indianapolis, Indiana were destined to go down in history as being two of the most hopeless drug addicts to ever frequent the halls of justice and the treatment centers in the city of Indianapolis and the surrounding environs of Marion County, Indiana.

What with two counts of dealing drugs already on the books, and also after having been incarcerated for a total of twenty-two months in the Marion County Indiana Detention Center, the pair knew full well that their drug dealing days were most likely behind them. So naturally, the self-proclaimed unlucky duo decided that they would have to find another way in which to support their expensive crack cocaine habit.

At first, it seemed as if that particular dilemma was about to be resolved when the husband, a young man by the name of Jonathon Bracket, who was the self-appointed brains of the outfit, decided that he and his wife, Marilee, would go into the (iron and steal) business; that is, his wife would take in other people's ironing during the day, but then during the evening, the two of them would steal scrap metal and then sell it.

To be sure, the risky enterprise of absconding with the highly sought-after copper guttering which can still be found in a few of the older houses certainly wasn't anything new; in fact, that particular type of theft had been going on for quite a long while. What was new, however, would be the thievery of a two hundred pound bronze portrait busts which had been fashioned into the bearded likeness of one of Indiana's most favorite adopted sons, Robert Dale Owen, who, in the year of eighteen hundred and twenty-five had migrated to the southwestern Indiana town of New Harmony, Indiana with his father, the well-known British social reformer, Robert Owen.

The Robert Dale Owen Memorial which was dedicated in the year of 1912 is still located at the south entrance of the Indiana Statehouse along Washington Street in the city of Indianapolis, Indiana; however, only the three stones where the bronze portrait-like bust of Owen once rested still remain. Luckily though, the seventy inch tall stones are still in place; and then along with them is the memorial plaque which is centered on the face of the top stone block.

The memorial plaque, which to this day still adorns one of the memorial's original three stones, most aptly describes Robert Dale Owen as an author, statesman, politician, philanthropist, social reformer, and a person who loved his fellow man. Yet not in a million years would the good people of Indiana ever believe that someone would have the gall to steal a bronze bust of a person who'd always stood up for the underdog whether they were our women folk, or the racially disadvantaged.

Nevertheless, when the average drug addict feels the need to feed his or her addiction, then something as foreign as "save our history" is almost certainly an anathema of lesser importance to them. Then also just as assuredly, their answer to a question of that type would have been; "well, if the price of bronze and copper hadn't risen to such great heights, then we might have stolen some other type of metal; and consequently, we most likely would have left that stupid old bronze bust where it was."

Yet when the local law enforcement agencies decided to turn up the heat on the thousands of petty thieves who reside in the capital city, Jonathon and Marilee simply removed their business enterprise a ways out of the city limits just so they could remain a tad less visible to the ever vigilant city authorities. Of course that also meant that the two semi-professional boosters would have to spend a lot more of their semi-valuable time on the byways and highways just getting to and from their next available window of opportunity which was thievery of course.

Of course if the investigators had only known, then they would have backtracked and then very diligently searched the soil in the backyards of every Marion County, Indiana home where the pilfering duo had formerly resided. Then too, if the authorities had only taken the time to interview the already documented scrap metal thieves of Marion County, then they might have located the missing bronze bust of one of Indiana's most favorite sons.

Though without a doubt, Jonathon and Marilee knew all too well that the purloined bronze bust of Robert Dale Owen was entirely too hot to sell for scrap metal; so as a result, they'd simply buried the famous bust a full six feet deep in the backyard of one of the numerous rented properties where they'd previously resided.

So unless a future property owner decides to drill a well, or else to dig a foundation for a new home in that same exact location, the missing bust will most likely go down in history along with the rest of the buried treasures of Indiana that have been lost to perpetuity.

Inherent Wickedness

Not very often had the small town of Brownsburg been recognized for any of its finer qualities; however, the town's latest bit of notoriety was something that the city father's could have certainly done without. For it was all too clear that the forty year streak of murderous free living in this very excellent little lakeside village had come to a sudden halt.

In an account which appeared in a special edition of the town's only newspaper, the Brownsburg Star, newspaper editor Bret Wampler affirmed the fact that it'd been forty years to the day since there'd been a recorded homicide in the normally peaceful and law-abiding community of Brownsburg.

Then during that ancient murder trial and the subsequent conviction, it was brought to light that a local farmer by the name of Jason Broward Sr. had killed a neighbor of his over a dispute which concerned the rightful ownership of a strip of land which had previously adjoined the two farms, but had subsequently been displaced by some extraordinarily high floodwaters causing the creek which runs between the two farms to alter its course.

Now it seems as if the convicted murderers son, a certain Mr. Jason Broward Jr., might just possibly be complicit in the disappearance, and the eventual discovery, of the dismembered and headless body which had been found lying on the eastern bank of the stream that separates the two farms which have historically been owned by the Broward and the Brown families of Wilmington County.

Also just as interestingly, the newly discovered corpse appeared to be none other than William Brown, who just happened to be the son of the man that Jason Broward Sr. had been convicted of slaying some forty years prior to that date. Then again, the authorities wouldn't know the true identity of the victim until the medical examiner had arrived from the county seat which was located some thirty-five miles northeast of the crime scene. In the meantime, however, the body would be released to the local undertaker who would have the unenviable job of reattaching the head and the limbs to the torso in the hopes that the next of kin would to be able to properly identify the remains; if and when, that is, the remainder of the missing body parts were ever found.

It goes without saying that while investigating any case of homicide, the law enforcement officers in charge of the case will almost always take a good look at the closest family members. Though in this particular case, the Wilmington County Sheriff, Major Keith Williams, thought that he already had a pretty good idea as to the identity of the killer; and that would be none other than the owner of the neighboring farm, a certain Mr. Jason Broward Jr.; or at the very least, that's what the sheriff was inclined to believe. Then too, they would know a great deal more about the case once the autopsy had been performed.

And even though Jason Broward Jr. was subsequently arrested by the Wilmington County Sheriff for the murder and the dismemberment of his neighbor, William Brown Jr., the longtime Deputy State Prosecutor for Wilmington County had expressed some concerns about her chances of being able to convict such a highly decorated Persian Gulf War veteran as Jason Broward Jr.

What with no confession coming forth from the defendant, and also with no eye witnesses to the grotesque and heinous murder of a member of the original founding fathers of the town of Brownsburg, the deputy prosecutor, Caitlin Burrows, figured her chances of convincing a jury of Broward's guilt were about 50-50 at best.

Though what happened next was so completely unexpected that it could have only taken place in the Old South of yesteryear. It seems as if three of Mr. Broward's old war buddies had suddenly remembered that the defendant had just recently accompanied them on an out-of-state fishing expedition at a lake which was located some five hundred miles away from the scene of the crime; and as an additional treat, they were willing to testify in court that all four of them were out of town on the day that the murder had supposedly taken place.

By then, of course, everyone on the prosecutor's team tended to feel a bit dejected and defeated; until, that is, when Deputy Prosecutor, Caitlin Burrows, remembered an old lawsuit that Jason Broward Jr. had filed in Superior Court approximately one year prior to the murder of William Brown. Thus after reviewing the old case file which had primarily dealt with the rightful ownership of a strip of land that lies just to the east of the creek that separates the two farms which are owned by the two longtime warring families, Ms. Burrows noticed in the old court file that Jason Broward Jr. had claimed to have photographic evidence to support his lawsuit.

Therefore, it was quickly assumed by everyone in the prosecutor's office that at some point in the past Jason Broward Jr. must have installed an onsite camera nearby to the creek that separates his farm from the neighboring farm which is owned by the Brown family. And if so, then Ms. Burrows was thinking that perhaps the camera might still be in place; and so naturally, she immediately obtained a search warrant from a somewhat friendly judge who not only would give her the legal right to reconnoiter the area surrounding the aforesaid creek, but the warrant would also allow her and the sheriff to confiscate any cameras that they happened to find the property.

Then luckily for the people in the prosecutor's office, the previously noted camera was still in place where it was sitting atop a fencepost on the Broward side of the creek; and so of course, it was then hurriedly rushed to a local photographer's shop where it could be properly studied.

The camera in question was a solar powered, bridge digital camera that was equipped with both a GPS and a large compact flash memory card. But one of the most intriguing features in the on-site camera was that it was equipped with a SASER type of device. And even though the device itself was still considered to be somewhat theoretical in design, the SASER was supposedly able to cause the camera to automatically record any action that was taking place in the front of the camera once some movement or noise had been detected.

Thus with the images of that brutal murder stored safely away in the memory flash card that was now safely in the hands of the prosecution, Jason Broward Jr. had no other recourse, then, but to plead guilty to a charge of first-degree manslaughter that would ultimately place him in the same state penitentiary where his father was still incarcerated.

As Shakespeare once said, "Truth will come to light; murder cannot be hid long."

Vigilantes

Throughout River City, it was common knowledge that Torres Philpot was the undisputed leader of the Southside Gang; so naturally, his word on the Southeast side of town was final. Yet even Torres was somewhat surprised when one of his latest efforts had succeeded beyond his wildest dreams. Simply said, Torres had hoped to duplicate what the American Mafia had accomplished in the twentieth century. For history will show that the U. S. Mafia was one of the first U. S. organizations to have perfected the practice of swapping favors with a criminal element from another city. Consequently, Torres Philpot had felt justified in making the first overture of a similar nature to the leader of one of the more dominant gangs on the Southside of Chicago, Illinois.

One year prior, while Torres Philpot was visiting some family members in the city of Chicago, Illinois, he'd spent a portion of the Fourth of July locked up in the Cook County Illinois Jail on a misdemeanor charge of public intoxication where he just happened to befriend a man by the name Clifford Mansfield, who as it turned out, was one of the highest-ranking members of one of the most powerful gangs on the Southside of Chicago.

Then once back home in River City, Torres had begun an almost daily dialogue with Clifford Mansfield as to how they could institute a similar arrangement between the two gangs which would be beneficial to them both. In the end, the gist of their final accord was that the two gang leaders would temporarily lend a few of their most trusted gang members to the other's organization for the sole purpose of eliminating any potential rivals or trouble makers in their respective cities. In other words, they would use each other's gang members as hit men.

Furthermore, since River City sits directly on the Ohio River, and since it's also located in the Midwest, it's only a three hundred mile drive by automobile from River City to Chicago; so theoretically, one of Clifford's gang members could murder one of Torres's rivals in River City on a given morning and then be back home in Chicago in time for supper. To their way of thinking, the new system of borrowing a hit man from another organization seemed like a dream come true; and especially since the imported gunmen would not be known to the local police departments.

At first glance, this new arrangement appeared to be an important new weapon in the gang's arsenal, for nowadays the act of eliminating one's business competition is not only considered to be de rigueur, but in the illegal drug trade it's an absolute necessity.

The problem was, however, what in the world would the River City authorities do with all of the additional dead bodies. Of late, the River City coroner, who was a woman by the name of Mary Simpson, had just recently requested some emergency support of not only her own county council, but she'd also submitted a supplemental request to the state treasurer's office to the tune of a quarter of a million dollars just so she could hire enough additional deputy coroners in the hopes that she could facilitate the proper disposal of the dozens of bodies that were currently in cold storage.

Of course a goodly number of those stacked up bodies in the River City morgue were the local citizens who'd either died from natural causes, or else their deaths were the result of fatal accidents; however, over a dozen of those bodies in the morgue were the direct result of the local drug war which was presently taking place on the Southeast side of town.

Yet unbeknownst to Torres Philpot, an equally powerful individual had just recently moved into the Southeast side of town. His name was Tom Trottier: and just like Torres Philpot he was also a longtime resident of River City. Tom Trottier had lived a very interesting life, for not only was he was a former member of the French Foreign Legion, but he was also a survivor of the famous Dien Bien Phu battle which had taken place in the North Western corner of Vietnam back in the year of 1954. The battle was eventually won by the Viet Minhand which then had precipitated the immediate withdraw of all the French Forces from Vietnam.

So upon his return to the United States, and then ultimately back to his hometown of River City, Tom Trottier had tried valiantly to absolve himself of the tremendous guilt and the responsibility that he felt for having killed all of those unknown numbers of people while serving with the French Foreign Legion. Unfortunately, though, he'd handled that devastating situation in the only way that he knew how; and that was by drinking alcohol to excess.

Eventually, though, the bottle had begun to cause Tom problems. So it was also at that point in time that Tom had made the decision to return to the religion of his childhood. In fact, Tom had decided to found a church on the Southeast side of River City where he very modestly adopted the secular title of religious leader. Though by most regards, his new church would be considered rather small; that said, however, it's steadily growing membership tended to lend itself to the people who were formally addicted to drugs and alcohol. Then once the word got out, the membership continued to swell with literally dozens of new church members who were also recovering from their various addictions.

Yet in addition to his work at the church, which had helped immensely to save him from a life of drunkenness, Tom had also been advised to submit to the more traditional forms of psycho therapy in order to rid himself of what he called the addictive habit of killing people which he thought was something that he'd picked up by osmosis while serving in the French Foreign Legion.

But then also luckily for Tom and the millions of other combat veterans in the U. S, the severe anxiety stress disorder from which he'd long suffered was beginning to receive so much attention from the U. S. Military establishment that the psychiatrist and therapist of today seemed to have a pretty good grip on the cause and the effect of the disorder which nowadays is more commonly known as PTSD. And even though there may never be an absolute cure for the disorder, it's fervently hoped by all that the veterans of today can somehow learn how to live in their own skin.

So with all things considered, it appeared as if Tom Trottier had finally learned how to live a fairly peaceful and productive life; and more often than not, he was happy joyous and free. That is, of course, unless he was subjected to some extremely loud noises such as gunfire; for then the old warrior in him was likely to emerge. But since he was currently living on the Southeast side of River City, he had only to venture outside to witness the almost daily violence that was the direct result of the local drug war for which Torres Philpot was largely responsible for.

Yet strangely enough, Tom Trottier had never had a meaningful conversation with the leader of the Southside Gang; and that was somewhat odd being that they resided so close to one another. In fact Tom's new church was located in a large two-story building that stood on the northeast corner of a Southeast side intersection. Then directly across the street from Tom's church and residence sat an old two-story redbrick building which had formally housed a grocery store on the first floor but the apartments on the second floor were used to house the owner and his family.

As in any neighborhood, parking can sometimes be a problem. So in order to supply the necessary parking spaces for their individual enterprises, it was required of both Tom and Torres to purchase and then raze the houses that were located directly next-door to their respective properties. Yet more often than not Tom's parking lot was only crowded on Wednesdays and Sundays when the church was holding services; whereas the adjoining parking lot belonging to Torres Philpot was filled to the brim practically every single hour of the day with the busiest times being between 3:00 o'clock in the afternoon to around 3:00 o'clock in the following morning.

Of course to the majority of the people living on the Southeast side of town it appeared as if the two completely different types of neighbors would have to eventually clash. For to them, it didn't seem quite proper for one group of people to offer love and salvation from one side of the street, while at the same time, the enterprise on the opposite corner was there to dish out death and destruction to the people who bought their deadly drugs. Then just as the early prognosticators had always feared, the problem of living in a drug war zone was about to be delivered to the front door of their church.

The tragic and almost inevitable event took place one evening during a scheduled baptismal service at the church while Tom was assisting the church's ordained minister by supplying him with clean and dry white handkerchiefs which are normally used to cover the member's faces as they are being lowered into the shallow water of the baptismal tank.

Then later on, it was determined by the authorities that the stray bullet which had struck and killed an elderly female member of the church had been fired from an AK47 automatic rifle. The police also reported that according to their forensics experts, the bullet which had killed Lisa Van Orman had most likely been fired from the parking lot located directly behind the two-story brick building from whence Torres Philpot held sway over the local drug trade.

Eventually, though, the investigation into the murder of Lisa Van Orman would go cold for without any eye witnesses to the shooting the police had their hands tied. For in the majority of these types of cases it's quite understandable that the average person is usually reluctant to testify against the violent gang members. There was, however, a well organized Neighborhood Watch Committee in the area which had a longstanding relationship with the River City Police Department; and coincidentally, their next meeting was scheduled to take place during the week that immediately followed the fatal shooting at Tom's church.

Tom sincerely believed that since one of his church's members had been gunned down in his very own building that the next Neighborhood Watch Committee meeting should be held n his church. Then once that the word got out, over one hundred members and nonmembers alike showed up for the next regularly scheduled meeting just so they could hear what the former Ligonier might have to say.

The truth be told, however, Tom always felt a little uneasy when he was asked to address such a large and vocal group of people; for in the past, he'd personally witnessed the violent aftermath of mob actions while serving with the Legion. So when Tom was asked point blank by a Neighborhood Watch Committee member if he believed in the biblical saying of an "eye for an eye;" he could tell that the committee members were itching to take revenge against the drug dealing neighbor of theirs that was headquartered just across the street from the church. There's supposed to be safety in numbers, Tom thought, but when serving as a sniper in Vietnam he'd usually worked alone.

Thankfully, though, the meeting ended on a somewhat peaceful note with an agreement being made that more volunteers would definitely be needed to man the streets at all hours of the day and night. Because harking back to the military training that he'd had received, Tom knew that the best way to resolve a violent situation was always with a superior force. Moreover, he'd recently been formatting a covert plan whereby he would begin an around the clock surveillance and reconnaissance of his drug dealing neighbor's enterprise.

Then not so surprisingly, Tom had only to rely on the arrogance of the neighborhood purveyors of death who'd come to believe that not only should they be able to deal their deadly drugs with complete impunity, but that they should be able to do so in plain sight of everybody. So for that reason, Tom felt that in the future he should be able count on the abject carelessness of their actions. Also to Tom's potential benefit, the gang didn't appear to have any standardized form of security in and around their base of operations. In Fact, Torres seemed completely oblivious to anything but his own greedy interest.

Therefore, with his extensive training and experience in the field of reconnaissance, Tom was easily able to pinpoint the exact time of day when the Southside Gang's drug dealing din of inequities was the least occupied which was around 4:00 o'clock in the morning. Then the next course of action would be Tom's eventual plan of attack. At first, Tom had tried to develop a plan that would keep him immune from suspicion. Though later on, he'd come to the conclusion that he was willing to commit his planned acts of violence without having to worry about the real possibility of getting caught by the River City Police.

Tom's thinking was that instead of the courts handing him down a severe punishment for eliminating such a murderous gang of thugs, the city fathers might instead offer him a key to the city for ridding the community of such a vile bunch of despicable gangsters. Therefore, he was beginning to think that he might just do the deed and then take his chances with a jury of his peers. Tom was also worried that a few of the more vocal members of the Neighborhood Watch Committee might decide to take matters into their own hands.

"That would be a terrible idea," Tom thought. For he knew from experience that a single individual would have a much better chance of executing a well rehearsed plan of vengeance than an unruly mob. Moreover, he didn't particularly want any of his church members to take the fall if things happened to terribly wrong. Tom also knew that he'd already lived longer than he thought that he would have. "So therefore, it was a simple matter of who was the most expendable;" Tom thought.

In the meantime, however, one of Tom's former church members had decided to return to the streets. And even more unfortunately, the lad that Tom had personally mentored had not only started using drugs again, but he was now working for Torres as both a lookout, and as one of the people who move the illegal drugs around from place to place. So by then, it was assumed by all that Torres most likely knew all about the neighborhood watch group's plans which called for increased foot patrols. Of course there was no way for Torres to know about Tom's own personal plans; however, it was also a given that Torres might just have a few secret plans of his own.

Accordingly, then, with the stepped up security systems that were assumed to be in place at the so-called (social club) across the street, Tom knew that his own plans of revenge would have to be tweaked somewhat. In fact, Tom was beginning to believe that perhaps it might just be for the better because he would then be forced to eliminate Torres and his lieutenants one at a time; and hopefully, those killings could take place just as far away from the neighborhood as possible.

Thus after giving the problem a significant amount of thought and meditation, Tom decided to borrow a sheetrock worker's pickup truck from one of the church members. "This provided good cover," Tom thought, because with the company owner's name and phone number on the doors of the truck it would allow him to follow Torres around town without having to drive one of the church's vans.

So from the amount time that Tom had already spent on reconnoitering the neighborhood, he knew for a fact that Torres almost always took his fully restored 1973 Cadillac Coupe convertible into the Cadillac dealership for its monthly checkup, service, and detailing. So then on the following Tuesday afternoon, Tom was waiting for them as Torres drove out of his garage which was behind the drug house. Yet by taking some shortcuts to the Cadillac Dealership which was located on the far eastside of town, it allowed Tom to arrive at the dealership a full five minutes before Torres. Then by parking a good distance away from the service department,

Tom was able to verify the fact that Torres had indeed left his car with the dealer.

Then as Tom continued to watch, another of the gang members picked up Torres at the service department entrance before then heading off for what Tom surmised would be another Tuesday of shopping, dining, and the running of personal errands. Or at least, that's what the gangster's routine had consisted of during the past several months.

Hence, it was also at that very moment when Tom decided to follow his instincts as to whether the social club would be completely deserted on this particular Tuesday. So after parking the borrowed pickup truck in the rear of his church, Tom crossed the street and then casually walked toward the rear of the redbrick two-story building.

Even Tom was a little surprised by how easily he was able 'to gain access to the social club; for he'd just naturally expected the rear door of the social club to be outfitted with the newest types of deadbolt locks. Instead, the hardware on the seventy-five year old entrance door was equipped with the type of locks that could easily be unlocked by using a credit card.

Then once inside, Tom's luck seemed to continue for the place appeared to be completely deserted. But then Tom had suspected, an operational video camera was pointed directly to the area around the computer desk. Of course all Tom had to do was to locate the fuse box which was conveniently located in a closet nearby to the rear door. Then, by simply flipping the main switch on the service box he was able to disable the electric power for the entire building; this then gave Tom the freedom to search the apartments without worry.

Nevertheless, excepting for the arsenal of weaponry which he'd located in the upstairs apartments, there was nothing else of great importance to be found; besides, he felt that his own personal supply of firepower was far superior and even more modern than the guns belonging to Torres. There was, of course, a good chance that the AK 47 Rifle that he'd found hidden under a bed was the same exact weapon which had been used to kill the elderly woman in his church.

Naturally, though, the only absolute way to prove that the automatic rifle in question was the murder weapon would be for him to turn it over to the police; and that wasn't about to happen because Tom had already made the decision that he would personally avenge the lady's death.

After turning the electricity back on, Tom very carefully then exited the rear of the building. Next, he'd planned on spending the rest of the afternoon by devising an exact timeline of the goings and comings of the members of the Southside Social Club. Then, he figured that he would simply wait for right time to strike.

Unbeknownst to Tom, however, Torres Philpot was busy formulating his own deadly plans of revenge against society. To be sure, violence was certainly nothing new to Torres for he'd lived in violence for most of his life. Of course that was somewhat due to the fact that all throughout childhood he'd been bounced from one foster home to another. So naturally, he greatly resented the fact that not only had his Latino mother and his Caucasian father divorced when he was a small child, but he also resented the fact that their failure to stay married had relegated him to either a life on the streets, or else in various orphanages and foster homes. Then also just as unfortunately for Torres, he'd accepted the violence that he'd witnessed as a child as being normal.

But then thanks to the former church member, Jamal Jones, who'd once again, picked up the needle and the gun, Torres would have a pretty good idea of just exactly what the Neighborhood Watch Committee's plans were.

All the same, the situation in the neighborhood was about to get a lot worse. And unfortunately, the newest outbreak of violence just happened to take place on a Sunday morning when services were being held across the street at Tom's church. It began quite suddenly when several small time drug dealers from another part of town were lying in wait with the plans robbing Jamal Jones, the former church member, and another one of the Southside Gang's major drug suppliers who'd just recently arrived in town with a rather large cache of drugs from the city of Chicago.

Then after parking their car in the rear of the social club, both Jamal and his cohort from Chicago were attacked from all sides as they attempted to climb the outdoors stairwell which led to the upstairs apartments in the rear of the building. So not only were Jamal Jones and the drug dealing man from Chicago brutally murdered, but the large shipment of drugs which had originated in Chicago was stolen by the members of yet another River City Gang.

Normally, a setback of that nature would not have been such a complete catastrophe for Torres Philpot; however, this incident had occurred on the heels of a trip to Orlando, Florida where he'd just purchased a multimillion dollar estate.

Of course if he'd had the time Torres could have sold off his newly acquired property in Florida; that is, if his business partner, Clifford Mansfield, the leader of one of the most powerful gangs in the city of Chicago, Illinois would agree to wait for his money.

Though as it turned out, Clifford Mansfield had decided not to wait for the money that Torres and the Southside Gang of River City owed him. For within only another forty-eight hours following the loss of that shipment of drugs, Torres Philpot, and the vast majority of the Southside Gang's members would end up dead. Moreover, the two story brick building which had once been home to the so-called social club would prophetically be burned to the ground.

Robert R. Railey

From Pillar to Post
From one place to another; hither and thither

While traveling throughout northern Iraq on a secret diplomatic mission with his father, Aydin he-Hasid had become an orphan at the age of twelve. His father, Judah he-Hasid, was a natural born citizen of Israel; however, he'd married a Turkish woman he'd met while serving as an Israeli Diplomat in the Turkish capital city of Ankara. So by custom, his son Aydin could claim citizenship from either Israel or Turkey.

The trick was, however, just exactly how a person with Israeli and Turkish bloodlines could be expected to travel throughout the northern parts of Iraq during a war which had been going on for what seemed like an eternity. Then too, the travel in the north could be made even more difficult by the fact that some of the Kurdish tribes in that part of Iraq weren't exactly keen on either the Turks or the Jews.

But then some eight years later, the twenty year old man of mixed nationalities had somehow made a home for himself in the northern Iraqi city of Mosul. And with the Turkish border being so near to the city of Mosul, Aydin's ability to speak fluent Turkish, Hebrew, Arabic, and Kurdish would definitely come in handy for a young man who'd not yet made his fortune

Though just exactly how Aydin was going to earn a living in that war-torn part of the world; he knew not. He was, however, well aware of the fact that he could always embark upon the highly dangerous and illegal career of smuggling arms from the relatively nearby border of Iran to the Kurdish tribes of northern Iraq. On the other hand, though, he knew that if he ever got caught that his life would definitely be over.

Even so, when a young man is in love he just might risk life and limb in order to procure some of the necessary worldly goods that he might require if he ever planned on gaining an Iraqi's father's permission to marry his daughter.

The love of Aydin's life was a beautiful young woman of some eighteen years of age who also resided in the Iraqi city of Mosel. Her name was Burcu Toran, and she too was of mixed bloodlines in as much that her father was Turkish and her mother was from a long line of seafaring people who'd migrated over from Greece.

So when it came to complying with the prenuptial traditions of the people modern-day Mesopotamia, Aydin had no problem in respecting his fiancé's family's ancient customs. Otherwise, everything else seemed to be progressing along nicely.

Yet before Aydin could allow himself to marry, there was an important situation that required his immediate attention; and that simply was his intent to make good on a promise that he'd made to his deceased father which was to give aid to the oppressed people of Syria. For it seems that even well before the so-called Arab Spring had unfolded itself upon North Africa, both the Turkish and the Israeli governments had long feared a political and a civil uprising in the autocratic nation of Syria.

Aydin knew, of course, that anyone caught spying for the state of Israel would be arrested and then almost assuredly condemned to death by the Syrian Government. Yet with at least two more years of schooling at the university facing him, and also with his wedding day rapidly approaching, he'd made the decision to honor the promise that he'd made to his dying father by redirecting a vast shipment of weapons which had originally been intended for the Kurds, but instead, would now be delivered to the revolutionary fighters in Syria.

Then luckily for Aydin, the prior arrangements that his father had made with the officials at the Iranian and the Iraqi borders were still in place; and therefore, it was simply a matter of covertly transporting the shipment of arms by-way of commercial trucking across the northern parts of Iraq and then finally on into the northeastern parts of Syria where the rebels would take control of the weaponry. Then also just as fortunately for Aydin, the payment for the shipment of arms had already been handled by the Israeli Embassy in Turkey.

Nevertheless, the trickiest part of this highly dangerous enterprise would be the transporting of those arms across the northern parts of Iraq which are controlled by the Kurds. For in that part of the world, the weapons of war are coveted above all else. Even so, Aydin had decided to stick with his father's original plan which had called for them to use a special convoy of trucks that ostensibly would be provided by the World Health Organization, (WHO); but in reality, it would be part of a larger and more covert operation which had tentatively been approved by both the United Nations and NATO.

But since the launch date was still fourteen days away, Aydin had plenty of time in which to visit a temple and then possibly even spend some time with his future wife. Of course when the time came for him to embark upon the mission, the plan was for him to use his student's visa in order to gain entrance into Iran where the arms were to be picked up. It was quite understandable that an exercise of that nature could prove to be an extremely dangerous proposition; then again, there were always a goodly number of greedy border guards and government officials who were willing to take a bribe.

"Nonetheless, the transporting of the arms across northern Iraq would most likely be the easy part," Aydin thought, and which then left the most difficult part of the journey which would be their attempt to avoid the various checkpoints that dotted the main roadways along the Iraqi and the Syrian border. So as a result, the original plan to transport the weapons of war by-way of a camel caravan across the less inhabited areas of northern Iraq and Syria had been reinstituted for the final leg of the journey.

To this end, Aydin was able to employ a sufficient number of Bedouins from the Al-Baggara tribe who primarily hailed from the northern Iraqi and Syrian provinces. Those same men would also be used to help unload the trucks once they'd arrived in the area around Mosel, Iraq. And according to Aydin's plans, the arms would then be transported by a camel caravan to the outskirts of a village by the name of Manbij which is located in a northern Syrian district and just to the west of the Euphrates River.

Yet in that particular part of the world, an attack on your person wouldn't necessarily come from the conventional armies of Iraq and Syria; but rather, from the various tribal chiefs of the area that will either charge you and your group an exorbitant fee for the privilege of traversing their lands; or else, they might just simply help themselves to your cargo.

Then too, there was another potential problem facing young Aydin and his group of coconspirators; for all throughout his previous dealings with the Al-Baggara tribe, he'd learned that there were more than thirty different branches; this then meant that each and every sheikh had the right to demand a tribute for the pleasure of traveling through his territory.

Yet for Aydin and his team of gunrunners, things seemed to be going along rather smoothly; until, that is, when an argument broke out in earnest amongst a few of the activist who supposedly represented the Council for a free Syria. But then just as Aydin was about to hand over that enormous shipment of arms to the Syrians, he had to wonder if there would ever be any real cohesiveness in the ranks of the Free Syrian Militia.

For at that very moment, one of the rebels had become so upset with some of his own countrymen that he began firing his automatic rifle indiscriminately into the crowd before he himself was eventually gunned down by the Bedouins.

In all, five of the Syrian Rebels and two of the Bedouins lay dead. Yet the worst was about to come; for after first disarming the remaining Syrians, the Bedouins had managed to take control of the entire shipment of arms. And yet to their dismay, the Bedouins were unaware of the fact that the firefight between the Syrian Militia and the tribesmen had caught the attention of an U. S. Air Force Colonel based in Texas, U. S. A., who then ordered a drone attack on the entire group which ended up killing every single person in the caravan, including Aydin.

Then just days later, the Kurdish Tribes of northern Iraq were able to salvage the majority of the weapons from the killing field. However, instead of celebrating the wedding between Aydin and his finance', Burcu Toran, the entire community of Mosel decided to host an elaborate funeral out of respect for one of their own.

Of course Aydin's tragic and untimely death meant that he would never fulfill his dream of making his way back home to Israel where he'd planned on finishing his schooling at the University of Israel before then eventually going to work for the Israel Security Agency from whence he would have gladly accepted any future assignments in the Middle East and North Africa.

Fortunes Lost

artin Eastman wasn't related to, or even vaguely associated with the owners of the highly successful Eastman-Kodak company. Even so, it was widely believed that he was the wealthiest person in Buckman County, Georgia; and that was plenty good enough for him. Yet just exactly how he'd managed to amass such a great amount of wealth would depend upon the people you asked. For example, if you were to ask any of the Southern Democrats to render their opinion as to how he'd accumulated so many assets, they would most likely relate to you the old timeworn story of how Martin Eastman had completely outsmarted the majority of the northern Republicans while serving his fifteen terms as a United States Congressman.

Then too, the exact details of just exactly how Mr. Martin Eastman had made his millions have always been a closely guarded secret; and as such, the facts were known only to a select number of friends and business associates. With the exception, that is, of his longtime mistress and confidant, who as a former stripper was better known by her stage name of Marylou.

Of course while Martin was faithfully serving the state of Georgia as a United States Congressman, he was obligated to supply the Government Accountability Office, or (GAO), with proof of his current financial net worth. Cagily, though, Martin was able to conceal a good deal of his enormous wealth by listing his mistress, Marylou, as the real and legitimate owner of a great many of his assets and holdings which included the great mansion in Georgia.

Though as a rule, just the placing of that much trust in another person could very well end up being an unwise decision for any married public servant; and especially since an ugly divorce could have easily exposed his under the table shenanigans. Nonetheless, Martin had somehow managed to live his life in a mostly unscathed fashion until the unfortunate and untimely death of his wife, Geneva Holbrook-Eastman.

Then notwithstanding the true and honest feelings of a great loss which he'd felt for his loving and devoted wife of many a year, Martin had made the egregious error of moving his longtime mistress into his mansion before the matrimonial bedcovers of his recently deceased wife had even cooled. Yet even a blunder of that magnitude might have been overlooked had it not been for a local investigative reporter's desire to win a Pulitzer Prize for journalism.

It seems that the publisher of a small-town Georgia newspaper had at one time been a major stockholder in a recently defunct manufacturing company that the Honorable Mr. Martin Eastman had purchased in order to purposely bankrupt just so he could then show a substantial loss on his Federal Income Taxes. But as the former congressman was about to learn, revenge would be the guiding factor behind this very persistent investigative reporter's inquiries.

The publisher's true name and identity was a man name named Thomas Steele. Although most of his friends and neighbors preferred to address him by his nickname which was, "Bulldog." Thomas was a pleasure alright, and as befitting to a man with a nickname like Bulldog, he just naturally had to own a season ticket that was smack-dab on the fifty yard line at the University of Georgia's football stadium in Athens, Georgia.

But since Thomas Steele has also led a shrouded, and somewhat less than stellar life. He would have had to have been especially careful in attempting to exact his revenge against one of the most powerful men in the entire state of Georgia.

That said, the Bulldog was fortunate in one respect since both he and Mr. Martin Eastman were members of a very old and prestigious fraternity known as the Kentucky Colonels. For as a member in good standing of that esteemed organization, both he and Mr. Eastman were entitled to be addressed as Col. However, that also meant that as members in good standing of that fraternity they must fervently attempt to perform both good and charitable deeds for the sake of the community and their fellow man.

Another blessing of sorts had befallen the "Bulldog" and that was the fact that he'd never personally met Col. Eastman; and so if the need ever arose, Col. Eastman would not even be able to pick him out of a police lineup. To be sure, however, Thomas Steele, AKA the Bulldog, had totally committed himself to bringing the mighty Col. Eastman down to his knees. So to that end, nothing less than the Honorable Mr. Eastman's complete ruin and utter disgrace would be acceptable; and if he were to be completely honest with himself, then the Bulldog wasn't any too sure that the Col. Eastman's well-deserved punishment might even result in an early departure from this old world.

The Bulldog knew, of course, that revenge can be a very destructive force: and he also knew that it really didn't matter so much as to whether a person was on the giving or the receiving end; for just the act of trying to exact your revenge on another person can sometimes take over a person's mind and soul.

Still, a man has to do what a man has to do: for after having been on this earth for a goodly number of years, the Bulldog had decided not to surrender quietly to the twilight of his life. Yet if there'd been a more loving and close-knit family in Mr. Steele's former life, then he might have regretted his plans to completely humiliate the person that he held most responsible for his terrible financial losses.

At the same time, however, the Honorable Colonel Eastman was having to deal with a desperate situation of his very own making. For it seemed that his longtime companion and lover, a woman by the name of Marylou Dodd-Hanson, had suddenly found her own voice; and to the Colonel's chagrin, it'd recently become a very loud and demanding voice.

They say that solace is what we seek when we're at our wit's ends. Consequently, then, Col. Eastman must have felt the urge to find a little more solace in his own life by committing at least a small part of his great fortune to help fulfill his obligation to the Kentucky Colonels' organization by throwing a fundraiser at his mansion for the less privileged children of Buckman County, Georgia. And of course, it would just naturally require of him to announce this generous deed in the majority of the local newspapers.

And since the announcement for the grand benefit would go out over the wire, it seemed only fitting that the Buckman County Journal, which was owned by no other than Mr. Thomas Steele, would be one of the newspapers that would run the article. Moreover, the Bulldog was utterly delighted that not only would he be able to officially cover the charity event at the Colonel's Mansion, but he would also get to meet the great man in person. But since Mr. Thomas Steele, AKA the Bulldog, was also a longtime member of the Kentucky Colonel's organization, then the charity event might even end up benefitting him.

The great charity event at the Colonel's mansion was scheduled to take place on the upcoming Saturday; and so naturally no expense would be barred. For according to all outward appearances it was to be a gala that would be written about for years to come. What's more, even the guest of honor, the lovely live-in girlfriend, Ms. Marylou Dodd-Hanson, had gone all out to make the party unforgettable. Though for reasons unknown at the time she'd secretly invited several of the local realtors, and even a real-estate appraiser, to attend the benefit which might have led some people to think that she must have had an ulterior motive.

So when the day for the gala and fundraiser finally arrived, it was none other than the mistress of the mansion, Ms. Marylou Dodd-Hanson herself, who took control of an impromptu press conference on the front steps of the great mansion where she proceeded to announce that not only was she planning to reunite with her former lover, a certain Mr. Thomas (Bulldog) Steele, but that she was also about to sever all ties with the Honorable Colonel Eastman. And as a matter of fact she would do so on that very day by serving a restraining order on the great man which would immediately evict the former congressman from his own mansion.

Corpus Delicti
Show me the body

By being an aggressive and progressively minded businessman, Justin Hobart was able to maintain his dominant position as the number one highway contractor in the state where he did business. But in his home town of River City, however, that has not always been the case. For in the past decade alone a number of other civil engineering firms had attempted to establish themselves in the Midwestern metropolis that Justin called home.

Generally speaking, the majority of those out-of-town engineering companies would usually just pull up stakes and leave town after failing to be rewarded a sizeable contract from any one of the local governments which might include the city, the county, the state, and even possibly the United States Department of Transportation.

Yet there was an exception to this unspoken rule of political dominance that certain public officials sometimes hold towards a favorite company; for it was beginning to appear as if one of the more recent arrivals of the architectural and engineering firms, an outfit by the name of Biggerstaff & Co., might just be able to survive on the smaller contracting jobs that it was able procure in the neighboring counties and states.

Even so, one would think that any sane and rational person could learn to live with at least a modicum of competition. The problem was, however, Justin Hobart wasn't quite right; as a matter of fact, he was far from being normal.

Yet if those mental images of what had transpired so very long ago were to ever be deemed correct, then it would be quite understandable for Justin to continue to reject the court's ruling of many years past that he was responsible for his parent's death; instead, he preferred to believe that as a very young child he'd had the grave misfortune of being a witness to the bloody slaughter of both his parents.

This then might just help to explain why Justin felt the need to continue on with those intense psychotherapy sessions for his nervous disorder. In fact, he was currently seeing the very same therapist that he'd used as an adolescent. That alone was no mean trick since the doctor in question was the original court appointed psychologist who'd been assigned to him during the interval between his parent's death, and the eventual move into an orphanage where the courts had ultimately placed him.

In Justin's mind, the enormous cost of having to pay for the relocation of his therapist from his childhood home back in Georgia, and then on to a metropolis in the Midwest was incidental; for in his way of thinking his relationship with the doctor who'd helped him all throughout those troubling adolescent years, and then eventually on into manhood, was that important to him. After all, Dr. James Metcalf was certainly a lot more familiar with the history of the person who'd been accused of killing his own parents, Henry and Sarah Jane Hobart, than any replacement therapist would ever be.

But since Justin's highway construction company had just recently been awarded a rather sizeable contract to build an extension onto one of the local interstate highway systems, he simply didn't have the luxury of time to try to figure out who'd not only murdered his parents, but who'd so callously left their lifeless bodies on the inside of the family home in Georgia before then burning it to the ground.

Then on top of everything else, the long hours that Justin was currently working in order to finish up this latest highway project had worsened his inability to sleep. This in turn was severely affecting each and every one of Justin's relationships. Additionally, his constant mood changes had so unnerved his wife Lorraine that she'd recently been forced to move into the spare bedroom just so she could get the sufficient rest that she needed in order to take care of the couple's two children and their busy household.

Yet regardless of the daily pressures that his hectic work schedule had placed upon him and his family, Justin still felt the need to maintain a good working relationship with his therapist Dr. Metcalf. For when all else failed, Justin had always felt that he could rely on the advice of one of his deceased parent's closet friends who'd stood by him all throughout the tumultuous years following the subsequent murder trial and the times in which he'd been incarcerated which had even included a stint in a mental hospital.

Though at times, Justin couldn't help but wonder if the drug-induced confession of a child of only eight years of age should have been allowed to stand; and particularly since the confession was obtained in the privacy of Dr. Metcalf's own office where the confession had been taped and transcribed without the benefit of an impartial witness. So looking back, it would have been fairly obvious to almost anybody in the know that a third party observer should have been present during the confession in order to protect the rights of such a young defendant.

Thus in light of everything else, there was simply no way of knowing for sure just exactly what other kinds of drugs that the doctor might have given Justin along with the truth serum which had been administered to him on the day that he confessed to killing his parents.

Therefore, Justin felt that he had no other recourse but to further investigate the events of that terrible evening some thirty years prior. Hence for that reason alone, Justin had felt justified in making the decision to hire an independent investigator back home in Georgia in order to try to discover the truth concerning the murders for which he believed he'd been so wrongly convicted. Justin was also beginning to wonder if he might have been framed by someone who would have benefited from his parent's death.

So then after diligently searching through a website provided by the National Association of Private Detectives, Justin was able to connect with a private detective named Everett J. Mansfield whose office was listed in a town that wasn't too far removed from Justin's old hometown back in Georgia. Of course Justin had always been of the opinion that a face-to-face meeting is more preferable than a long distance phone conversation; so therefore, he immediately advanced the detective a major part of his proposed fee just so the investigator would then make the trip to River City for a meeting of the minds.

The newly hired private investigator just happened to be a retired veteran of some thirty odd years of service with the Fulton County, Georgia's Sherriff's Department where he'd spent a good deal of his time working old homicide cases. And not so surprisingly, the former deputy sheriff, Everett J. Manfred, clearly remembered the double homicide and the subsequent fire which had destroyed the antebellum type of structure which had been home to the Hobart family for several generations.

The retired deputy Sheriff Manfred had also reported to Justin that he vaguely remembered hearing some rumors concerning Justin's deceased father, Henry Hobart. For during Henry's drastically shortened lifetime, it was widely believed that he was somehow related to, or at the very least, he was known to have been on very good terms with a man by the name of Richard Brevard Russell Jr. of Georgia who'd served in the U. S. Senate for a period of several decades. That said, excepting for the fact that Justin's father had received numerous government contracts for the manufacture of various military vehicles which were then being produced in the state of Georgia, the close relationship between those two prominent Georgians appeared to be primarily social.

Then once the detective had completed a cursory look into the facts concerning the thirty year old case, Justin then straight away asked his newly hired private investigator to once again go over his findings. Of course this caused detective Mansfield to dig even deeper into the life of Justin's psychologist, Dr. James Metcalf. In the end, however, Justin was completely overwhelmed with emotion when detective Manfred revealed that he'd found some evidence linking his mother, Sara Jane Hobart, to none other than Dr. James Metcalf.

It seems that the previously unknown relationship between Justin's mother and the therapist, Dr. James Metcalf, had purportedly begun even well before Justin was born. Accordingly, then, the affair had supposedly continued unabated until just shortly before the death of both of Justin's parents. Even so, the only evidence that supported the possibility of such a relationship came from an illegal wiretap that Justin's father, Henry Hobart, had authorized when he'd first become suspicious of his wife's therapist who just happened to be Justin's current therapist.

Of course the meager amount of evidence which the private investigator had provided to Justin wasn't nearly enough for him to go to the authorities with; but to Justin, it was more than enough to prompt him to ask Dr, Metcalf to meet him at the highway construction site where an unfortunate accident was about to take place.

Thus with a little help from Justin, the therapist, Dr. James Metcalf, wound up lying face down in a very deep hole which had previously been dug for the pilings of the bridge supports for the new highway. Of course once the still warm body had been covered over with a few shovelfuls of dirt, the excavated hole would just simply wait for the concrete truck to arrive which would be at approximately 7:00 o'clock on the following morning.

Then several weeks later, the inevitable investigation into the disappearance of the therapist would undoubtedly end up focusing on Justin Hobart, who as a previously convicted murderer would almost assuredly be suspected of having done away with his longtime therapist.

Though at the trial, Justin's attorney would successfully defend his client by applying the time-tested tradition of one of the oldest criminal defenses ever recorded in the history of law by filing a writ of *Corpus Delicti* which we all know was borrowed from the original English Bill of Rights. That particular piece of jurisprudence is more commonly known as, *"show me the body."* And since there was no body to be found, Justin Hobart walked out of the courtroom a free man.

Black Widow

Unlike the female member of the black widow species of the spider family which purportedly eats its partner after they've finished mating, the female of the human species has also been known to kill its mate; though as a rule, she doesn't usually devour the corpse.

It's long been said that practically every person on earth is capable of killing another human being; and especially if they feel as if their own life is in danger. And yet the so-called black widow of the human variety has been known to kill for monetary gains.

So as a testament to one of our nation's darkest moments, one of the worst case scenarios ever recorded concerning a female serial killer occurred a few years back in the Midwestern metropolis of River City. And considering the fact that the area had already seen more than its fair of violence and mayhem, that one singular piece of history was deemed most unfortunate by the residents of that particular community.

For when America was still a young nation, River City was situated handedly on the outer edge of one of the first major westward expansions which had followed closely upon the heels of the American Revolution; and therefore, the would-be thriving community was one of the first of the frontier towns to be located on the north westernmost banks of the Ohio River. Consequently, then, the early inhabitants of River City had to first learn how to live alongside of the Native Americans, who for hundreds of years prior to the encroachment of the Europeans, had called that particular part of the Ohio Valley their ancestral home.

Yet after only a few decades had passed following the settling of the community on the banks of the Ohio River, which would ultimately become as known as River City, the descendents of those original pioneers had found themselves living directly on the Mason Dixon Line, which in theory, would separate the Union North from the Confederate South.

Then all throughout those four terrible years of the American Civil War, and even up to the present time which had included two world wars, the residents of River City had hoped that they would finally be immune from any more violence.

Though just prior to the city's modern-day era of peace and prosperity, Patricia Smithhart had decided to travel north to River City from her home in Middle Tennessee in hopes of finding work in one of the manufacturing plants which were running full tilt in that bustling community. Then once settled in, Trish arranged for her children's maternal grandmother to make the two hundred mile trip from her home in Middle Tennessee in order to transport Trish's two young children which were the product of a marriage which had proved to have disastrous consequences.

Then notwithstanding the rigors of having been a single mom who'd migrated to the north in hopes of finding gainful employment, the twenty-three year old mother of two was an exceptional beauty. What with her long black hair that was properly accentuated by high cheekbones, and the so-called Roman nose of legend which had caused many people to associate her with the Native Americans who for hundreds of years prior had lived and thrived in the bountiful Tennessee Valley.

Also just as fortunately for Trish, she'd learned to take great pride in her new position at one of the factories in River City where she helped to manufacture the various machine parts which would eventually be assembled into those enormous General Electric jet engines which help to power a great many of our U. S. Military planes. Even so, it was inevitable that a beautiful young woman such as Patricia would attract the attention of some of the men that worked at the plant.

For as a matter of fact, there were a total of five men in her department alone that were actively vying for her interest. Out of those five, Trish felt that only her immediate supervisor, a gentleman by the name of Marlin Strophe, was deserving of any real consideration.

So thus began one of the most unlikely relationships that anybody working at that particular plant could ever recall; excepting, perhaps, for the age-old rumors of those stormy relationships which had pervaded the break rooms and the assembly lines during the World War II era when the likes of Rosie the Riveter had held sway over many of our American manufacturing plants.

Still, it was generally ceded by practically everyone at the plant that Marlin Strophe might just be a bit too laid back, and very possibly even the type of man that would end up being henpecked and dominated by a woman who was as beautiful as Patricia Smithhart. But then expressly to place an exclamation point behind everybody's private, and even sometimes not so private concerns, it was duly noted that Trish had accepted a marriage proposal from none other than her supervisor, Marlin Strophe.

Nonetheless, just shortly after a brief engagement period of only a few months the two lovebirds were married in a small church in Middle Tennessee just so Trish's father and her three brothers could have a chance to properly dictate to the northern boy just exactly what would be expected of him after he'd been accepted into a Southern family.

Then luckily for the two newlyweds, life in the Strophe household had turned out to be reasonably happy and uneventful; with the exception, that is, for one minor detail. For after only about three months of harmonious matrimony Marlin had become overly protective and somewhat jealous of his extremely beautiful bride.

This was also around the same point-in-time that Marlin had decided to unveil one of his previously unmentioned plans by telling Trish that she should immediately quit her job at the plant just so she could then spend more time with him and her two children from a previous union.

At first, Trish could certainly appreciate the logic behind a decision of that nature, but then after seriously meditating on the long-term consequences of never again being able to draw a paycheck, she became somewhat worried that if she were to resign her position at the plant then she might just miss out on one of the most important possibilities of her future; and that would be her inability to be able to contribute to the Federal Government's Social Security retirement program.

So for that reason, Trish was terribly afraid that if she ever decided to quit her job at the plant that she might just end up like her loyal and dutiful mother, who after being the perfect stay-at-home mom while raising her four children, she'd ended up divorced and penniless to such an degree that she'd eventually become a ward of the State of Tennessee.

Secondly, if Trish were to be completely honest with herself, then she would have to admit that she would also miss being looked upon as one of the most beautiful women who'd ever worked at the plant where she was presently employed. Trish would also freely admit that not only did she enjoy the envious looks from the other women at the plant, but she also appreciated the appraising glances that were frequently showered upon by her male coworkers.

It was a conundrum alright: in the end, however, Trish decided to trust her husband's judgment enough to quit her job at the factory in order to become a fulltime housewife. Yet the new routine of not having to work outside the home had given her more time to think and to worry about her own personal affairs. Moreover, the worries about the new arrangement with her husband seemed to be especially apropos to the situation at hand when Marlin started working late at the plant.

Then as if to make matters even worse, Marlin had leveled yet another major source of worry and bedevilment on top of Trish's already troubled head when he decided to commit two of his otherwise free evenings in order to help out his old college fraternity, which he said, was having financial problems. Unfortunately, though, it wasn't long before Trish and Marlin had stopped enjoying any quality time together; and therefore, their sex life during those trying days had become almost nonexistent.

Still, Trish continued to try her best at being the trusting and believing housewife any time that Marlin was forced to go out at night on his so-called company business. Then in addition to that terribly unfavorable scenario, Trish was becoming more than a little suspicious about the two evenings a week that Marlin was supposedly spending with his old college chums.

What to do, she mused, for this brand new event at home had occurred well after she'd been properly advised by her mother on how best to handle a husband that might be tempted to stray. So then as a result of receiving that invaluable bit of advice from her mother, Trish had made a determined effort to rekindle the spark which had suddenly disappeared from their marriage.

The next plan of attack that was slowly emerging from the depth of Trish's mind was something that she'd always felt was beneath her; and that would be for her to spy on the husband who was rarely at home. Of course the act of spying would be no easy trick to manage since they lived on a small farm that was situated approximately seven miles from the city where Marlin's place of employment was located.

Nonetheless, Trish did have access to a very old extended cab, Ford pickup truck, which she occasionally used anytime that she was forced to make an emergency trip into town with the two girls. So then the very next time that Marlin called to say that he had to work late at the office, Trish was able to safely secure her two young daughters in the smallish backseat of the old pickup truck by the using seatbelts and the mandatory children's car seats before she headed off to town.

Trish knew, of course, where Marlin's plant was located; for she had also been employed there. And since the two of them had made love on the top of the desk in his office, she knew precisely that his office was the last one to the rear on the easternmost side of the building. Thus after walking toward the rear of the building with her two young girls in tow, Trish could readily see that there no lights burning in Marlin's office.

So basically, there was nothing left for Trish to do but to head on back home where she'd planned on putting the girls to bed before then patiently waiting up for the man that she now suspected of being a wayward husband. And she would have gone on back home as planned if she hadn't seen what appeared to be her husband's brand-new shiny red truck pulling into a rather large apartment complex which was located only about two blocks from the intersection where she was waiting for a stoplight to change.

"She'd come that far," she thought, and so she quickly then decided that she might as well finish up what she'd started by very cautiously turning into the rear of the same parking lot of the apartment complex that her husband's red truck had just entered. Then after turning off her headlights, she noticed that the lighting in the parking lot was so excellent that it wasn't difficult for her to confirm that her husband and a rather youngish looking woman were preparing to enter one of the ground floor apartments.

Then after sitting there for a little while longer, Trish was feeling so angry and betrayed that she risked doing some irreparable damage to the engine of that old Ford truck by asking everything out of that antique vehicle as she proceeded to slide dangerously out onto the street where she just happened to be observed a patrolling police officer who then pulled her over about a block away from the apartment complex.

By then, of course, the two young children were crying and screaming so loudly that the officer simply checked Trish's driving license and her insurance status before letting her off with an oral warning that she should never again drive in such a way that might endanger the lives of those two young girls.

But even before she'd arrived back home, Trish had made the fatal decision that on the upcoming holiday she would invite Marlin to accompany her and the two girls back to the family's homestead in Middle Tennessee where she would then very happily introduce him to the family's private cemetery where she'd already disposed of the other three men who'd treated her badly.

Unfortunately for Trish, however, Marlin's disappearance, and the eventual investigation that would just naturally ensue, would ultimately place her at the top of the list as the primary person of interest in the missing person's case. Also just as regrettably for Trish's sake, a River City Policeman just happened to remember that he'd pulled her over for driving recklessly somewhere near the parking lot where Marlin's mistress was known to reside.

Robert R. Railey

Across the Thames
A mild case of fiction

At the time, their intention was to locate a suitable indoor playhouse where their company of actors could perform their plays during the seven months of winter. Then during the remaining five months of the year, the King's Men theatrical group of London, England would continue to produce a variety of their plays at the old Globe Theater which was located on the south side of the Thames River. Then luckily for the owners of the King's Men, the newly renovated Blackfriars Theater became available; it was, however, located on the north side of the Thames.

Above all, the new group of shareholders would forever be grateful to the impresario of the King's Men, Richard Burbage, and his father, James Burbage, who'd not only been the impresario of a previous acting group called the Lord Chamberlain's Men, but he'd also built the new Blackfriars Theater for the considerable sum of 600 pound sterling. It was also around that same point in time that Richard Burbage decided to invite several well-known playwrights and entrepreneurs to become shareholders in this great artistic venture of his.

Originally, the seven sharers in the newly reorganized theater were listed as: Richard Burbage, William Shakespeare, Henry Condell, John Heminges, and William Sly, all members of the King's Men Theatrical Group, plus Cuthbert Burbage and Thomas Evans, who was the agent for the theater manager, Henry Evans. Unfortunately, however, William Sly died shortly thereafter and his share was divided among the other six.

So with great fanfare, the 1609 debut performance at the newly renovated Blackfriars Theater would be a play which had been written by one of their fellow actors and shareholders, a certain Mr. William Shakespeare, who would present his humble interpretation of, "The Tragical History of Hamlet, Prince of Denmark."

Then shortly thereafter, Henry Evans, the lawyer who'd held the lease for the remodeled Blackfriars Theater for the past three years, and who'd also been among those ejected from the theater some fifteen prior, now privately requested an immediate audience with the playwright William Shakespeare.

"Dear Will, as your friend, but then also as the lawyer for the King's Men acting group, I wholeheartedly advise you to have all of your wonderful work published," said Henry Evans.

"Well Henry, I'm sure that would be mightily sound advice; and particularly since there are rumors floating around the city of London saying that several other members of the community may have actually written some of my very own material," said William Shakespeare.

"Yes, I've heard those rumors too, and the names that come readily to mind are the now deceased Christopher Marlowe, and then along with, of course, William Stanley, 6th Earl of Derby; Sir Francis Bacon; and even Edward de Vere, 17th Earl of Oxford who tends to head the list," said Henry Evans.

Amazingly, though, not one single person had the audacity to sue William Shakespeare for plagiarism during his lifetime; and as a matter of fact, it wasn't until the middle of the nineteenth century before any halfway credible claims were made. And even those couldn't be substantiated with any hard evidence. However, that's not to say that the subject matter will ever fade into obscurity. For one thing, the thoroughly unsubstantiated rumor which had floated around a number of European parlors and drawing rooms had put forth the supposition that Mr. William Shakespeare himself might have added some fuel to the fire by purposely publishing some of his own work under a pseudonym.

Only time will tell, however, but at the rate we're going it might take us another hundred years or so before we'll be able to finally close the book on this very frustrating subject.

From Cow Town to Appomattox

Chapter One
Out of England

The farmlands located nearby to the Southwestern English communities of Fardel and Hayes Barton have been occupied by my ancestors for well over a thousand years, whereas a few of my kinsman have chosen to reside closer to the larger community of Exeter, England. Also according to an old family tradition, some of those far-distant relatives of mine had procured their parcels of land within the counties of Devon and Dorset with the intention of owning properties that were located close by to the new Sherborne Castle which had originally been owned by one of England's most famous adventurers and courtiers, Sir Walter Raleigh.

Yet as unfortunate as it may be, it was during the early part of the sixteen hundreds, that King James the 1st of England handed over the Sherborne estate to the Digby family, who to this day still holds title to the property. This bit of ancient history occurred just shortly after Sir Walter's trial for treason and his subsequent execution which had come about because of the erroneous belief that not only had he been involved in a plot against the state to depose the king, but also because of the disastrous outcome of a battle in which Sir Walter had foolishly instigated with the Spanish Garrison at Ft. Thomas which was located in the South American Country of Venezuela.

During Sir Walter's trial for treason, the prosecution asserted that he'd attacked the Spanish outpost in Venezuela while in search of the mythical golden kingdom of Eldorado. In the end, however, the tragic outcome of Sir Walter's fateful expedition into Venezuela had turned into a tragedy of multiple consequences since his eldest son, who was also named Walter, had been killed along with approximately one hundred and twenty-five of the Spanish Soldiers at the garrison.

But then only as providence could provide, it was during those years when Sir Walter was imprisoned in the Tower of London that he was afforded the ample opportunity to write the several volumes of his critically acclaimed, "The History of the World."

It's true, of course, that the incidents involving Sir Walter Raleigh had taken place in the long distant past; and so it was only natural that in the year of eighteen hundred and forty-nine that the people of Devon Shire, England were for the most part concerned with holding on to their farms. For it was during that very same year that a severe drought had taken a stranglehold on many parts of South West England. And then as if to make matters even worse, a steady stream of rumors had begun to flow downward from the north about a new type of animal sickness that was capable of destroying entire flocks of sheep.

Although luckily for the local residents of that area, this strange new disease was thought to be transferable only from one sheep to another, and not to human beings; or for that matter, it wasn't believed to be harmful to any other livestock. Nevertheless, for the farmers who derived as much as fifty percent of their annual income from the raising of sheep, the resulting situation had become extremely disastrous. So then as a result of this threat, the majority of the sheep owners in the South West counties of England felt as if they had no other recourse then but to get completely out of the wool business.

Even so, some of us farmers continued to make regular visits to the port city of Plymouth, England from where we could ship any excess farm produce to the major ports in Great Britain. And so it goes without saying that those usual and customary visits to the port city of Plymouth were always a pleasant diversion from our normal routines.

Yet during those regular visits to the English Channel a strange feeling of nostalgia would occasionally overwhelm me. And being that I am a native son of South West England, I was well aware of the historical fact that the men of Devon had always been seafaring adventurers. Therefore, the lure of the open sea was a constant urge that I had to resist on a daily basis. I knew, of course, that I could take to the sea at any time I wished; and this was particularly true since I was a twenty-three year old man who was still unmarried.

Nevertheless, it was during one of those seemingly unparticular trips to the port city of Plymouth while I was in the act of shipping some of my excess farm produce to another one of Briton's major ports that I couldn't help but notice the headlines on an American newspaper that one of the local ship's captains just happened to be reading. Then after noticing my interest in paper's cover story, the captain most graciously offered me the opportunity read his newspaper.

If memory serves, the headline on that particular newspaper was printed in bold and stark letters which read; ***Gold has been discovered near Sutter's Mill, California***. "It sure causes a person to pause," I thought, and since I was traveling by horseback and wagon back to my home which was located just to the outside of the village of Hayes Barton, it meant that I certainly had an idle hour or two in which to daydream about the amazing situation that was then taking place in America.

Then once back home I made the fateful decision to discuss this new turn of events with my good friend Johnny Devon, who not only was a old school chum of mine at the university, but who also happened to own a farm just down the road from my meager holdings at Hayes Barton, whereas Johnny's farm was located closer to the village of Fardel.

In the past, the Devon and the Carew families had formed a personal and a military alliance that not only was beneficial to the ruling monarchy in London, but it was also good for the West Country. According to the local church records, and even my own family's oral histories, the Devon and the Carew families had been living in the Devon Shire area for a period of several hundreds of years before Duke William of Normandy decided to invade England. Of course William the Conqueror, as he would later become known, had been victorious over the English armies of King Harold in the battle of Hastings which had occurred on the 14th Day of September in the year of ten sixty-six.

Even so, it wouldn't be until the year of ten eighty-eight before the new ruler of England would get around to ordering the first ever true census of England to be taken. Then curiously enough, the new census was prophetically titled, "The Doomsday Book."

In due course, Johnny Devon and had I entered into a rather lengthy discussion about the real possibly of selling off our properties and then migrating to America. And in time, these thoughts actually materialized; for in the end, both Johnny and I had made the momentous decision to put our minor estates on the open market and then embark upon the greatest adventure of our young lives. We decided that we would indeed travel to America where we were extremely confident that we could make our fortunes in the goldfields of California.

Of course it took several months of intense negotiations in order for us to get a fair market price for our properties. In the end, however, Johnny and I had sold off our entire holdings. So with a little more than 15,000 pounds sterling each in our pocketbooks, we proceeded to the port city of Plymouth, England where we'd previously made reservations to board an English ship by the name of Exminster.

Just prior to that date, Johnny and I had discovered that the ship that we were about to sail to America on had been hired by a consortium of English businessman to deliver a shipment of the finest quality of English furniture to the Pacific Coast city of San Francisco, California. Then upon its return voyage to England, the Exminster would sail back home with a shipment of various animal pelts, such as beaver skins and buffalo hides, which at the time, were being widely used in the hat and the clothing industries in Great Britain.

Chapter Two
The Voyage

At times, the crossing of those two thousand miles of open sea from South West England to the eastern shores of America could prove to be a treacherous and most dangerous proposition; and this was especially true during the winter or early spring months when the icebergs presented a real navigational hazard. Yet luckily for us Brits, our ship didn't leave the port city of Plymouth, England until the 15th of August in the year of eighteen hundred and forty-nine; and therefore, the majority of the ocean ice had already melted away.

Nonetheless, some of the more experienced seafaring types of folks on our ship stated that the months of July, August, and September were in the middle of the hurricane season; and consequently, it could be a perilous for those of us who dared to venture upon the coasts of North and South America in a sailing ship during those three months. We were also told that some of the most dangerous storms had been known to occur in the month of October.

Of course we passengers and the crew alike were also well aware of the inherent dangers of having to navigate around the southernmost parts of South America while attempting to sail to the west coast of America; for it'd been well documented that the ferocious storms in that part of the world could at times be almost mythical.

All the same, the crew, and even the majority of the more traveled of our seagoing passengers, didn't seem to be too overly concerned about the possibility of running into any extremely foul weather that might be lurking around out there on the far distant horizon; and this was mainly due to the expertise of the captain of the Exminster who was certainly a well qualified and experienced man of the seas who'd made the trip around the southern tip of South America numerous times; and, he'd done so without incident.

Regrettably, though, it was beginning to appear as if the captain's luck might have run out. For as we were about to sail past the Florida Keys we suddenly became a great deal more concerned when the wind velocity began to increase in intensity; and shortly thereafter we found ourselves being blown towards the center of the Gulf of Mexico where we were told that there should be smooth sailing ahead.

Also just as interestingly, a few of our more seaworthy travelers had previously told us that approximately sixty percent of all the major storms that cross North America tend to originate in the south westernmost part of the continent. On that particular day, however, the wind was not only coming out of the southeast, but it was blowing directly towards us at a strong and steady clip. And by then, even Captain Ferrell Munford had begun to worry.

Even so, we were told that we needed only to sail another two hundred nautical miles to the south in order to reach the shores of Central America; and with any luck at all we would once again be in much safe waters. Unfortunately, however, the wind from the southeast began to blow at full hurricane strength; and as if we weren't already terrified enough, the captain told us that the storm we were witnessing was without a doubt one of the worst ones that he'd ever tried to sail through.

By then, I was inclined to agree with the ship's captain. In fact, the very next time that I dared to venture out of my cabin I observed the ship's main mast sway and then suddenly snap into. Thus within another moment or two, our ship had lost all three of its mast. So by then, we were completely at the mercy of a most terrible storm that seemed intent upon pushing our severely damaged ship completely across the Gulf of Mexico and onto the shores of Texas.

On that day, however, providence must have been shinning down upon us Englishmen for even though our ship had become helplessly wrecked and stranded upon a sandy and rocky shoal just off the shoreline of Houston, Texas, the ship's crew was able to safely row us passengers and our luggage ashore in the longboats they'd rescued from the broken ship. In the end, the ship's cargo would eventually have to be salvaged and then sold at a public auction by the ship's owner's insurance company, Lloyds of London.

Naturally, though, we were all quite happy to just be alive and well: and then once we were finally ashore with our lives and our luggage intact, Johnny Devon and I joined the ship's officers and a few of the other passengers in a crowed dining room in the largest hotel that could be found anywhere in that hot and humid southwestern American community of Houston, Texas.

Though at that point in history it was abundantly clear to the stranded passengers of the Exminster that the city of Houston, Texas would eventually become a major shipping port. For as we'd all been told, the city had already prospered immensely from the exportation of cattle, both legal and illegal, which had been made possible by the Mexican Nationals and the American cattle ranchers who operated out of the southwestern states of America.

Then once we were all properly seated at a table in the city's largest hotel, we had only to wonder if the hotel's management could satisfactorily serve the sudden influx of well over fifty additional mouths to feed. Luckily, though, Johnny and I were indeed fortunate enough to be able to take possession of the last two vacant chairs left open in the hotel's main dining room. Also just as interestingly, we found that we were sitting alongside of what I believed to be one of roughest looking characters that I'd laid eyes on since we'd made our early arrival upon the shores of the United States of America.

In due course, the formal introductions at our table were eventually over and done with: and after Johnny and I had both shared our names and nationalities with the man we honestly believed to be a genuine American cowboy, we were told us that his name was Captain Thurston McQuinn and that he was a retired Texas Ranger; and which then meant to us that he was an ex-policeman of sorts.

"Where are you boys headed"? McQuinn asked.

"Well Mr. McQuinn before our ship ran aground we were headed for California where we'd planned on making our fortunes in the gold mines," Johnny said.

"The California gold mines, huh, well boys let me tell you a thing or two about wealth: it's in the cattle business in Central Florida, that's where; and by the way, y'all can call me Captain McQuinn or just plain captain if you prefer," McQuinn said.

"But from what little I've read about Florida, it seems that the entire state is made up of nothing but swamps, alligators, and Native American Indians," Johnny said.

"Well I suppose Florida does have its fair share of swamps: but from what I've been told the state is also blessed with a good deal of excellent pasture land; and interestingly enough, a few of those Native Americans that you spoke of just happen to own some of the largest herds of cattle in the entire state of Florida. Although unfortunately for them, if the white man continues to push them further south, then they'll most likely end up in the southernmost swamps of the Everglades," McQuinn said.

"So Captain, do you personally own some land in Florida," Johnny asked.

"No sir I don't: but I've just recently been contacted by ship's mail with an offer of employment from one of the biggest cattle ranchers in the entire state of Florida who just happens to be a man who'd previously migrated to Florida from the West Indies. His proposal would entail of me to travel to central Florida and then hang a few of the more troublesome cattle rustlers for him and several of the other big ranchers," the captain said.

"Do you plan to accept his offer," I asked.

"Yes sir I believe I will; and if you boys are smart then you'll come along with me," the captain said.

"Well on a proposition of that nature I'm sure that we'd have to talk it over amongst ourselves; and possibly even sleep on it," I said.

"Would tomorrow morning be too late for us to give you our answer?" Johnny said.

"But no later than that, for that's when I plan on heading out," McQuinn said.

"What a tough predicament we'd suddenly found ourselves in," I was thinking. What with the shipwreck and all, and then on top of everything else we were being asked to make a snap decision on such a strange offer from an ex-lawman whom we'd just met. For it goes without saying that a decision of that nature could very well affect our entire future.

As advertised, the sun did rise on that very next morning and since Johnny and I had decided to take the captain up on his very exciting offer, we then obediently headed for the city's main horse and cattle corral; of course we'd also brought along our shipping trunks and valises.

Then upon arrival, Captain McQuinn was already at the corral: and strangely enough, his first question to us was whether or not we were in possession of any firearms, and if so, were we proficient in the use of them.

Since Johnny and I had previously read everything that we could get our hands on concerning the perilous conditions that the men in the gold fields of California were facing, we'd decided to purchase a small arsenal of the finest firearms to be found anywhere in the whole of Europe. Our armory included four, six shot, ball and percussion cap English made 38 caliber pistols which we were told were similar to the U. S. Navy Colt revolvers that were then being produced in America.

Plus, we'd also brought along with us two of the finest 58 caliber German made long guns with rifled barrels. We'd also purchased a substantial quantity of a brand new type of ammunition called a mini-ball which had been named for the Frenchmen who'd invented that modern marvel.

Then in addition to the pistols and rifles that we had in our inventory of personal protection, we'd also brought along two of the finest Swiss made double-barreled shotguns with a sufficient quantity of gun powder and lead birdshot which is needed for the downing of fowl. And in addition to the bird shot, we'd also purchased a substantial supply of the larger pieces of lead-shot which were approximately the size of a .25 caliber pistol round.

So after first making a few slightly derisive remarks about the enormous amount of luggage that Johnny and I had brought along with us on this little adventure of ours, the captain noted that the transportation of our personal effects wouldn't be a problem since he'd previously purchased practically every head of stock that was available in the Houston area. This magnificent inventory of his included some fine riding horses, several pack horses, and sixty-four mules; and then along with, of course, some beef cattle for us to eat along the way.

Chapter Three
The Excursion

In addition to some sixteen muleskinners, the captain had also brought along a half dozen Spanish speaking vaqueros who he said were needed to drive our herd of beef cattle. Then without any further explanation as to why we needed all of the additional horse flesh, mules, beef cattle and the extra men, we were soon headed back out to the shoreline where the captain informed us that there would be a steam engine paddlewheel boat waiting for us at the wharf which would ferry us across the gulf to the northwestern shore of Florida to a spot called Apalachee Bay.

Then shortly thereafter, we arrived at the bay but it wasn't until after we'd put in a grueling first day's journey of a goodly number of miles on horseback that the captain had grudgingly allowed us make camp under some willow trees on the bank of a small stream which had apparently been named by one of the Spanish explorers who'd traversed the area some three hundred years prior to our time. Yet even to this day the name of the stream escapes me.

Interestingly enough, however, when Captain McQuinn finally decided to disclose the ultimate objective of his travel plans to Johnny and myself, we would have left the party right then and there except for one very important reason; we had no earthly idea as to where we were. For at that point in time it was obvious to us Brits that we were just barely cognizant of the approximate latitude and longitude of where we'd camped.

So for all practical purposes Johnny and I were hopelessly lost. But then later on that same evening when Johnny and I began in earnest to insist upon being treated as equal partners in this grand adventure we were finally able to get a full disclosure as to just exactly what the former Texas Ranger had in mind for the whole lot of us.

It was then that Captain McQuinn had somewhat reluctantly agreed to let us in on the general picture; and which was, of course, that he was determined to continue on a northerly course until we arrived at a city named Atlanta, Georgia, where he said we would be able to have sixteen of the finest types of wagons manufactured to his own specifications. This, then, would help to explain the need for the troop of Mexican cowboys, the muleskinners, and the herds of horses and mules which we'd brought along with us.

Then as the captain continued on with his lengthy dissertation on some of the major goals of our little expedition, he explained in detail that once we were in possession of the new wagons, we would then continue on a northwesterly direction until we reached the area around the city of Chattanooga, Tennessee where we could purchase, and then have felled, a significant quantity of native hardwood trees which we could then have sawed to the exact and correct sizes so as to fit comfortably into our newly manufactured wagons.

"Hardwood of this nature is in great demand in central Florida," McQuinn said." "The fact being that the native oak groves in Florida don't grow to the enormous heights as the trees in the mountainous regions of the country known as the foothills of the Blue Ridge and the Appalachian Mountains: and if you're so inclined, then half of the profits made from the sale of the timber will be yours; that is, of course, if you're willing to put up half of the money for the original investment," McQuinn said.

"So that's his devious plan?" I was thinking. Now, it was abundantly clear that Captain McQuinn was planning on making profits on two separate fronts. First, he would be paid for the capture of, and then the hanging of, the cattle rustlers in central Florida. Secondly, he would make a handsome profit from the sale of the sixteen wagon loads of the sawn hardwood that we would be purchasing in an area somewhere near the Tennessee and Georgia border.

By that time, however, a meeting of the minds was definitely called for: and after only about thirty minutes of secret negotiations, Johnny and I came to the conclusion that we would have had to spend at least that much front money in the gold fields of California before we even wet a pan in the now famous American River at Sutter's Mill. So therefore, it was agreed that we would be better off if we paid our fair share of the total cost of this great adventure of ours.

Chapter Four
The Atlanta of the Old South

As compared to the majority of the people that we'd met in Texas, and then along with, of course, the change of climate and topography, there were many other stark differences in the populace of the people we'd met in the Atlanta, Georgia area. For without a doubt, we'd seen some interesting sights in our trek across the south-central part of the country.

But after having traveled on up into some of the southeastern parts of the United States, we couldn't help but notice what the American's called their "peculiar institution" which existed primarily in the southern states and was most intriguing to us Brits; and that very simply was our being able to see firsthand the American custom of slavery.

Johnny and I knew, of course, that by the latter part of the seventeen hundreds, and then on into the early parts of the eighteen hundreds, Great Britain had abolished the terrible yoke of human slavery. Although slavery had been tolerated in a few of her colonies for several more years to come; in time, however, even that enterprise would be eliminated.

This then made us realize just how fortunate it was that we were white Europeans. But since Johnny and I had not as yet taken the necessary steps to become naturalized American citizens, we felt as though we might be well-advised to stay out of the complicated mix of American politics which had become so controversial. Even so, Johnny and I felt as though we would most likely follow the lead of a few of our relatives who'd been living in the United States for well over two hundred years by Americanizing both our surnames and our politics.

Having said that, we also felt that we should start afresh in America by burying our old resentments from the past; for as the histories of those original Devon families go, some of the members of those founding families still resented greatly the actions taken by King James the 1st of England, who in the early sixteen hundreds had ordered the beheading of Sir Walter Raleigh.

But since a United States District Court Federal Judge just happened to be holding court in the city of Atlanta, Georgia on one of the days when we were being forced to wait on the wagons that Captain McQuinn had caused to be manufactured, Johnny and I took advantage of the delay by applying for, and then actually receiving some documents which stated that from then on, we were to be considered naturalized American citizens. Then also while we were stranded in the city of Atlanta, I decided to change my surname; and from that day forward, my old surname of Raleigh would be a distant memory from the past.

Thus following those tumultuous days in that Southernmost American city, the time literally flew during the rest of our hiatus in the exciting city of Atlanta, Georgia which seemed to be a very interesting place to visit; and especially since the city had become the hub for many of the fledging railroad companies that were just beginning to spring up all over the South.

Then after only another three days of waiting, the sturdily built sixteen wagons which the captain had ordered were finished and ready for us to pick up. So naturally, we were once again ready to hit the trail which would ultimately take us up into the foothills and the forests of the Blue Ridge and the Appalachian Mountains.

Thus for several days straight, we'd been traveling on the old wagon and game trails through some of the more mountainous parts of Georgia when just shortly after camping for the evening of the third day out of Atlanta, Johnny and I were more than a little concerned when Captain McQuinn suggested that it might be a good idea if we unpacked a few of the firearms which we'd brought along with us.

Admittedly, I was a little taken aback by such a statement. But then as we were about to learn, the Indian

Removal Act of 1830 had caused the Native American Indians who were then living in the southern and the southeastern American states to be relocated to the west of the Mississippi River into what was then called the Indian Territory but was actually part of the country which at the time was known as the Oklahoma Territory.

But then according to Captain McQuinn, President Andrew Jackson's Federal Troops had failed in their attempt to roundup every single group of the native American people; and consequently, some of the holdouts could still be found living in the mountainous regions of Georgia and the Carolinas; and therefore, it was quite understandable that some of those Native Americans had become more than a little hostile to the white people who lived in the area.

Eventually, though, we arrived safe and sound in the Chattanooga area; and as luck would have it, we'd experienced no trouble at all from the so-called hostile natives. Then next, we proceeded to make a trade with a man by the name of Estes Reynolds who purportedly owned an entire half of a mountain in addition to a large valley which had supposedly been deeded to his ancestors from the state of North Carolina for fighting on the line in the American Revolution. Also not so surprisingly, the local lumber king was most happy to fulfill our request to fill our sixteen wagons with loads of rough sawn hardwood lumber; and even more curiously, he'd done so for a reasonable amount of money.

Yet because of the torrential rains which had fallen after our cargo of lumber had been loaded onto our new wagons, we were understandably forced to spend an additional two days and nights in the beautiful foothills of the Blue Ridge and Appalachian Mountains before being able to bade them farewell.

On the other hand, though, our trip southward through the state of Georgia had taken only ten days of travel time instead of the twenty days that McQuinn had first estimated; then again, that was after the numerous heated arguments we'd had with our business partner about whether we should avail ourselves to the services of the railroads which were operating only part of the time.

Ultimately, though, by riding the flat cars on the rails, and then by also driving the wagons over the extremely hardened red clay earthen roads, we eventually ended up in a town named Valdosta, Georgia which sat squarely on the northwestern Florida and southern Georgia border; and while there, we learned that we would be wise to travel across the westernmost part of the state of Florida which, as a rule, the land is usually a lot drier than the northeastern parts of the state which were a good deal more swampy.

So by then, or at least according to his own reckonings, and then along with, of course, the use of some military style maps, Captain McQuinn informed us that we were closing in on our target which was a town in Central Florida known locally as Cow Town; and with any luck at all we had only another week or so of travel time before we would come upon the place where Captain McQuinn's benefactor lived.

Chapter Five
The Oak Grove Hammocks

With very few fences to be found anywhere in the entire state of Florida, it was easy to see why they called it a cattle rustler's paradise. Then too, Captain McQuinn had been right on target when he told us that the trees in Central Florida were certainly slight in stature when compared to the giants that we'd seen in the hardwood forest of the southern states of Tennessee and Georgia.

Still, we quickly discovered that we had much to learn about the local customs; for according to the local cowhunters, or crackers, as the cowboys in Florida were then being called, the settlement named Cow Town was indeed a lively place; but then on, we would learn that the town wasn't nearly as rough as some of the other little settlements which were spread out all across Central Florida.

Then next, a meeting between Captain McQuinn and his benefactor, the Cattle Baron who had originally hailed from the West Indies but had newly immigrated to Florida, was immediately arranged. It was said of him that when discussing business matters he was the type of man who most generally came directly to the point. So with his beautiful singsong voice which appeared to be a melodic mixture of both the Spanish and the West African tongues, Orleans Caracas, the cattle rancher and our benefactor from Central Florida, proceeded to fill us in on the nature and the customs of the local cattle rustlers.

The way that the cattle business in Central Florida was explained to us was that the major cattle ranchers had paid for the erection of a series of camps which began in the northern parts of Florida near St Augustine and the St. Johns River, and then continued on southwards until they reached a huge lake which was called Lake Okeechobee. The camps, which were called hammocks by the locals, were normally placed in the Oak Groves.

As a rule, the camps were strategically spaced around fifteen or twenty miles apart, which at the time, was considered an average day's ride on horseback. The camps, which were plentiful throughout much of the state, were also interspersed with multitudes of meadows and the fertile grass lands which were abundant throughout Central Florida.

So after having driven their herds of cattle for some distances, the cow hunters, (cowboys) both legal and illegal, would then ultimately drive the cattle to a place on the west coast of Florida called Punta Rassa which was located across the river from Ft. Meyers; and from there, the cattle would most generally be sold to the Cubans for a very a handsome price.

Captain McQuinn, being the wise old ex-lawman of the West, had decided that the best way to catch the rustlers would be for us to stake out the main trails which led directly to the shipping port where the stolen cattle would eventually be sold.

Of course it would also help matters if we knew just exactly who the bandits were. So to that end, that particular problem was solved when Mr. Caracas suggested that we hire a few of the Native Americans who were also in the cattle business. For as a rule, the local natives would have a much better grip on the comings and goings of the cow hunters than the average person in Central Florida; and as we were about to learn, that was partly due the fact that a tribe of their very own brethren just happened to live close by to Fort Meyers.

So after having spent only a short amount of time and effort in the pursuit of a guide, we settled on a local Indian who was a member of the Cacema tribe. This particular group of Native Americans had been driven out of the Carolinas by the encroachment of the white settlers who not only had been streaming steadily southward from the east coast of America, but also from Europe. And even though our newly hired Indian guide stated that he preferred to be addressed by his ancestral name, which was Montok, Mr. Caracas preferred the Americanized name of Monty; and therefore, the Indian's ancestral and tribal name was summarily then changed for our benefit.

So within only a few more days of constant surveillance on the most heavily used cattle trail in that part of Florida, our party of five had detained a total of six suspected cattle rustlers which included the most notorious bandit of the them all; Tombstone Bob. Oddly enough, however, not a single person in our party of dozens had shown even the slightest bit of interest into how the well-known bandit and rustler had come to own such a moniker as Tombstone Bob.

To the wealthy cattle ranchers, however, the only thing that really mattered to them was that the captured rustlers should immediately be transported to a town in Central Florida by the name of Allendale which was located on the Kissimmee River but was better known as Cow Town where it was widely assumed by all that the bandits would then be brought up before a kangaroo court which would make short work of their so-called trial. More importantly, though, the rustlers would then very quickly be hanged by the neck until dead.

Then not so surprisingly, both Mr. Caracas and the native called Montok knew exactly where the hanging should take place. Apparently, there was a particular Oak tree just south of Cow Town where several hundred years prior some Spanish soldiers had hanged one of their prisoners; and even to this day the tree is rumored to be haunted by the ghost of the poor dead man who'd died there while swinging from one of its limbs. So then after only a five minute trial in the newly named community of Cow Town, all six of the convicted rustlers were sentenced to die by hanging.

Yet to this day, I occasionally experience a twinge of conscience; but more than anything else, most of us were simply glad that the necessary but sordid ordeal was finally over and done with. That said, it was widely believed that we had indeed hung the guilty parties; because soon thereafter the cattle rustling in central Florida had slowed considerably. Albeit, whether we'd actually hung the right men was never absolutely clear to me, but to the legitimate cattle ranchers of Central Florida, just the idea of having a former Texas Rancher in their presence was certainly a plus.

Chapter Six
The Seminole Wars

For hundreds of years prior to their relocation to the state of Florida, Tetautan's family had lived in the Piedmont Plateau region which is located in the northwestern corner of South Carolina along the base of the Blue Ridge Mountains. His family's tribe was part of the larger Cherokee Nation which had been moved steadily southward by the steady influx of European settlers. In fact, the southern migration of the white man had intensified even greater since the beginning of the American Revolutionary War which began in the year of 1775 and which was then followed by the war of 1812.

In view of that, Tetautan and his father Chief Seneca, and their extended families had first migrated to the state of Florida during the 1820s in order to try to escape the white man's constant invasion into their tribal lands back in the Carolinas. They'd also discovered that even yet another expansion of white settlers and farmers had already begun to sweep down from the north. So by then, the constant influx of Europeans and Americans had almost completely inundated the entire state of Florida with thousands more of white families which consisted primarily of farmers and cattle ranchers.

Although back when Chief Seneca and his tribe were still living in South Carolina, he'd had a vision of the white man's eventual migration into Northern Florida; and so to him, it was only a natural continuation of the same old problem which they'd previously faced back home in the Carolinas. Therefore, both Tetautan and his father were content with the fact that, as a people, they would continually be moving on southwards and possibly even deeper into the more swampy parts of Florida.

Eventually, though, their hopes and dreams were somewhat buoyed by the fact that when they'd eventually reached the central parts of Florida they discovered that the Seminole Native Americans who were living in that part of the state were actually doing quite well for themselves; and as the new comers were about to learn, a few of the Seminole people were the owners of some of the largest herds of cattle that could range up into the thousands of heads.

Of course that doesn't mean to say that the relationships between the ever encroaching white man and the Native Americans who'd already been residing in the state of Florida for a number of generations were always peaceful. But then also just as regrettably, the tensions between the white man and the Native Americans were unhappy reminders of the same types of hostilities that Tetautan and his father Chief Seneca had faced when theylived in South Carolina.

What's more, a few of the older chiefs in the central Florida region, such as the great Seminole Chief Osceola, who before his death in the year of eighteen hundred and thirty-eight from a bout with malaria, had resented the white man's intrusions into Central Florida even more so than the rest of the Native Americans.

Consequently, then, in the year of eighteen hundred and forty-nine, when Captain Thurston McQuinn and Johnny Devon and I made our initial foray into the general area of what was then called Cow Town, it was readily apparent to us that future hostilities with the natives would almost certainly be a real possibility. Even so, Captain McQuinn stated that his main obligation was to the man who'd hired him to come over to Florida in the first place; and that, of course, would be the wealthy cattle rancher, Orleans Caracas.

Yet fortunately for those of us who'd planned to make our homes in Central Florida, the Indian wars that would take place during the next few years were somewhat brief in their nature and not nearly as severe as the first two Seminole Wars; of course that's not to say that they weren't bloody.

Epilogue

With the expert help and advice from Captain Thurston McQuinn, and also because of our having toiled so relentlessly for a full six years which included several years of extreme hardships and personal danger before we were finally able to erect a well-protected stockade from whence we could feel safe and secure from the elements and the local natives, Johnny Devon and I were fortunate enough to have ended up owning several very successful cattle ranching businesses.

Then the next visual step in my optimistic ten-year plan of outward success was for me to become a married man. Of course that situation would hopefully be rectified at the conclusion of a planned sojourn to the northern state of Pennsylvania. This particular excursion would be the end result of a chance encounter which had taken place several years prior when we'd temporarily resided in the Southern City of Atlanta, Georgia as we anxiously waited for the manufacture of our sixteen wagons to be completed.

And coincidentally, it was at that very same point in time when Johnny Devon, Captain McQuinn, and I had been formally introduced to a U. S. Army civil engineer by the name of George Gordon Meade, who at the time, was living in the city of Atlanta, Georgia, but who'd originally hailed from the state of Pennsylvania.

By reputation, Meade had fought with distinction in both the Seminole War in Florida and the Mexican American War. Although in his earlier life, he'd served in the army as a junior officer. Ultimately, however, he would go on to become one of the most highly decorated generals in the entire Union Army.

It seems as if some things in life are destined to be, and so later on it was suggested that I should travel north to the state of Pennsylvania in order to meet a young woman who might just possibly become my bride. The lady in question was a friend of George Gordon Meade's widowed niece. This of course was the same General Meade whom I'd met while dining at the Meade Mansion in Atlanta, Georgia.

So when planning the trip up north it seemed only natural to invite my good friend and business partner, Johnny Devon, to go along with me on the boat trip to Pennsylvania. Unfortunately for Johnny, however, there were no more available women living in that particular part of the state.

So with my new family now solidly intact, and also with my cattle business booming, life should have seemed perfect; and it would have been if it had not been for the constant disagreeable dialogue which had accompanied the eighteen hundred and sixty presidential elections.

The daily news from the Northern leaders which consisted primarily of a constant barrage of rhetoric which implied that slavery would no longer be tolerated in the United States of America. Then of course, that dialogue was immediately followed with a much sterner form of rhetoric from the Southern leaders. Therefore, a civil war between the Northern and the Southern states seemed almost inevitable.

Modern Antiquities

"Let's parade the troops past the newly elected president," said the Commanding General of the United States Army.

"Yes, let's do: for its times like these that we must continue to profess our total commitment to the defense of our country," said the newly appointed United States Secretary of Defense."

"Unfortunately, though, the new president isn't nearly as enthusiastic about the idea of expanding the size of our standing army as we are; then again, that's politics, and that's where your power lies," said the general.

"Well if my influence resides is in the political arena then your power must lie on the battlefield. By the way, a tremendous military victory on your part might just go a long way in swaying the American public and their elected congressional servants in Washington to go along with our plans of doubling our present military budget. And who knows, if the victory on the battlefield were truly great enough then they might even build you a triumphal arch at the edge ofWashington D. C. in as much as the way that the Romans did when they erected those monuments to glorify their successful generals," said the secretary.

So as a result of their highly secretive collaboration, it was unilaterally decided by only a few of our most trusted military leaders that the United States would take the war against global terrorism to the shores of the country which had allegedly trained the suicide bomber responsible for the recent slaughter of those two dozen innocent Americans who'd perished in an explosion aboard a ferryboat licensed out of Washington State but had departed from a port in Western Canada.

To their credit, however, the idea of taking the fight to a foreign land could not be placed entirely upon the shoulders of the current Commanding General of the United States Army; or even the brand-new United States Secretary of Defense. For in reality, the modern-day cowboy approach which intends to punish each and every one of the countries that the U. S. has deemed to be a terrorist nationwasn't anything new at all; in fact, the program had been previously established by one of our former presidential administrations.

Also just as interestingly, the superhot topic of nation retaliation had been sharply brought to the forefront during one of the last presidential debates when both the current president and his unsuccessful opponent had pledged to exact a most awful retribution for the loss of those two dozen innocent American lives.

Having said that, the American public seemed to be growing increasingly intolerant of all types of war; and that was particularly true of the ones that seem to go on forever. Yet all throughout history the warmongers have more often than not been able to find a way in which to garner the support they needed in order to make a case for yet a another war. Thus a case in point would be when one of our former presidents was able to persuade the U. S. Congress and the American public of the need to build up our troop strength in Southeast Asia following an event in which one of our navy's ships had allegedly been fired upon by components of the North Vietnamese Navy.

Although it was beginning to appearas if the Commanding General of the United States Army, and then along with, of course, the United States Secretary of Defense, would need all the help they could muster if they ever hoped to convince the President of the United States and the Speaker of the House of the need to spend tens of billions more of the taxpayer's dollars in order to feed the ever hungry military machine.

Yet all was not lost, for at that point in time both the directors of the F. B. I. and the C. I. A. had secretly agreed to work towards gaining the support of the White House and the U. S. Congress in order to help them implement a program named "Stopgap" which was the code name used for the plan to severely punish every single one of America's modern-day enemy nations.

The plotters knew, of course, that as a last resort they could always attempt to corrupt the proceedings of the nation's electronic surveillance system which is under the auspices of the National Security Agency, or N.S.A., where one well placed double agent, or mole, could feed enough erroneous information into the daily operations at the National Security Council so as to warrant an immediate military action against an enemy nation of their choosing.

So after only a few short weeks following their decision to punish the country of origin of the terrorist who'd been identified as the "Ferry-Bomber," it appeared as if the war hawks had their man. The person they chose was a retired Special Agent of the F. B. I., who with some twenty-five years of service under his belt would be the ideal person to do their undercover work at the National Security Agency.

Of course the main reason they'd chosen that particular man was the fact that he held a degree in electronic engineering and so naturally he would know his way around the war room, where as a rule, the intelligence experts went about their daily business of disseminating the enormous amounts of electronic information that came in on a regular basis.

Then just days later, the self-styled patriots, which included the Secretary of Defense and the Commanding General of the U. S. Army, and then along with, of course, their newly imbedded spy at N. S. A., were more than ready to put their brazen plan into action.

First of all, the team of plotters would have to convince the few remaining members of the president's Security Council that weren't already in on the plot to go along with their scheme. In reality, though, the only people that weren't a part of the covert team consisted of the Secretary of State, the special advisors to the president, the White House lawyers, and of course, the president himself.

So all in all it was beginning to appear as if there would be nothing but clear skies and smooth sailing ahead for the members of the underhanded cabal which could almost assuredly be proved to be illegal; and especially since their inside man at the N. S. A. had found a way to create, and then forge, some false and fictitious electronic reports which had supposedly been composed by some of our real live C. I. A. agents on the ground in North Africa and the Middle-east.

In retrospect, however, it would be rather difficult to see how a normal person, or even a super patriot such as the commanding general, could have condoned a plot that intended to destroy as much as one fourth of the world's population. Yet considering the fact that the general's famous family had produced five generations of highly decorated and greatly admired military leaders it was somewhat understandable that the current Commanding General of the United States Army might have believed that he was acting in the stead of Patrick Henry, who as one of our greatest American Revolution War heroes had proclaimed, "Give me liberty or give me death." This then is very similar to what our present-day commanding general had said many times over; "Americans will never agree to live under the threat of terrorism."

Amazingly, then, just shortly after all of the various parts of the plan had come together the leaders of both of the major U. S. political parties had not only agreed to double the size of the military budget, but they were also willing to bring back the military draft which had been discontinued in the year of nineteen hundred and seventy-three just shortly after the long drawn-out Vietnamese War had wound down. But to the anti-war doves, and then along with their watchdog types of compatriots, it'd become all too obvious that our military leaders were seriously considering a plan to mobilize the country.

Nonetheless, the sitting president had steadfastly vowed to veto any bill that would increase the amount of money which had already been allocated for that particular year's military budget. This meant, of course, that the advocates of the emergency military bill that the plotters had hoped to pass through congress would need a two thirds majority in both houses if they had any hopes of overriding the president's veto. And since their bill to increase the military budget had passed the House of Representatives by only the narrowest of margins, both the general and the secretary feared that their cause might be dead in the water.

Therefore, the plotters were beginning to believe that the only way that they would ever be able to procure the necessary funds to finance their campaign against global terrorism was to find a way in which to embarrass the president to such an extinct that he would be forced to resign rather than face the possibility of being impeached. So as a result, the immediate question before the cabal was where they should start digging if they hoped to find anything in his background as sinister as the Watergate Scandal which had toppled President Nixon's administration back in 1974.

Though dig as they might the plotters were unable to find any evidence of felony wrongdoing against the sitting president. And aside from his being slightly embarrassed by the actions a few of his family members, at least none of the current president's relatives had relieved themselves on an airport tarmac.

So in view of those findings the members of the cabal had decided that if there wasn't any real evidence to be found against the sitting president, then they would just have to invent some.

Their plan was simple and straightforward in its very nature: for in the immediate future they would begin to keep two sets of books. In the first instance they would compose a compendium of false and fictitious reports which had primarily been prepared by their man inside the N. S. A.; and so naturally, those books would be shown to the president. Secondly, the true and factual reports would be kept in a separate set of books in case the U. S. Congress ever got around to calling up the members of the cabal to testify.

The commanding general had also suggested that the members of the cabal should attempt to install a coconspirator in the White House in the guise of a beautiful female intern in order to try to seduce the president. But since a similar situation had taken place back in the latter part of the twentieth century which had almost led to the downfall of a sitting president, they doubted seriously if a ploy such as that could ever again be replicated.

But then not to be outdone another not so brilliant plan had been posited by the Secretary of Defense. His extremely dangerous and highly treasonous suggestion was that the F. B. I. should attempt to install an undercover person in the White House just so that they could then have access to the food that was prepared daily in the White House kitchen. Of course that particular idea would have never been implemented; for after all, Americans would never stoop so low as to commit the types of crimes that the people in Hitler's Germany or Stalin's Russia had perpetrated on their own people, would they?

To an outsider, however, the machinations that were then being carried out by some of our highest ranking government officials couldn't help but to remind us of the type of treachery which had been played out in Shakespeare's playPrince Hamlet which was centered around his mother the queen, Gertrude, and Hamlet's uncle Claudius, who together had conspired to kill Hamlet's father, the King of Denmark.

Of course all throughout history there have been many examples of various leaders around the world which have been assassinated; or at the very least, they'd been overthrown by a military coup. In the United States alone we've suffered through the results of four presidential assassinations; and on top of that, an even dozen attempts to kill the sitting president have failed. And that's not even counting the deaths of four of our presidents who supposedly died of natural causes while in office; though at the time, it was widely rumored that two of them had been murdered.

In the end, however, the hard-won democracy that our forefathers had fought and died for would eventually win out. Thus with the help and the protection of the president's own personal bodyguards, which included the men and women of the Secret Service, both the Commanding General of the United States Army and the nation's Secretary of Defense were summarily then summoned before a joint session of congress where they were forced to resign their posts in lieu not having to face either a military court martial or a civil trial.

What's more, since the directors of the F. B. I. and the C. I. A. serve at the president's pleasure, they too were fired.

Then immediately following one of the most turbulent times in our nation's history, an Executive Presidential Order was issued which stated that for the first time ever, the President of the United States would have the legal authority to order the assassination of an American Citizen.

A Sad Carpet

On a specific and particular morning, Arnold Roebling was somewhat keener than he normally would have been; and that was primarily due to the fact that it was going to be the very last day that he would ever again have to personally manhandle those heavy and somewhat awkward steamers and vacuum machines that his company used to clean their client's carpets with.

Then just as interestingly, it was also going to be last day that Arnold's employer was planning on using the hot water extraction "steam cleaning" system which is a lot more labor-intensive than the newer dry-cleaning system which has a fast drying application; and not so surprisingly, the new system is steadily gaining in popularity with the general public.

And on top of that, Arnold had just recently been promoted to a supervisory position by the parent company where he'd been employed for the past nine years. Furthermore, he'd also been recognized by one of the leading carpet cleaning industries' journals as being the number one rated commercial carpet cleaning technician in the entire Midwest.

So on the very last day that Arnold Roebling would ever again have to personally manhandle those long hoses from the truck mounted carpet cleaner, his work schedule on that particular day had called for him to visit only two separate establishments; and one of which just happened to be an empty, but recently remodeled doctor's office where Arnold's work had progressed like clockwork; and therefore, the crew was finished working by 11:00 o'clock that same morning.

Yet after he'd surveyed the filthy and heavily stained carpet on the floor of their next scheduled stop, both Arnold and the members of his crew had collectively bemoaned their bad luck of having to explain to the general manager of the building that housed a not-for-profit organization that not even a well-respected carpet cleaning company, such as, "The Luck of the Irish," could ever hope to bring the sheen of life back into one of the most horrible looking floor coverings that Arnold had ever had the misfortune to observe.

In truth, however, it wasn't just the dirt and the stains that detracted so heavily from the carpet's former grace and elegance; for it seemed that the real culprit was the fact that the carpet had been stitched and sewn so many times that the caretakers of the building had finally given up on using a needle and thread, and instead, they'd resorted to applying an ungodly amount of duct tape on the ragged seams and edges in what had ended up being a losing effort in order to coax a little more life out of the old and worn-out carpet.

Nonetheless, the general manager of the building that housed the filthy and worn-out carpet had decided to reveal to Arnold the fact that the current managing board of directors had just recently expressed hopes that the cleaning of the carpet would only have to be a temporary and stopgap measure until such time as they would able to replace the old carpet.

Nevertheless, the building's general manager likened the board's recent statement as being somewhat similar to the old adage of, "When pigs fly,"; for he was well aware of the fact that one of the club's long-time members had faithfully promised to replace the crummy old carpet with a rather expensive floor tile just as soon as Hollywood decided to turn one of his stories into a major motion picture. But since the manager was a realist and not a dreamer, he tended to view the writer's hopes and desires of one day becoming rich and famous as nothing more than pipedreams.

In the end, however, the board was somehow able to find the money to replace the old worn-out carpet with an eye dazzling collection of multicolored colored, 2 foot by 2 foot, squares of brand-new carpeting which featured some very unique and eye-popping designs.

Files From Above

Since the beginning of time, every generation of humans has produced a few remarkable individuals that seemed to have been blessed with what appears to be some supernatural powers of insight. And during their time on earth, these extremely gifted people have not only given us many beneficial aids such as the Holy Bible, which includes the laws on how best to conduct our daily lives, but some of those same individuals have also developed a wide variety of antibiotics and other types of medications which have helped us to eliminate a great many of the deadly bacteria that used to shorten our life spans by decades.

So then one might ask, is it reasonable for us to believe that there really is a zipped file hidden away somewhere out there in this giant universe of ours; and if so, is it possible that this ultra secret document can only be unzipped by those of us who are the especially appointed caretakers of our time? Naturally, then, our very next question might be what would we do if a person were to find a way to unlock the files that might just possibly be stored someplace out there in this vast cosmos of ours.

Oddly enough, however, the answer to such an intriguing question would more than likely shock the average person for when that brilliant modern-day physicist, Josh Spearman, was completing his graduate studies at M. I. T., he claimed to have found the answer to that particular riddle while attempting to provide evidence that the, "String Theory," was supposedly the driving force that holds the universe together.

Then along these same lines, that same renowned scientist, Dr. Josh Spearman, published a stunning declaration that the answer to the unlocking of the "Files From Above" was relatively simple. However, he then proceeded to confuse the issue even further by suggesting that the solution to this proposition might be found in Einstein's famous formula; $E=MC2$. Of course a statement such as that might cause a person to wonder just exactly what the unlocking of the "Files From Above" would have to do with the subject of energy, mass, or even the speed of light.

Yet in response to such a complicated question, the very knowledgeable Dr. Spearman reiterated what he'd said many times before; and that was simply that man's destiny, religion, and even the world's social and financial structure could be defined by the mathematical equation which had been given to him while he was asleep.

Furthermore, it's been noted that it was when Dr. Josh Spearman was compiling his master's thesis at M. I. T., he was driven to promulgate this earthshaking theory of his as to how the science of mathematics had helped him to unlock the secrets of the "Files From Above." And therefore, Dr. Spearman has since decided to share his earthshaking findings with us normal people here on earth.

First of all, the plans which were allegedly given to him for a unified and peaceful takeover of the world by the followers of the author of the "Files From Above" would require us to develop a specific type of a caste system.

Secondly, every person born in the current century would be exempt from the rationing of foodstuffs. They would, however, be forced to undergo a specific surgical procedure, if as a married couple, they ever produced more than one child.

Next, every type of the world's currency would be pooled together in a global trust fund that would only be accessible to a few select members of the United Nations Security Council who'd been democratically selected from the twelve most industrialized nations on earth. Yet another dictate of the "new world order" would be that no further spending on any types of luxury items would be permitted.

Then finally, every nation on earth would be supplied with a copy of the "Files From Above" which clearly states that anyone found guilty of breaking any one of the, "Seven Deadly Sins" or the "Ten Commandments," would automatically be put to death by means of, "Fire From Above."

Furthermore, the last part of this highly subjective treatise succinctly states that any groups of persons, or any one of the City State Members that happens to violate any one of the tenets of this proclamation, would immediately be subjected to the same type of punishment that was meted out to the inhabitants of the ancient cities of Sodom and Gomorra, which according to the Bible, were all destroyed by fire and brimstone sent down from Heaven.

If a person is not familiar with the names of these two cities, then it's suggested that they might want to read the biblical Book of Genesis.

The End